A FATAL FAMILY FEAST

By Lynn Cahoon

The Farm-to-Fork Mysteries
Fatal Family Feast
Killer Comfort Food
Deep Fried Revenge
One Potato, Two Potato, Dead
Killer Green Tomatoes
Who Moved My Goat Cheese?
Novellas
A Pumpkin Spice Killing
Penned In
Have a Deadly New Year

The Tourist Trap Mysteries
Picture Perfect Frame
Murder in Waiting
Memories and Murder
Killer Party
Hospitality and Homicide
Tea Cups and Carnage
Murder on Wheels
Killer Run
Dressed to Kill
If the Shoe Kills
Mission to Murder
Guidebook to Murder
Novellas
A Very Mummy Holiday
Mother's Day Mayhem
Corned Beef and Casualties
Santa Puppy
A Deadly Brew
Rockets' Dead Glare

The Kitchen Witch Mysteries
Two Wicked Desserts
One Poison Pie

Novellas
Have a Holly, Haunted Christmas
Murder 101
Chili Cauldron Curse

The Cat Latimer Mysteries
A Field Guide to Homicide
Sconed to Death
Slay in Character
Of Murder and Men
Fatality by Firelight
A Story to Kill

A FATAL FAMILY FEAST

A Farm-to-Fork Mystery

By Lynn Cahoon

LYRICAL PRESS
Kensington Publishing Corp.
www.kensingtonbooks.com

To the extent that the image or images on the cover of this book depict a person or persons, such person or persons are merely models, and are not intended to portray any character or characters featured in the book.

This book is a work of fiction. Names, characters, businesses, organizations, places, events, and incidents either are the product of the author's imagination or are used fictitiously. Any resemblance to actual persons, living or dead, events, or locales is entirely coincidental.

LYRICAL PRESS BOOKS are published by

Kensington Publishing Corp.
119 West 40th Street
New York, NY 10018

All Kensington titles, imprints, and distributed lines are available at special quantity discounts for bulk purchases for sales promotion, premiums, fund-raising, educational, or institutional use.

Special book excerpts or customized printings can also be created to fit specific needs. For details, write or phone the office of the Kensington Sales Manager: Kensington Publishing Corp., 119 West 40th Street, New York, NY 10018, Attn. Sales Department. Phone: 1-800-221-2647.

Lyrical Press and Lyrical Press logo Reg. U.S. Pat. & TM Off.

First Electronic Edition: January 2022
ISBN: 978-1-5161-1105-3 (ebook)

First Print Edition: January 2022
ISBN: 978-1-5161-1106-0

Printed in the United States of America

DEDICATION

To my middle school librarian, who knew that books were a perfect place to hide in an imperfect world.

ACKNOWLEDGMENTS

River Vista is a fictional town with roots in the real small town I lived outside of for most of my childhood. The town had three bars and twice that many churches. When I placed the County Seat on Main Street, I knew exactly where it was located, across from the small city park. Now there are a lot of farm-to-fork restaurants in the area, headed by local chefs, but back when I was growing up, there was the drive-in. So what better business to add to my imaginary hometown as Angie and Felicia's restaurant. Thanks for all the support to my editor, Esi Sogah, and my agent, Jill Marsal.

Chapter 1

Spring in southwestern Idaho is fickle. One day, the weather could be soft and perfect. The grass in your lawn turns a bright green, and the daffodils in your flower bed start to bloom. Then, a week later, you wake up to a late storm that freezes the ground and covers all that spring green with an inch or two of white snow.

Angie Turner wasn't sure Felicia Williams, her best friend, had made the correct decision to hold her spring wedding on the Turner farm. The driveway was dirt, so the chance it could turn to mud and ruin not only Felicia's dress but everyone's shoes was a real possibility. Holding it in the barn was an option, but then she had to think about what to do with Mabel and Precious. She didn't want to tell Felicia and Estebe Blackstone, who was the groom and also Angie's sous chef at the County Seat, no, but it might be the smartest thing to do.

They could hold it at the restaurant. The floors wouldn't be muddy, and with the beams and white fairy lights they'd installed last summer, the eatery would be a beautiful place for a wedding. Now all she had to do was convince the bride. She picked up her phone and dialed Felicia's number. The call went straight to voice mail.

"Hey, call me when you get this. I was looking at next week's forecast, and I think we're going to have to go with plan B on the wedding site. We've closed the restaurant for that week anyway, so we'll be able to decorate starting on Sunday. I'm sorry about the farm, I just don't think it's a good idea." The voice mail beeped, and Angie hoped she'd been fast enough to deliver the bad news without actually talking to Felicia directly.

Dom woofed from his bed, and Angie reached down and rubbed the Saint Bernard's head. "I don't need any comments from the peanut gallery. Besides, what would I do with you around two hundred people?"

The door opened, and Ian McNeal stepped inside. She'd been dating Ian for a while now, and he was a frequent visitor to the farm. "Talking to Dom again? You must be discussing the pros and cons of holding the wedding here."

"Actually, I've decided against it and called Felicia already." Angie stood and turned on the gas under the teapot. "Do you have time for some tea and coffee cake? I made a cinnamon apple version this morning."

"I'm going to gain so much weight being with you that I'll need to go up a few sizes. You always bake when you're stressed." He leaned in and kissed her. "I'd love to stay for tea. What did Felicia say when you told her? Was she upset?"

Angie got down cups and plates. She cut the coffee cake and served slices on the plates, which she set on the table. "I don't know."

"What do you mean, you don't know? What did her voice sound like? You called her, right?" He flipped through the tea bags in a basket on the table and pulled out an Earl Grey packet. "I need to order you some proper English tea. Maybe I'll pick some up this summer when I go back to see Mom."

"Oh, you're visiting your mom this summer? That's nice." Angie changed the subject while she took the screaming kettle off the stove and turned off the heat. She poured hot water in the cups and then sat down and fiddled with the tea bags.

"You didn't answer my question. What did you do, email her? Or worse, text?" He was staring at her.

She felt the heat on her face. "I called her. She just didn't answer, so I left a voice mail. I'm sure she'll call back soon."

"You are going to be in so much trouble. If this was such a big deal, why did you say yes when they asked you to hold the wedding here?" Ian took a bite of the coffee cake and groaned. "I love it when you're conflicted. This is fun to watch."

"Thanks, I think. Anyway, I didn't think it would be a problem, but then I got thinking about the driveway and how it turns to mud after a rain. And Mabel, you know she doesn't like strangers. And she's so old. What if someone didn't see her and ran her over? I'd be heartbroken. And there's no way Precious wouldn't try to get out and see what was going on. Then she'd eat something, like Felicia's bouquet, and Felicia would cry." Angie stuck a tea bag in the water and started dunking it. "And that's not even taking into consideration Dom. He's so big, he'd probably sit on one of Estebe's nieces and squish her."

"You have been putting this to a lot of thought." Ian looked out the door window. "Well, at least we'll get this over with. There's Estebe's Hummer now."

Angie sank against the back of her chair. Either Felicia had heard the voice mail and was mad at her...or she hadn't heard the voice mail and she was going to have to break Felicia's heart now. "Great. Now I'm going to get yelled at in person."

"She's not going to yell," Ian assured her.

But when the door banged open, Felicia stormed into the house and flopped into a chair. "My wedding is ruined."

Angie and Ian shared a look.

"It's not ruined, my love." Estebe closed the door and put a hand on Felicia's shoulder. "Let's just talk this out. I know you're hurt. But let's have some tea and do some damage control."

"I'm sorry, I just didn't want your dress to get all muddy. And Precious would want to eat the bouquet," Angie blurted out as Estebe moved around the kitchen to get two more cups. The four of them had cooked in Angie's kitchen way too many times for her to play hostess. "Then there was Dom to think about."

Felicia lifted her head from where she'd laid it on the table, her blond hair pooling around her tear-stained face. "Angie, what the heck are you talking about?"

"Why you can't have the wedding here. That's what ruined your wedding, right?" Now Angie was confused. She looked at Ian, who shrugged, but Estebe wouldn't meet her gaze. "Why are you upset, then?"

"Don't worry about the farmhouse. I knew we couldn't do the wedding here when I heard the forecast for next week. I don't want to be pelted by rain during my ceremony." Felicia wiped the tears off her face. "The problem is my family."

"Aren't they coming to the wedding?" In all the years Angie had known Felicia, she'd never met anyone from her family. And when she'd confessed that they were East Coast wealthy, Angie felt better about it. She might cook upscale food, but she'd hate to have to do the whole socialite thing. Even for her best friend.

"Mom says she's coming. She says Dad is as well, but he refuses to give me away." Felicia snuck a look at Estebe. "He's..."

"He's afraid she's marrying beneath herself," Estebe clarified. He puffed up his chest. "I am proud of my Basque heritage, and if it's about money,

I'm very well suited to take care of Felicia and myself. I probably have more money than a lot of those boys they wanted her to marry when she was just a child."

Felicia grinned and patted his hand. "In Dad's defense, I was of legal age before he started bringing over suitable dates. He never set up an arranged marriage for me, even though he tried."

"I want to send him copies of my accounts and a list of real estate I own, but Felicia says she loves me for me and won't let me." Estebe shook his head. "I tell her she doesn't understand men. This will make him happy his daughter is marrying someone who can take care of her."

Angie wondered if it was Estebe's money that was bothering Felicia's father or something else. Like Estebe's heritage. "Look, we'll figure something out. Maybe Allen will walk you down the aisle. He's going to need the practice when Bleak finds the one."

"From what Bleak's told me, she's going to elope." Felicia sipped her tea. "I can't believe I let him get into my head again. There's a reason I don't go home."

"This is your wedding. If it's not exactly as you pictured it, maybe that might be a better thing." Angie patted her friend's arm. "So let's talk about the reception. Have you finalized the menu? With the wedding being at the restaurant, that will help in keeping things cold before, and we can hire some temps to cook the day of so we're not too stressed out."

"You want temps to cook for my wedding?" Estebe shook his head. "Maybe I can find some friends to come over the morning before."

"They won't have anything to cook if we don't finalize the menu. Do you have final numbers? The restaurant can hold up to three hundred, but that's a stretch." Angie walked over and took out the notebook that held the notes they'd taken as they planned this wedding for the last three months. "We have to get the order in tomorrow."

Estebe pulled out his list. "My family has responded. However, several others from the community would like to be invited if we have room. A Basque wedding is very large."

"Yes, and typically held in June. Which we could have done if you hadn't chosen March 23rd for the wedding date. At least it's a Saturday. Why on earth did you insist on March?" Felicia pulled out her own list. "We could have had it here on the farm."

"Too late to change your mind now." Angie tried to push past the discussion, but Felicia smoothed her list.

"Seriously, Estebe, why March 23rd?" Felicia wasn't letting the question drop. She turned toward her soon-to-be husband.

He smiled and pushed a lock of hair back out of her face. "You wouldn't remember, but it's the day I knew I was going to marry you. One day."

"That's so sweet." Angie glanced at Ian, who was sipping his tea.

He shook his head. "Don't look at me. I'm still making up my mind about our future."

She swatted at him with the notebook and turned back to the happy couple, who were now staring deeply into each other's eyes. "Come on, guys, no matter why the date was chosen, it's in a little over a week. Let's get this planning finished."

They worked for a couple of hours on the menu, and Angie made up an order list from the plans. As they were finishing, Felicia's phone beeped with a text. She picked it up, read it, and set the phone down. Upside down.

Estebe, who'd been talking to Ian about the local college basketball team and their chances in the tournament, turned back. Something in her face must have alerted him to a problem. "Who was that?"

"The dress. I need to go in for another fitting tomorrow." Felicia tucked her phone into her jeans pocket. "Angie, do you want to go with me?"

Angie nodded, but she was totally confused. The final fitting had been last week, and they'd gone to Boise and had lunch at Copper Creek to celebrate. Something was definitely up with her friend, and she didn't want Estebe to know. "I was going to play with some recipes in the morning, but I can do that next week."

"Great." She put her hand on Estebe's shoulder. "If we're going to your parents' for dinner, we need to leave now. I'd like to change."

He stood and gave her a kiss. "I don't know why. You look beautiful as you are."

She grinned at Angie. "I told you the last time we went to the Blackstones' for dinner and Estebe said it was casual, I wore jeans and everyone else was in dresses."

"That is not true," Estebe deadpanned. "I was not in a dress, and neither were my father or brothers."

"You know what I mean." She leaned into his arm. "He's so exasperating at times."

"And yet you love him," Angie told her friend. Felicia would explain what they were doing when they were alone. "Do you want me to pick you up, or do you want to drive?"

"I want to drive." Felicia lowered her voice. "You haven't seen my wedding gift from Estebe yet. It's on fire."

"I hope not," Ian said, glancing between the two women. "You don't want to lose it so soon."

"I didn't mean real fire...." Felicia pointed her finger at Ian. "You're teasing me."

"Guilty as charged. But I didn't think you'd fall for it so quickly." He slapped Estebe on the back. "I need to head back into town as well. I'll walk out with you."

Angie followed everyone to the door, where she got hugs from Estebe and Felicia and a kiss from Ian. She watched as everyone left. It was almost dinnertime, and she had a recipe she wanted to try. Ian had already fed the zoo, as he called Mabel and Precious. Dom sat next to her, watching out the window as everyone left.

"I hope Felicia's family realizes what a gem Estebe is and how much Felicia loves him," Angie told Dom.

Dom woofed his support, then left her standing at the door. He went and cuddled back into his bed. He hadn't gotten his afternoon nap since there were too many people here to play with him. He laid his head on the edge of the bed and watched her shut the door and go to the fridge.

Estebe might not be a trust fund baby, but the guy had money. And he'd do anything to protect Felicia. That much Angie was certain of. She took out the chicken breasts and started pounding them flat. Cooking was a perfect way to deal with emotions.

Chapter 2

Angie climbed into Felicia's brand-new cherry-red Jeep and tucked her tote on the floor behind her. She pulled on her seatbelt and whistled. "Now you have to marry him. This is a great wedding present."

"Estebe's the best, but I'm not marrying him for the money. I could have bought my own Jeep, but it makes him happy to do things for me." She pushed a few buttons on the dash. "I wouldn't have gotten the fully loaded version, though. This model has heated seats and a heated steering wheel."

"There's some vehicle brand that has massage seats. I'd fall asleep driving and kill myself." Angie leaned back as the seat started to warm. "This is like having your own personal heating pad."

"I know, right." She pulled the Jeep out of the driveway and onto the road.

Angie turned toward Felicia and watched her face. "Do you want to tell me what we're really doing this morning? And who sent you the text?"

"Crap, was I that obvious?" Felicia glanced over at her.

"For someone who has known you for years, yes." Angie paused. "I don't think Estebe questioned your motives, however."

"He is a trusting soul. Probably too trusting in this case." Felicia sighed and focused on the road. "I'm, I mean, *we're* having coffee with Jason Anderson Roberts, the Third."

Now that was an answer Angie hadn't been expecting. "The guy you were engaged to back home? He's here in Boise?"

"The one and only. He heard about my wedding from my dad and wanted to congratulate me in person." Felicia stared straight ahead at the road.

Angie tried to read between the lines. "You don't think he's here to congratulate you on the wedding. You think he's here to stop it."

Felicia nodded. "He's going to try. He works for my dad. He was one of Dad's fix-it guys. He takes care of problems." Felicia added, "Problems like me."

"Why did you two break up, anyway?" Angie wasn't sure seeing this guy was the best decision, but she wanted to have enough information beforehand to stop anything from happening. "You never told me that part."

"It was going too fast. He and my folks planned everything. Like I was some chattel that my family could pass on to him. I got mad and told him I wanted a say in my own wedding. Then he went behind my back and changed something that was very important to me. When I confronted him, he tried to placate me and told me that no one who was anyone wanted that sort of thing at a wedding."

"What did you ask for? A three-ring circus?"

"I was working with a choir from a local public school. I asked them to perform at the wedding. He decided the school they came from was in the wrong part of town. Not classy enough for our wedding." She laughed at the memory. "Like I cared about the optics of my own wedding. He was such a jerk. I dumped him that same day. Then I took off to attend school at Boise State the next week. There was no way I was going to be tied to someone who measured worth in the size of their wallet."

"I'm glad he showed his true colors early, then. So...why are we meeting him?" Angie didn't like the guy at all.

"One, because he'll buy us breakfast while he tries to convince me to listen to my father and move back home. And two, because he has my father's ear. Maybe I can get him to tell us why Dad's refusing to give me away. If I knew, maybe I could fix what has Dad so riled up." Felicia sighed. "You don't have to be part of this. I kind of tricked you into coming anyway."

"I don't want you to be alone. I'll stay in the car if you want me to, but if you need an anti-wing woman, I can be that person too," Angie pledged. "Besides, I like a free breakfast, especially if it comes with a show."

"Oh, this one probably will." Felicia turned onto the highway that would take them into Boise.

By the time they got downtown to the upscale hotel and found parking, it was almost ten. Felicia smoothed her hair down as they took the elevator to the top floor of the hotel to the panoramic restaurant.

"Did you know there was a different Top of the Hoff down on 5th Street? The building was the Hoff, but the chef who owned the restaurant closed that one and moved here. He didn't want to change the name of the restaurant, so now the Top of the Hoff is at the Grove Hotel." Angie chatted, but she could tell Felicia wasn't listening. "And so when Santa comes on Christmas Eve, he knows where to find the chef's children, who live behind the stove."

"That's interesting." Felicia checked her hair for the third time in the elevator mirrors.

"Are you sure you're not interested in this guy anymore? Why do you care what you look like?" Angie pointed out the obvious.

Felicia glanced at herself again, then turned toward Angie, her shoulders dropping. "I don't. It's just an old habit. He didn't like it if my hair was out of place. He preferred it being up in a bun and me in a dress. I can't believe I'm still worried about what he thinks."

"That's a discussion between you and your therapist. I just want to know, do you love Estebe?"

Felicia's face broke into a smile for the first time that morning. "Of course I do."

"Then it doesn't matter what this guy thinks or that he likes his women to look like they stepped out of the fifties. You are here seeing an old friend. That's all." The elevator doors opened, and Angie stepped out into the lobby. "Let's get this breakfast going. I'm hungry."

They walked up to the hostess stand, and Felicia nodded to the man sitting by the window. "We're meeting him."

"Oh, we were expecting a table of two. Carol, please get a third setting." The hostess nodded to the woman next to her, who scrambled back into the restaurant. "Come this way, please."

They wound their way through the tables and finally reached the table where the man stood and greeted Felicia. He leaned in for a kiss, but she moved just as his lips came close, and he kissed her cheek instead. Then he focused on Angie. "I'm sorry, Felicia didn't mention she was bringing a friend. I'm Jason. Any friend of Felicia's is a friend of mine."

"I'm Angie Turner. I'm Felicia's partner at the County Seat." Angie studied the man. He was handsome in a suit-and-tie kind of way. He'd make a good model for a billionaire romance. She sat in the chair at the end of the table, putting herself between the other two. "And I'm famished. Thanks for inviting us to breakfast."

Jason's eyes twinkled as he caught the implication. Of course, he hadn't invited Angie to breakfast, but now he was the host. A role he probably enjoyed. Being in charge. "My pleasure. I hope you don't mind long, boring stories of the old days. I'm afraid Felicia and I go way back."

"I'm sure you're more interested in what I'm doing and who I am now than rehashing old ground." Felicia sat and took a sip of her water. She studied the menu, ignoring the man across from her. "Angie, what are you having?"

Angie took the menu that Jason had set aside and started looking. "I'm always interested in a croque monsieur. Or eggs Benedict. Most places can handle a good omelet. What about you?"

"I was thinking the prime rib and eggs." Felicia met Jason's gaze. "Or maybe the lobster eggs. You should try them. They're supposed to be quite good."

And they're also the most expensive thing on the menu. Angie wondered if this gameplay had always been a part of their relationship. Neither saying directly what they wanted, both just taking shots under the belt. Given how Felicia was acting, money must be Jason's weak spot.

After the waitress took their order and brought more coffee, Jason leaned back and studied Felicia. "You have grown into a beautiful woman. You were always pretty, striking even. But now. Now, you're amazing."

"Thanks." Felicia sipped her coffee. "Are you still working for Dad?"

"Guilty as charged. I believe I'm the employee with the most tenure at the company besides your father. And with his temper, that's quite an accomplishment." He picked up a spoon and polished it with a napkin.

"Well, except for Carter. He's still Dad's right-hand man, I take it." Felicia didn't watch the reaction to her words, but Angie saw him grip the coffee cup a little tighter at the mention of the man's name.

"Your father has a soft spot for people like Carter. Believe me, he'll screw up, and without anyone behind him supporting his actions, your father will drop Carter like the bad penny everyone knows he is. I'm sure I'll be moved up to senior leadership when the time is right."

"And yet Carter made it when he was only twenty-four. Aren't you in your midthirties now?" Felicia asked sweetly, taking a drink of her orange juice as she waited for the verbal punch to connect.

When it did, Jason's face went beet red. He wiped his mouth and forehead where beads of sweat had formed. "You always were blunt and to the point. Anyway, you need to move back to Boston. It's time to come home, Pooks."

"I didn't like that nickname when we were dating, and I don't like it now." Felicia's eyes burned bright as she glared at Jason. "Besides, I have a business here. And a life. Tell my father we talked, and as usual, I was uncooperative. That answer, he'll understand."

"I'm not leaving here without a commitment from you to move home, P—" He met Felicia's gaze and dropped the nickname. "Fine, Felicia. Tell me about your life here. Make me a true believer in the magic of Idaho.

And your business. You help run this County Seat? What kind of food do you serve? Fast American?"

"We're a farm-to-table restaurant." Angie stepped into the conversation, as she wasn't quite sure how Felicia was going to answer. "It's one of the reasons we opened here. The availability of fresh food is a perfect supply chain. How long are you in town? You should come by the restaurant. Estebe, Felicia's fiancé, is my second-in-command. We have a ton of his recipes on the menu right now."

"Hopefully, I won't be here that long. Felicia, we need to talk about this in private. You know your parents miss you. They're getting older. They need someone to watch over their best interests." He was interrupted by the waitress, who delivered their meals.

After the food was set on the table, Felicia picked up her fork. "Anything you have to say, you can say in front of Angie. I won't be meeting with you again."

Jason started on his prepared lecture. "Your father asked me to try to talk some sense into you. We think it's time you moved home and started a proper job. You can come work under me. I know you and I had our issues as a couple, but maybe after a few years, you'll learn to love me again. Besides, you can't be happy out here in the sticks."

"I love my life here. I hike, camp, hang out with my friends—*real* friends, who aren't paid to be close to me. I knew about Kari and her arrangement with my father. I'm glad she got a full ride at Bryn Mawr just for hanging out with me in high school." Felicia moved the food around her plate with a fork. "The people I hang around with here love me for who I am, not who my parents are or what they can do for them."

"Felicia, be reasonable. You can't marry this guy. He's not from a good family. He's a nobody. He was born in Idaho, for God's sake," Jason blurted out. He met Angie's stare. "No offense."

"What's wrong with being born in Idaho?" Angie asked, not really interested in his reasoning, but now she was very glad she'd ordered the lobster scrambled eggs. If the waitress would ever come back, she'd order the croque monsieur too and have her put it in a to-go box. Maybe she'd order two. She wondered if this place even had to-go boxes.

Then again, Felicia didn't look like she was eating much, and from the way she was staring at Jason, she couldn't stand to be here much longer.

A voice came from behind her. "Felicia is very happy here. You should not be trying to force her to do something she doesn't want to do. She and my cousin will be happy together."

Angie turned around and looked up at Javier Blackstone, Estebe's bad-boy cousin who also ran the tomato farm that supplied the County Seat with a lot of their fresh produce. "Javier, it's fine. Felicia's just talking to an old friend."

"He is not much of a friend if he is pressuring her to break promises she's already made." Javier pointed a finger at Jason. "You should leave before something bad happens to you."

Jason stood. "Is that a threat?"

"No, man, it's a promise."

They stood, staring at each other until a man in a black suit hurried over. "I'm sorry, is there a problem?"

"No. I said what I needed to say." Javier stepped back to the woman who was behind him, watching in fascination. "Let's go, Maria. We can eat somewhere else."

"But I wanted to eat here."

Angie thought the girl was going to stamp her foot, but Javier wasn't watching. "Miss Angie, Miss Felicia, if you are all right here, I will take my leave."

"We're fine, Javier. Thank you for your concern." She met Felicia's gaze. Yep, the drive home was going to be interesting. Maybe they should stop at the Ice Cream Palace and get a treat since breakfast looked like it was going to be called for stormy weather.

After Javier left, Jason pointed to his retreating back. "This guy just proved my point. They're savages here. What are you thinking?"

"I'm thinking that I'm well taken care of, and I've never had an issue with anyone except you since I've lived in Idaho. I'm thinking *you're* the problem here. Maybe your shine hasn't worn off enough for my dad. But I don't want you to feel compelled to stay somewhere so beneath you. I think you should go back to Boston." Felicia finished her orange juice and stood. "Sorry, Angie, I think it's time to leave."

Angie set her empty juice glass down and picked up a croissant that was in the bread basket. She told Jason, "Nice meeting you. Have a safe trip home."

"Felicia, stop. Family means everything. You need to come back with me." He stood and took a step toward her but stopped when Felicia shook her head.

"Angie?" Felicia turned away from Jason and called to her from the hostess stand.

Angie hurried after Felicia and met her at the coat room. "Wow, he's full of himself."

"Jason is only concerned with one thing: Jason." She took the coats from the coat check attendant and handed one to Angie. Then she gave the attendant a twenty-dollar bill. "The problem is my dad hasn't seen the weaknesses in him. My parents were sure we'd be married and Jason would be taking over the company. Now that I ruined that plan, they're having issues turning the company over to someone who they don't see as family. Which is why Carter bugs him so much. Carter is actually my half brother. Long messy story, but I think Dad's just using Jason for his experience, and when the time comes, Carter will be the one to take over the company. It definitely won't be me."

They stepped into the elevator. Angie pushed the garage button and turned toward Felicia. They were alone in the elevator. "Okay, one pressing question."

"Only one? I'm kind of disappointed." Felicia smiled and leaned back. "Hit me, I want to know what has you curious."

"Jason? How in the world were the two of you ever engaged?" Angie watched the numbers light up above the door. She mentally cheered after each one passed by without slowing to pick up new passengers.

"Jason Anderson Roberts told me we were the perfect couple. And what can I say, I was young. He's a tool, but he's good to my dad. So there's that." Felicia stepped out and handed the valet her ticket for the Jeep. "After that meal, I'm just so aware that I dodged a bullet. If I'd married him, I would have been the woman doing shots by noon."

"That wouldn't be a pretty look for you." Angie hugged her friend and hoped she'd seen the last of Jason. One almost meal with the guy was more than enough for one lifetime.

Chapter 3

As they drove back to River Vista, Felicia answered a call on her hands-free Bluetooth. She rolled her eyes at Angie before picking up the call. "Estebe, I'm glad you called. Angie and I are just heading back to the farmhouse."

"I think you should come by the restaurant. You have company waiting for you. I am making lunch for everyone. Bring Angie along. I will feed her as well. I hear you didn't have much of a breakfast at your meeting."

Felicia and Angie shared a look. "I take it Javier already called. I was going to tell you when I got home."

"Meeting an old flame is not an issue. There are many women around who have thought they had claim to me that have been upset since I am off the market. Don't worry so much. Just come here and see your guests. I think you are going to be pleased." He paused. "Barb Travis is here as well. She's entertaining your guests."

"Which is your way of telling me I need to get there faster than normal." Felicia grinned. "Love you, we'll be there in fifteen minutes at the max."

"Ten would be better. Barb is *very* entertaining." Estebe chuckled. "I'll see you soon."

After she hung up, Felicia turned to Angie. "I was going to tell you after the wedding, but we've had some interest from *Boise Foodie* to do a story on the restaurant. I didn't think they'd be out here so quickly. I've heard sometimes it takes months just to get a 'no thank you' when you submit an application. Sorry it's short notice, but I'm pretty sure that's what Estebe was trying to tell me. Barb's always wanted a feature in the magazine, but they rarely do bars. Especially..."

"You can say it, especially dive bars like Barb's. The Red Eye really isn't a tourist draw." Angie checked her makeup in the mirror. "Good thing I keep an extra set of chef whites at the restaurant. I can change into those before they do any photos. I want to look like an up-and-coming chef, not one that doesn't know her stuff."

"I've got some makeup stashed in the office along with a dress that will photograph sharper. I didn't really want to dress up for Jason. He'd just see it as one of the many signs that I was missing him." Felicia negotiated the curve into town. River Vista had been growing, which meant more businesses around, so you didn't have to leave town to shop, but the speed limit dropped as soon as you made the curve. She put her foot on the brake to slow the Jeep. "This thing can fly if you let it. Estebe's such a sweetheart."

"Well, maybe I'll use *your* year-end bonus to get me a new car." Angie snuggled into the warm seat. "I've decided I need heated seats."

Felicia pulled into the lot and parked the car in her spot. She grabbed her tote and hurried toward the back door, locking the car as she went.

Angie ran to keep up. She was excited for the magazine coverage, but she wished Felicia had mentioned that she'd applied for a slot in the upscale magazine. She knew the County Seat was ready for attention like this, but Angie wasn't sure she was. She liked being the new kid in the valley. It gave her some leeway in trying new things. She could make mistakes and learn from experiences. If the County Seat was on the map with the rest of the high-end restaurants in the valley, she'd have to standardize some things just to make sure they kept their rating. Or to get a higher one the next time they were tested. "What's done is done," she said to herself as she was catching up.

Estebe was the only one in the kitchen. He was behind the stove, working on something that smelled amazing. He pointed with his spoon. "They're in the dining room. Hurry before Barb runs them off."

"Barb wouldn't do that," Felicia started; then she shook her head. "You're right, what am I thinking."

Angie followed her into the serving area and almost ran into the back of her friend. "Why did you stop? What's Barb doing?"

Angie glanced around Felicia and saw a conservatively dressed couple who appeared to be in their sixties sitting at a table, studying Barb like she was an errant child, telling a story. "Oh, I was expecting someone... younger. I know, that's ageist of me. Wait, no—I've *met* the columnist for *Boise Foodies*. That's not her. Last time I saw her, she had dyed her hair purple. Who are these people?"

Felicia took in a deep breath and took Angie's arm to drag her along to the table. "Angie Turner, I'd like you to meet my parents, Royce and MaryEllen Williams. Mom, Dad, this is my business partner, Angie."

"It's about time you got here. I've run out of stories to tell your folks about life here in River Vista." Barb stood and hugged Felicia. "You've got yourself one lovely daughter here. I've recently reconnected with my daughter after giving her up for adoption when she was younger. Worst mistake I've ever made."

"Thanks for entertaining them, Barb." Felicia smiled at her. "I'm sure you need to get the bar ready to open."

"Yeah, you're probably right. Bubba will probably be standing at the front door banging to get in. He likes to start early." Barb waved and headed out the front door. "Come by and have a beer before you take off. My treat."

"We can't wait," Mrs. Williams said, then exhaled deeply when Barb disappeared out the door. "I don't know if I could have stood for one more story. Life really isn't that bad out here, is it, pumpkin?"

Felicia slipped into the chair Barb had vacated. "Barb's just colorful. Her life experiences are colorful too. I can't believe you're here. I didn't think you were coming so soon."

"I, we, wouldn't miss your wedding. Besides, we want to meet this young man of yours." Mrs. Williams squeezed Felicia's hand. "Tell us all about him."

Angie frowned as Estebe came out with a tray. He set plates in front of the three who were sitting and then added two more. "My chicken marsala, with a Basque wine substitute. I hope you enjoy. Angie, please sit. I'll take this chair by Felicia."

Mr. Williams blinked at the food. "We really didn't come to eat. We have reservations at the Sandpiper later."

"Then this will be an appetizer. It's good to see you again, Mr. Williams." Estebe held the chair out for Angie, and she sat, meeting Felicia's gaze. "Of course, our food is better than what you'll get there. I'm sure you'll agree."

"So are you the chef here?" Mrs. Williams gave her husband a questioning look, but he shook his head at his wife. She followed his lead, picked up a knife and fork, and cut into the chicken. "This smells divine. All we've had today was a muffin and coffee at the hotel."

"Angie is the chef. I am just her humble servant," Estebe said. "I'm afraid I didn't mention our—"

"I was hoping we could take Felicia somewhere private to chat and have lunch." Mr. Williams interrupted Estebe. Then he shook out his napkin.

"I guess this is as good a place as any. Felicia, not to be rude, but what on earth are you thinking?"

"Mom, Dad." Felicia's voice held a little warning. A bit of ice Angie had never heard her friend use. "Estebe isn't just a chef in the restaurant. He's my fiancé."

* * * *

After a tense lunch, Mr. and Mrs. Williams left, and Felicia promised to meet them the next morning for breakfast. Angie helped Estebe clean the plates as Felicia walked her parents outside to their rented BMW. She glanced up at Estebe and saw the storm clouds in his eyes. "That went well."

"They barely ate. Food is a way to someone's mind, to their heart. They are closed to a relationship between Felicia and me. This makes things difficult. I knew her father didn't approve, but I'd thought maybe he'd change his mind." He put the last plate in the bin. "Never mind, I will clean up the kitchen before I leave. I will see you tomorrow night for service. I think Felicia can drive you home; if not, maybe Ian?"

"I'll find a way home, don't worry." Angie put a hand on his arm. "Felicia loves you. Don't let her family's narrow minds make you question that one ounce."

He smiled and nodded. "You are a good friend, Angie Turner. Thank you for your kind words."

"I don't say things that aren't true." Angie watched him retreat to the kitchen. Felicia was still outside saying goodbye, so Angie stripped the table of linens and went back to the staging area and put the dirty ones in the laundry basket. Then she pulled a clean set of linens and four wineglasses and went out to reset the table.

She'd just finished with the silverware when Felicia came back into the room. She surveyed the new setup and nodded. "Good job, but you didn't have to do that. One dirty table isn't going to slow down the servers setting up tomorrow."

"I know, but I wanted to be busy. Your folks are...nice." Angie tested the word out.

"Really?" She glanced at the kitchen door. "They treated Estebe like he was hired help."

Angie shrugged. "After meeting Jason, I wasn't sure what to expect. Your mom is nice, but she looks to your dad for direction. A lot."

"She's always been that way. Any question I asked would be answered with a maybe. Which meant Dad needed to agree. I'm shocked they're here. I guess they are staying through next Sunday, so they plan to be here for the wedding."

"That's wonderful." Angie clapped her hands, then stopped when Felicia gave her a hard look. "What, am I missing something?"

"They're staying to try to talk me out of it." Felicia closed her eyes. "Typical. Now I have a migraine."

"I hate to mention it, but should I ask Ian to drive me home?" Angie nodded to the kitchen. "Estebe is a little distracted."

"I'm surprised he's not in here demanding his ring back after the way my parents treated him." She walked over to the counter where she'd left her purse. She held out the keys. "Take the Jeep home. You can bring it back tomorrow."

"I thought you were meeting your folks for breakfast." Angie didn't reach for the keys. "Do you need me to come in early?"

"Estebe will come with me." She nodded to the kitchen. "They all need to learn to get along. And Estebe and I are a package deal now, no matter what they want. Besides, I have a feeling they're going to try to ambush me with Jason. I need some backup here, and I can't keep dragging you all over the valley to protect me from my past."

Angie finally reached for the keys. "Okay, but I promise to not let Dom joyride in it. He'll drool all over your pretty leather."

Felicia smiled. "Maybe I need my own Dom after Estebe and I tie the knot. His house and land are big enough for a flock of Doms."

"I'm not sure they're a flock. Herd might be a better grouping name. Like a herd of buffalo." Angie leaned over and hugged her friend. "We'll get you through this. In a little over a week, you'll be Mrs. Estebe Blackstone. And then you're his problem."

"Thanks for your support, I think." Felicia laughed.

They walked into the kitchen, where the dishwasher was running and Estebe was in the walk-in. Angie glanced at the open walk-in door and nodded to Felicia. "I'll see you both tomorrow. Bye, Estebe," she called out as she left the kitchen. She didn't hear a response.

Angie opened the Jeep doors and climbed inside. It was high. Felicia was taller than Angie; Angie had to pull herself up into the driver's seat. She started it up, said a prayer for a safe drive home, and backed out of the lot. She drove down the street, surprised at the number of people who waved then realized it wasn't Felicia behind the wheel. Angie waved back, but she was sure Felicia would get a few calls checking in to see if Angie had permission to be driving her brand-new car around town.

When she got home and inside the house, she checked twice to make sure the car was locked. Dom watched her from his bed with suspicion. "What? We don't want anyone taking off with Aunt Felicia's new car. Not on my watch, do we?"

He barked and then settled back into his bed. He wasn't done with his midday nap. The dog had priorities. Angie went into the living room and turned on the television. She found a movie channel that ran old movies and sat with a cup of cocoa to think. Felicia's parents might be able to cause hurt feelings while they were here, but she didn't think they'd be able to break up the couple. Not in a week. Heck, not in a month.

Her cell rang, and she realized it was still in her purse. She ran into the kitchen to grab it before it stopped ringing, but failed. She looked at the missed calls and realized Ian had called three times. She hit his number, and he picked up on the first ring. "Hey, sorry about that. My phone was in my purse."

"I was starting to get worried. I talked to Barb, and she told me Felicia's folks were in town. I thought maybe they'd kidnapped the both of you and sent you to a brainwashing clinic in Arizona." He paused before asking, "Is she all right?"

"She's hurt. They talk to her like she's a child who doesn't understand what she's doing. And they talked down to Estebe during the meal, speaking slowly and enunciating every word. It was painful to watch." She refilled her cocoa cup and went back into the living room to sit down. She muted the television. "Tell me your day went better."

"Not much. Angry farmers about a potential rise in booth fees from the board. Who knew five dollars could make or break a season? And neither side wants to move a penny." He sighed. "I know it's Tuesday and you're home, but I need to work tonight. We have a board meeting tomorrow, and I want to run new numbers on lowering the increase."

"No worries. I think I'm reheating something and watching television with Dom." She thought about the Jeep in the driveway. "One good thing, Felicia let me drive Lucy home."

"Lucy? She called her Jeep Lucy?"

"Yep, and she's a dream ride. If I wasn't so short, I'd think about getting a lower-cost model."

"Don't be thinking I can keep you in gifts like Estebe keeps Felicia. Remember, I'm fighting for five dollars."

She laughed, and it felt good. They were on the same wavelength. Now, all she had to hope was his mom liked her. "No worries. I can buy my own car."

"I like an independent woman." A beep sounded over the phone. "Sorry, I've got to go. I'll stop in for dinner tomorrow night, and you can feed your indigent boyfriend."

"You're not indigent. You're a do-gooder. Those types of guys never make money." She said her goodbyes and set the phone down on the table. Dom looked up as if to say, is everything all right?

"That was your buddy Ian. He's not coming by tonight because he has homework." She watched as he dropped his head. He wasn't happy with her or Ian. But she was the one who was here to get his frustration. She leaned back and sipped her cocoa.

Felicia had some roadblocks trying to keep her from going down the road to happy ever after. The only thing they didn't realize was she was an excellent driver, and she had a plan.

A car pulled up in the driveway about nine that night. Angie had just finished washing dishes and was folding laundry. Not an exciting activity, but one that gave her comfort. And she'd thought she'd had enough excitement for one day. She looked out and saw Estebe's Hummer.

She unlocked the door and left it open a bit. She filled up the coffeepot with water and coffee but waited to start it. Estebe and Felicia came through the door.

"Hey, guys, do we need coffee?"

Felicia looked at Estebe, and he nodded. "That would be nice, Angie. We came to get Felicia's car, as she'll be needing it tomorrow to meet with her parents."

"I thought you were going with her?" Angie pushed the button on the coffeemaker, then went to her purse to grab the keys. She set them in front of Felicia and went to pull cookies out of the cookie jar. "What made you change your mind? I thought it was a good plan."

Felicia took a napkin and set a chocolate chip cookie on top of it. Then she looked at Angie. "We're not meeting for breakfast. We're meeting at the police station. Someone shot Jason. Angie, he's dead."

Chapter 4

Wednesday morning, Angie sat at her kitchen table watching the news for any mention of Jason's death. She felt bad she'd had such a negative reaction to the man now that he was dead, but on the other hand, his death might have been a result of his bad attitude. Of course, that didn't give anyone the right to kill another person, but Angie had to be honest—she could list a few that should be on the list if the law was changed. When the morning edition turned to local sports, she turned off the small television she kept in the kitchen and focused on her weekly plan.

The County Seat would be open tonight through Saturday, then closed all next week for the wedding events. Normally, she wouldn't think of closing for an entire week, but with most of the kitchen crew part of the wedding party, it made it hard to open the restaurant anyway without hiring a ton of temporary help. And without either her or Estebe in the kitchen, Nancy would be next in line, and she was one of Felicia's bridesmaids. Closing completely was more practical and kept the standards up where she wanted them. Especially with Felicia throwing the County Seat's proverbial hat into the mix for a *Boise Foodie* review.

No, even with the loss of income, this was a better alternative.

She started making plans for the closure, including trying to cost out if they could pay a salary to the full-time employees even though they weren't open. After an hour or so of manipulating numbers, she had a plan to take to Felicia tonight.

Last night before they'd left, Felicia said she'd call when she got back from meeting with her parents. Angie hoped they wouldn't put any pressure or guilt on her because of Jason's death. But from the short time Angie had spent with the Williamses, she didn't hold out hope.

She glanced around the kitchen, and her stomach growled. Pulling out one of her grandmother's cookbooks, she flipped through it until she found a recipe she wanted to play with. Then she tied on an apron, washed her hands, and got lost in the magic that is cooking.

By noon, she was sitting down to a spring stir-fry that she thought she might bring to a family meal next month to see if the recipe was strong enough to get a trial place on the menu. She opened the book she'd been reading last night and got lost in the story while she ate.

When she finished, she just had time to get the kitchen cleaned up before she needed to feed Precious and Mabel. On workdays, she fed them as soon as she got up and then just before she got ready to leave for the restaurant. And with the days being shorter, they went to sleep earlier than in the summer when they could graze the pasture for an evening snack if they were hungry. Having animals was a responsibility, but she enjoyed spending time with them. Especially Precious.

The goat bleated a greeting, then looked around Angie to see if Dom had ventured out into the barn as well. Precious liked Dom. Dom, on the other hand, didn't think much of the now adult goat Angie had brought home from a trail walk. "Hey, girl, it's just me today."

She got the food down and fed Mabel first. The hen was old and moved slower these days, but she still seemed to get around without any pain, so Angie was happy for that. Mabel was the last of Nona's hens, and losing her would be hard. She filled the water dish by the doorway and then filled a can with the goat feed. Precious had been watching, and when she saw Angie bringing the food over, she made three circles in her pen and then came back to the fence to poke her head through the slats. The vet had dehorned her when she was a baby, a process Angie had felt uncomfortable about, but Ian had insisted. The lack of horns made it harder for the curious goat to get stuck in the fence line, which was a blessing. Angie poured the food into the bin and turned on the faucet that filled her water trough. She knelt beside the fence to stroke the goat's back as she ate.

"Hey, how have you been today? It's a workday for me, so I'll be heading into town. If anything happens, I'll call Ian and have him come rescue you. But you have to be responsible."

The hen clucked her disbelief that the goat could even know the word *responsible*, which made Angie laugh.

"I know the two of you can't really understand what I'm saying, but sometimes, you make me feel like you can." She gave Precious one last rub and turned off the water. "I'll see you both in the morning. Stay warm tonight, Mabel."

She shut the barn door and headed back to the house to get ready. She'd left her phone on the table, but when she checked for a call, there was nothing. Felicia was probably on her way back into town. She'd talk to her when she got to the restaurant. She said a prayer of comfort for her friend and went to get ready.

An hour later, she pulled into the lot. Felicia's Jeep wasn't in her spot. Estebe's Hummer was there as she parked and went inside. The kitchen was already filled with good smells, indicating that Estebe had been there for a few hours, not just a few minutes. He wasn't in the kitchen when she entered. She paused at the stove where a warm stew bubbled in a pot. The man made excellent soups and stews. She took out a tasting spoon and took a small bite. "Yum." The word fell out of her mouth without thinking.

"I also made sheepherders bread to go along with the stew. I thought it could be a special tonight." Estebe stood in front of her, a pile of clean towels in his hands. He went and stocked the cooking area behind the stoves. "Do you want me to make you a bowl? Did you eat?"

"I was upset; of course I cooked and ate. But I could have a small bowl to tide me over through service." She pulled out the recipe card she'd made for the stir-fry. "I'm thinking about presenting this at the family meal. Can you make it one night and let me know what you think? Or are you too busy?"

"I am like you. When I have things on my mind, I cook. I will try it. You should also give a copy to Nancy. She needs to start expanding her role here at the restaurant." He tucked the card into the pocket on his chef coat. "I will eat with you."

"Let me drop this off in my office, and I'll be back. I'll make a copy of the card I made for myself, and I'll give it to Nancy. That's a good call. Now that her ex is out of the picture, again, she has a little more free time to take on some more responsibility here." Angie headed out of the kitchen and into her office. She grabbed two bottles of beer from the bar and headed back inside. She set them on the table before sitting down herself. "I have a feeling you might need one of these while we eat."

"The world is a hard place. If I drank every time I was sad, I wouldn't be able to stand up most days." He set a small loaf of bread on the table with a pat of butter, slicing the loaf before he sat down. The soup was already on the table. He opened the twist-off caps and handed a beer to her. "But today, I will make an exception. Thank you, Angie Turner, for being an amazing boss and a good friend. I was afraid when I took this job that I would be gone in a few weeks. Most people don't get my sense of humor."

"I don't think it's your humor that loses you jobs." Angie grinned, thinking of Estebe's past issues with anger in the kitchen. Especially when things weren't cooked to his standards. "But I'll let that slide."

"You have softened my rough edges." He smiled as he lifted the beer bottle in a toast to her. "You and my lovely Felicia. I am worried that this morning did not go well for her. She hasn't called me yet."

Just then a text came over Angie's phone. She picked it up and read it. "She's on her way."

"Yet she texted instead of calling. She is hurting and doesn't want us to see it. I will get her something to eat when she gets here. That should ease her pain, at least a little." He glanced at the clock.

"Don't focus on the time. She'll be here when she can. And just a heads-up, Felicia doesn't eat real food when she's upset; she bakes and eats sweets."

Estebe stood and went back to the kitchen. He brought out a pan of apple cobbler crisp. "I do know the woman I'm going to marry. There's even ice cream in the freezer."

When Felicia arrived, Estebe set the soup, bread, crisp, and ice cream in front of her. As Angie had predicted, she dumped the ice cream on the crisp, then dug in. "This would be better if we kept it in a warming oven tonight so the ice cream melts over the top when it's served."

"I'm having Matt make fresh ones every hour when service starts. He needs practice on his pastry chef skills." Estebe watched Felicia eat. "Do you want to talk about this morning?"

"No," she said quickly. Then she took a bite of the stew. "Probably I should, though."

"Do what you want. No pressure." Angie took a slice of bread and buttered it.

"Carter has already arrived. Mom's furious, but she's not talking about it. Carter is a love child from Dad and his first secretary. Mom's never forgiven Dad *or* Carter for that indiscretion. Of course, it's hard when he's a living, breathing reminder. Carter's nice, but I see why it's tough for her." Felicia took another bite of the stew. "Anyway, Carter's handling all the press and police discussions. He's an attorney. He's actually Dad's attorney, so him being here makes sense. I don't know who the police think did this, but the questions they asked me were all focused on yesterday's breakfast and my past relationship with Jason. They asked about you, Estebe. Asked if you were upset that my old flame was in town. I think you're going to be questioned."

"After the stunt Javier pulled yesterday by confronting Jason, I was already expecting it. I'm having my attorney make inquiries." He shook his head. "Do not worry. I did nothing wrong. They can't say that I did."

A knock came at the back door, and Estebe frowned. "Maybe Nancy forgot her keys."

He walked over, and two men in suits came inside, followed by two Boise police officers. One man showed his badge, then put it back in his suit pocket. "Estebe Blackstone?"

"Yes."

"We need you to come downtown and answer some questions about the death of Jason Anderson Roberts. Please come with us." The man turned toward the door.

"I am preparing for our dinner service. Can't this wait until tomorrow morning? I would come in on my own then." Estebe glanced over at Angie and Felicia, who had come to stand beside him.

"I'm sorry, but no, we need you now. It shouldn't take long." The detective held out an arm to direct Estebe to the door.

"Please wait a second." He turned toward Felicia. "Call my attorney. I left his name and number on a notebook on the table. Have him meet me downtown. Angie, please call in a temp to help with dinner. We have a full seating tonight. You may want to have him come tomorrow night as well."

"Surely you'll be done by then," Angie said; then she nodded. "Okay. Just be safe."

He smiled. "I will not let my humor get the best of me."

"Are you ready?" The detective glanced from Estebe to Angie and Felicia.

"Can you get my coat?" He nodded to the rack by the door. "The leather one. Please take out my keys and give them to Felicia. Someone will have to come get me when I call."

The police officer closest to the coatrack reached for the only coat there, then pulled out the keys. Estebe's wallet was also in the coat. "What about this?"

"I don't need that. Give the wallet to Felicia as well." He leaned closer to her and kissed her gently on the lips. "I'll see you soon."

As they left, Felicia stood watching the door. Angie took her arm and moved her toward the table. "We need to get busy. Estebe needs our help."

"I have a bad feeling about this. If this is my family pulling out all the stops to keep me from getting married, I'm going to be furious. I can get them being upset, but framing Estebe? I may never talk to my family again." She moved to the table and found the notebook. "And the worst part? He expected this. I never would have guessed, but Estebe was prepared for this situation."

Angie watched her dial the number, then left the kitchen to go to her office and make her own calls. She called the temp agency and luckily got a woman to come who'd worked for her before. Hallie was fun to be around and an excellent chef. Not quite up to Estebe's level, but she would keep the crew going for a couple of days. Especially if the mood was affected by Estebe's situation.

She also called Nancy Gowan, one of her line cooks, and asked if she could come in early to help with prep.

"Of course," Nancy answered quickly. "Let me call Matt and Hope too. We'll get through this and get Estebe back in the kitchen before you can even miss him."

Angie hoped Nancy's optimism was predictive. Of course, since Estebe didn't kill Jason, they couldn't really charge him with anything, could they? She picked up the phone one more time and hoped she'd get an answer.

"Chief Brown, how can I help you?"

Angie sighed in relief. He'd picked up. "Hi, Allen, it's Angie. Wait, you have my number in your contacts. You knew it was me. Why the formality?"

"Yes, I'm aware of the situation. In fact, I'm down at the county station right now getting ready to go over the case file. I'll have to call you back when I'm on my way back into town. Will you be available then?"

Angie tried to put all the clues he was giving her together. He knew Estebe had been brought in for questioning, and he was checking out the situation. "I've got to get prep ready for tonight's service, but I'll have my phone on me. Thanks, Allen. I appreciate your help."

"No problem at all. I'm happy to help out a member of the River Vista community. I'm sure we can count on your support during the Christmas toy drive." And with that, Allen Brown, police chief of River Vista and Ian's uncle, ended the call.

She tucked her phone into her chef whites and tied up her hair. It was time to stop worrying about things she couldn't control and handle the things she could. Like feeding people. Tonight's service was totally booked, and after word got out about Estebe being questioned, the rest of the week would fill up fast. People loved gossip, and coming to the County Seat would give them a front row seat.

Felicia was just hanging up when Angie came back into the kitchen. She glanced at the clock. "I've got an hour before my servers show, can you put me to work?"

"Of course. I've got a temp, and Nancy's pulling in the rest of the team to come in early. I also talked with Allen. He's at the police station now checking out the situation." Angie found the prep notebook and laughed after she opened it. "Estebe has already set up what we need to do for today's and tomorrow's menu. The guy was prepared for this."

"More than you know." Felicia washed her hands, then pulled on one of the extra chef coats they kept in the closet. "His lawyer is not only already down there to participate in the interview, he hired a private detective to check into Jason. I guess there might be someone who had words with him Monday night at the bar when he arrived in town. This guy is serious about keeping Estebe out of jail."

"Which is a good thing, right?" Angie handed Felicia part of the list Estebe had already made of prep items.

Felicia nodded, her face tight and a worry line creasing her brow between her eyes. "I'm just a little concerned that Estebe started this look into Jason before his death. The lawyer said they've been working on this since Tuesday morning."

Angie knew that look. "He probably wanted to be prepared for anything after Javier got into a shouting match with him at the restaurant. You know Javier is a hothead. If something had happened, he'd be the first one they'd look at."

"The second one," Felicia corrected.

Angie paused on the way to the walk-in to get out a bin of vegetables to clean and chop. "I'm sorry, what?"

"Something did happen. Jason is dead, and Javier isn't being questioned about it. Estebe is." Felicia leaned against the counter and stared at Angie. "Oh my God, Angie. Is it possible that Estebe did something to Jason?"

Chapter 5

After assuring Felicia that her fiancé could no more hurt Jason than he could a fly, Angie and Felicia started cooking. She could see Felicia's mind easing as she focused on the tasks in front of her rather than Estebe's current situation. As she'd expected, the phone started ringing off the hook, and the few reservations that were left for the week were quickly filled.

Bleak Hubbard, their hostess, had come in early and dealt with the reservations. Now that the servers were setting up the dining room, she was in the kitchen talking to her friend and Angie's newest chef, Hope Anderson. Bleak had a bowl of Estebe's stew in her hand as she leaned against the counter, waiting for Hope to come back from the walk-in. "Angie, we're booked through the next week too. Not next, next week, since we're closed, but the week after. I'm setting up reservations into April's calendar. Anything I need to know about dates? Are they all open?"

"One could only hope," Angie muttered, but then she paused, thinking. "Go find Felicia and see when they're getting back from the honeymoon. We may need to limit seating that first week."

Hallie held up a hand. "Angie, if you need me, I'm not booked in April at all. This is a slow period for part-time chef gigs. Now, summer, I'll be working all the time, but man, the pickings are slow in the winter, early spring."

"Good to know. Bleak, don't bother Felicia. We'll run a full service through the month of April. Hallie, I'll call your temp agency and have you assigned to us until then. After that, we'll reassess. If you're looking for something a little more permanent, maybe we can talk. Summer is always crazy around here." Angie glanced at the prep list. "If you all are okay finishing this up, I'm going to check the office and make sure we're set for the week."

As she left the kitchen, she tried not to run. Having Estebe out for a couple of days was one thing. Figuring out what they'd do without him if he was actually charged would be something else entirely. She'd been strong when she'd told Felicia not to worry. That Estebe wouldn't do something like this, but the man did have a temper. And if Jason had threatened Felicia at all? Who knows how Estebe would have reacted?

She closed her door and hung her jacket on the hook, just in case she got called back in. She'd need to expedite tonight, but that wasn't anything new. It was her normal job. She hadn't heard from Allen yet, and the longer it took for him to call her back, the more worried she'd gotten.

A knock at her door had her lifting her head off her hands, where she'd been for longer than she wanted to think about. "Yes? Come in."

Ian came in and closed the door behind him. "Sorry I'm late. I had to run to Boise to pick up one of your chefs."

"You got Estebe?" Angie felt her face and her mood lift. "They let him go?"

"Of course they did. He didn't kill anyone. And you know it." Ian sat in the chair next to the desk. He took a drink of a soda. "And he had his ducks in order. He was with his parents at a restaurant for an early dinner on Tuesday; then they went to the community center, where he helped serve drinks for bingo for over a hundred people. Unless the man could be in two places at once, he's covered."

Angie slumped in her chair. "I didn't think he could do it, but you know his temper. He has a reputation of being a hothead. I almost didn't hire him because of it."

"Have you ever seen him mad? Really mad?"

Angie tried to think back. "Actually, I don't think so. He's been arrogant. He was a know-it-all when he first came to work for me, but he never snapped at the other cooks. I just heard rumors."

"And you know that nothing flies as fast as rumors around here. You would think we were a small town instead of as big as Boise and the surrounding areas are now." He paused. "My uncle apologizes for not calling back, but there was a break-in at the high school that he had to go handle."

A quick knock on the door and Bleak stuck her head in. "Oh, hi, Ian. Angie, I'm supposed to ask if you're expediting tonight?"

"Tell Nancy I'll be right in. Ian, do you want to eat at the bar or in here?" She reached for her chef jacket.

He stood to follow Bleak out to the dining room. "I'll eat at the bar. I've been doing numbers alone for way too long this week. It will be nice to chat with Jeorge for a bit while I eat."

"Bleak, get him a menu." Angie slipped on her coat. "Time to make the donuts."

Bleak turned around and grinned. "We're having donuts? Save me one."

As she disappeared into the dining room, Ian laughed. "She's too young to get the reference. Now she's going to be disappointed."

Angie just shook her head and started for the kitchen.

* * * *

Allen Brown was sitting with Ian when Angie finally came out of the kitchen after service that night. He held up a fork. "This meatloaf is amazing. Don't tell Maggie."

"Maggie can have the recipe anytime she wants it. Jeorge, can you get me a club soda with lime?" Angie slipped onto a stool next to Ian. "Did you find the culprits?"

"From the high school? Unfortunately, yes. The mayor's son and his hoodlum friends were trying to figure out what to write on the gym wall. They were arguing about the spelling of 'sucks' when I walked in." He focused on the mashed potatoes. "His friend swore it was spelled with an *x*. They'd come to blows about it."

"Sounds like remedial English should be part of the punishment." Angie sipped the drink. She was always so dehydrated after a service. She needed to start drinking more water during service rather than waiting until she was done. "What did you find out about Jason's killing? Any suspects now that Estebe's off the list?"

"He's not quite off the list. The new theory is he hired someone. His lawyer's working on getting that one debunked. I don't know what he did to this detective, but he really doesn't like Estebe." Allen's gaze went over Angie's shoulder. "There's the man of the hour himself."

Jeorge pulled out a large bottle of water and handed it to Estebe without comment or being asked.

He took the bottle, opened it, then pulled out a stool to sit closer to the other three. "Roland went to school with me at Bishop Kelly. He tried out for football all four years but never was put on the team. That is only one of the long list of grievances he has against me."

"You didn't pick the team, the coach did," Ian pointed out.

Estebe smiled a little. “The little weasel thought he’d frame me for cheating. Then he could take my place during sophomore year. I retook the test with all new questions on the spot and still aced it. My interest in American history is a little obsessive. He was given detention, and I went on to win the championship game that year. He’s still a little bitter.”

“I’m just glad you’re back.” Angie lifted her glass. “To Estebe, thank you for being part of our team and our family.”

The others lifted their glasses.

Allen sipped his coffee. “I’m afraid this Roland doesn’t give up. He’s like a dog with a bone, so make sure your lawyer keeps on him. He’s known to be a little less than scrupulous with his investigation techniques.”

“I did not kill this man. I am not to blame for his death.” Estebe sipped his water. “But I will heed your warning. Angie, I see you pulled in Hallie to work tonight.”

“She’s a good chef. I was happy to see she was available.” Something about Estebe’s tone had Angie wary. “Is there a problem? I told her we might use her until the end of April. That won’t be a problem, will it?”

“Hallie and I have worked together before. She asked me out several times, but I turned her down. I was not interested then or now. I’m hoping she is over the issue, but sometimes the heart holds on to the wrong thing for too long.” He glanced at the kitchen. “I sent her home when service ended. Nancy and Matt are doing the cleanup. I will talk to her tomorrow and make sure everything is clear and she understands my current commitment. I would hate to hurt Felicia or Hallie because of a misunderstanding.”

Angie smiled. Sometimes Estebe’s machismo poked through. “I’m sure she’s not carrying a torch, but yes, if you could talk to her, that would be appreciated. If I need to get someone else for next month, I’d rather know early.”

“Now that that’s settled, I am checking on Matt and Nancy, kissing my future bride good night, and heading to my house. I’m beat. Being questioned all day is surprisingly tiring.” He shook Ian’s hand. “Thanks for the ride home. I appreciate you fitting me into your day.”

“No problem. I’d say anytime, but let’s hope you’re not going to need a ride from the police station again.” He stood and slapped Estebe on the back. “Go home. You look beat on your feet.”

After Estebe left, Bleak came over, finished with her shift. Allen said his goodbyes along with something about Bleak’s math homework, and then it was just Angie and Ian. Jeorge had cashed out the till and left right after Allen. Ian leaned against the bar and looked around the empty restaurant. "I feel bad for Estebe. He wants to be sympathetic to Felicia, but on the other hand, this guy was here to break them up. I'd be mad too."

"But she wasn't interested. And she'd already handled it. No one can blame Estebe for his protective feelings, but Felicia didn't need saving. I just don't understand who would have killed Jason. Besides anyone who'd ever met him. I swear, he was a total jerk." Angie finished her water and leaned over to get the gun to refill her glass. "He just oozed privilege. And come to think of it, he didn't like Felicia's half brother very much."

Ian held up a hand. "Wait, Felicia has a half brother?"

Angie explained the situation and then drained her glass. "I'm grabbing my stuff and checking in with the kitchen. Then I'm heading home. Will I see you tomorrow?"

"Probably. I'm interested in seeing how this turns out. And I need to keep your naturally strong investigation habits in check." He stood and kissed her on the cheek. "I'll walk you out. I'll be in the kitchen."

"I'll just be a minute." Angie rubbed her eyes. "I'm going to drive with the music blaring and the windows down just to stay awake."

"Call me if you get sleepy. I'll talk you through it." He brushed a crumb off her chef jacket.

"I will, but I want to think about Jason and what could have happened to him. I know your uncle doesn't like me getting involved, but if this detective really has Estebe in his sights, I think we should do something, right?" Angie stared out into the night through the restaurant's windows. A chill ran up her arms, and she rubbed them without thinking. "There is no way Estebe could have killed that man, and I'm going to prove it."

"You're going to get yourself in a situation where you're going to get hurt," Ian corrected her. "Look, I know you like Estebe, but for once, could you just let law enforcement do its job? You're a cook, for gosh sakes, not some television crime fighter. And this isn't a fictional little town where everyone's on your side. There are bad people out there, Angie. And one of them killed this Jason guy. I don't think he'd hesitate to kill you if you got too close."

"Fine, Ian. I'll just pretend my best chef and friend isn't in trouble, and I'll be the happy cook ignoring real life and real problems." She headed to her office. "And don't worry about walking me to my car. I'm sure I can ignore any 'bad' guys for the few feet from the door."

"Angie, don't be mad," Ian called after her.

She held up a hand, stopping him from following her. If Ian really thought she was too stupid to know better than to get in some killer's line of sight, he didn't know her very well. And if he thought she was just going to let

Estebe be railroaded into a jail cell by a kid from high school who didn't like him, he *really* didn't know her very well.

She grabbed a bottle of water from the fridge in the staging area and retrieved her coat and purse from her office. Locking it after her, she hurried into the kitchen.

Nancy looked up from where she'd been cleaning the stove and froze. "Angie, are you all right? Your face is beet red."

Angie put the water bottle up to her cheek to cool off some of the anger. "I'm fine. You guys okay? If so, I'm heading home. Big day tomorrow."

"We're good." Nancy glanced over at Matt, who was cleaning the flat top. "If slowpoke would hurry up, we could get out of here and I could go home to my kids. I'm sure the younger ones are fighting Elna about bedtime. It's a nightly ritual lately."

"Well, hurry and go home, then." Angie paused. "How did Hallie do tonight?"

"She was awesome. She's sharp, easy to direct, and a fast worker." Nancy paused from her cleaning. "She did say she and Estebe had history. Is that why you're asking?"

"Yeah, maybe. I hope she can put whatever feelings she had for him away if she wants to stay on. I like her, but Estebe thinks she's hanging on a bit." Angie got her keys out of her tote. "I don't want to have any drama in the kitchen. We've grown too close for that."

"From what she told me, she's aware of the engagement and happy for him. So maybe he's just overthinking it. You know how literal he can be at times."

Relief filled Angie at Nancy's evaluation of the situation. Having Hallie around for at least the month would fill some holes and give them time to get prepared for their busy season. And if she fit into the group, that would make it even easier to get through the next three months. "I'm glad to hear that. See you all tomorrow. Are you coming in early for prep?"

Nancy nodded. "Estebe's a little concerned that he might be called for a second interview, so he asked for both Matt and me to come in early. I hope that's all right with the schedule."

"Of course. Whatever we need to do to get through this week is what we need to do." Angie waved and headed out to her car. She started the engine remotely and then got into the driver's seat. Locking the doors once she was inside, she opened her water bottle before pulling out of the parking lot. Her phone buzzed, but when she saw it was Ian, she let the call go to voice mail. She didn't want to talk to him. Not right now. Even if he was apologizing for upsetting her, she still was mad and didn't want to continue the conversation *or* the fight.

Angie pulled the car out of the parking lot and made her way through the two blocks out of town and onto the country road that would take her home to the farmhouse. As she drove, she thought about Jason and his motives for being in Boise.

He'd wanted to get Felicia to break off the engagement. He clearly thought if he snapped his fingers, Felicia would come running back to him. When that hadn't happened, what would have been his next step? Looking into Estebe? Trying to get some dirt on him that Felicia didn't know about? Maybe he questioned some of the people who hung out at the community center. Would any of them say a bad thing about Estebe? Maybe someone there had a grudge.

Angie thought about the bars near the Basque community center. Most of them were preppy and focused on the college crowd just down the road from Boise State. You could walk from what used to be the girls' dorms to a lot of the bars in the same area as the community center. But there were a few that were old-time dive bars. Just on the fringe of the area. Closer to the freeway than the college. If she was looking for a working-class bar in the area, where would she go?

The Vista Bar and Grill popped into her mind. She'd gone there when she'd attended BSU, but they hadn't stayed long. The regulars didn't like strangers in their bar. At least not college-aged know-it-alls. She glanced at the clock then instead of turning left to go toward home, she turned right. By the time she reached the bar, it would be close to midnight. She'd chat up the bartender, see what he or she knew, then head home. With any luck, she'd be in bed by one at the latest.

She wasn't expected in the restaurant until three. She could sleep until nine and still get her eight hours in. There was really no reason not to check out her theory. Well, besides being in a strange bar an hour away from home on a worknight. Alone.

She chose not to acknowledge that maybe this was the kind of behavior Ian was worried about.

She thought about Dom sleeping in his kitchen bed, waiting for her. Then she thought of Estebe standing in a jail cell for something he didn't do. As soon as she left the city limits, she pushed on the gas. In and out. That was the plan. "I'll be home soon, boy," she whispered toward the house. "I've just got to make one stop first."

Chapter 6

Walking into the bar, Angie decided she'd made a good choice. It was filled with working-class people. No crazy disco patterns on the clothes or on the bar. Neon signs lit the room, and the two pool tables were in use. People gathered around the dart boards laughing and playing too. This was not a bar where the sole purpose was to be seen and network with other business types. This was a fun, drinking bar. She sat on a stool, and the bartender slid over to her. "Coffee, please."

"So what's Angie Turner doing in Boise at this time of night? Meeting someone?" the young man asked as he poured a cup of coffee and set it in front of her.

Angie noticed a name tag. "Tracy. I guess I know you, or do you just know me?"

"I subbed in for Jeorge in July when he went to California to help his brother for a few days." He scanned the bar, but no one seemed to need anything, so he poured his own cup of coffee. "You were only there on Wednesday; then you went out for a vacation too. I enjoyed serving at your place. I'm looking for a more upscale position. This is fine, for now. At least I don't have to deal with the college frats here. I think they're scared of my regulars."

"And that's why I'm here." Angie sipped her coffee. Not a bad brew, and it hadn't been sitting for hours.

"The college crew?" Tracy frowned. "I don't understand."

"No, I'm looking for any information on anyone who might have a grudge against my sous chef, Estebe Blackstone?" Angie figured if Tracy had known her, he would know Estebe. "Maybe you have people from the Basque community center that come in here?"

He shook his head. "Those guys drink there. I guess you didn't know they have their own bar in the building. I tried getting on with them last year, but they only hire people who have a connection to the heritage. Unfortunately, my ancestors came from South Dakota."

"I didn't think they could hire that way?"

"They claim to be open, which is how I got the interview, but the references killed me." He shrugged. "It's fine. I make good money here. But if Jeorge ever leaves or you hear of an opening somewhere, I'd love a heads-up."

"Okay, I guess that's all I need to know." She opened her wallet, but Tracy shook his head.

"Don't worry about it. I can buy you a cup of coffee."

She smiled and put her wallet away and stood.

"Aren't you a pretty little thing." A whiskey-laden breath came on her left side. "Why don't you let me buy you a real drink?"

"No thanks, I'm on my way out." She glanced over toward Tracy to see if she could get some help, but he'd left and was at the other end of the bar, filling shot glasses for what must have been the winning dart team.

"Sit down and drink with me. You can't just show up and leave. We don't get a lot of women who look like you around here. What will you have?" He put a hand on her shoulder, pinning her to her stool.

The guy was strong, Angie could tell that. She'd just wait it out and he'd leave her be. "I really have a long way to drive home. I can't be drinking."

"Well, I've got a solution to that. You can come home with me." He moved closer to the bar, and his body enveloped her.

A kiss from her other side that hit half on her cheek and half on her lips made her turn away from the whiskey guy to see what new man was invading her space.

She was looking into Javier's face. He winked at her.

"I'm so sorry I'm late, dear heart." He pulled her off the stool and into a hug next to his body and away from the other guy. "Who's your friend?"

"Actually, I didn't get his name. He was kind enough to offer to buy me a drink, but I told him we were leaving soon and driving home." Angie leaned into Javier and met the other guy's gaze. "This is my boyfriend."

"Whatever." The guy moved around them and bumped into Javier's shoulder, trying to get a reaction.

"Have a nice night," Javier called after him as whiskey guy made his way toward Tracy and the shot the bartender had just poured and was holding up to get his attention.

Tracy nodded toward the door, and Angie got his point. "We need to leave, now."

"I'll walk you to your car. I just stopped in for a quick drink, but I think I'll let my friends know I'll meet them another time." He put his arm around her and led her to the door.

When they were outside and next to Angie's car, she took a deep breath and dug for her keys. "Thanks for the assist back there. I was afraid I was going to have to fight my way out."

"You're not built to be a fighter." He narrowed his eyes. "Why are you here, and where is Ian? It seems like we're running into each other a lot the last few days."

"I wanted to see if anyone here had a beef with Estebe." Angie got into her car and turned on the engine and the heat to take the chill off her. It had been a close call. She had been foolish to just show up at a bar near closing time alone. It sent the wrong message to the inebriated.

"Okay, but why here?" Javier looked confused. "I don't get it."

"I thought maybe some of the Basque guys came here. I didn't know they had their own private bar." She rubbed her face. "Can we talk later about this? I need to get home before the adrenaline wears off."

"May I call you tomorrow? I'd like to talk more about your theory on who killed Felicia's friend. I'm afraid Estebe is being typecast into a prison cell." He shut her door and nodded to the road.

Angie rolled down her window. "Call me tomorrow. And you need to get out of here before the whiskey guy gets some friends behind him." She put the car in gear and watched in her rearview as Javier hurried to his truck. He'd taken her suggestion. She pulled out onto the almost deserted street and headed to the freeway.

She had a lot of time to think before she arrived home. And she spent the entire trip thinking on why someone would kill Jason.

* * * *

The phone rang at nine on the dot. She grabbed the cell from her bedside and croaked, "Hello?"

"What you did last night was dangerous." Estebe's voice echoed in her ears. "I cannot understand your motives. If Javier hadn't been there..."

"Hold on, if Javier hadn't been there, I would have gotten out of there with the help of the bartender. I wasn't in danger. Your cousin shouldn't have called you and ratted me out." That discussion she would have with Javier the next time she saw him. "I'm not a delicate flower."

"That is true." Estebe chuckled and lowered his tone. "However, you are putting yourself in danger to help me when I have the situation under control."

"If that were true, you wouldn't need an attorney anymore. Even Allen's worried about this Roland guy. And he never shows his hand." Angie got up and walked downstairs to start coffee. "I think we need to bring the Scooby gang into this discussion. Can you get Felicia over here by noon? We won't have a lot of time before we have to go open the restaurant, but we could set up a plan."

"I will if you tell Ian about what you did last night."

Angie hesitated. "Actually, I was hoping you'd call Ian. He and I got in a tiff last night."

"So he already knows about the visit to the bar. That's good."

Angie stared at the coffee cup that was slowing filling with the lifesaving liquid. "Well, no. We had the fight before I went to the Vista Bar. Anyway, can you call him?"

"No. I will not. And we need him, so you need to call and work it out *and* tell him about last night. Felicia and I will be there at noon, and we'll bring food."

"I wasn't—" Angie protested, but Estebe had already hung up. He knew she'd call Ian. But she didn't have to like it. She sat in her PJs and drank her coffee. She took a muffin out of the bag that she'd made on Sunday. She'd put them out for lunch as a treat. If they didn't get eaten, she'd freeze the rest.

Angie rubbed her face after she'd stalled long enough. Dom was watching her from his spot on the floor.

"Fine, I'll call him." She dialed his number, and when she got voice mail, her breath caught. "Hi, Ian. We're getting together here at the farm at noon if you want to come. Estebe and I have some things to talk through about this murder. Maybe we can solve it before the wedding so the groom won't have to spend his honeymoon in jail."

She paused, thinking about how to tell him about her adventure last night. "There's something else I need to tell you. I'm fine, but Estebe thinks you need to know."

The recording shut off, and a mechanical voice asked her if she was satisfied with her message. She could call and leave a second message. Or she could just wait for him to show up and she'd tell him then. That was her plan.

She set down the phone and jumped when it rang. It was Ian. She picked it up and put it on speaker as she made another cup of coffee. "Hi there."

"I figured I needed to be the one to call since I was such a jerk last night." Ian's voice was warm and friendly. "But you took the first step. I'm sorry I didn't call earlier."

"I just got up," Angie admitted. "I needed to say something besides I'm sorry we had the fight."

"I listened to your message. I can be at the farmhouse at noon, but I'll need to come back and do some bookwork after we have our meeting." He paused. "Sorry, someone just walked in. Can we talk later?"

"Sure, but don't be mad at me, okay?" Angie said, but then she realized she was talking to dead air. She'd been hung up on again. She looked at Dom. "I tried, right? That's what matters."

Dom hid his head under his paws.

Angie knew the universe wasn't on her side when even her dog didn't listen to her excuses. She needed some food, and then she'd draft a list of questions she had about Jason's death. Maybe once the others got here, she'd have some direction for everyone to go. And she could explain away the mistake she'd made last night. She wasn't beating herself up for going, but she should have told someone or even taken someone with her. And her timing had been an issue. She knew that from driving past Barb's Red Eye on weekend nights. She walked in somewhere looking for rational answers when most of the patrons were less than rational.

No use going over it again. She was sure Ian would have his say when he got over to the house. She fried some eggs to go with the sugar in the muffin and started working on her murder notebook.

The first thing she did was an internet search on Jason. Jason Anderson Roberts had gone to Harvard for both his undergrad and his MBA. His sightings that were on the internet typically were during the summer in the Hamptons. From what she saw, he was typically on the beach or at some big fundraiser with a very pretty girl on his arm. But she never saw the same girl more than a few times. Had Felicia known she would be a passing fad for the guy? Or had he carried a torch for her all these years?

Angie surfed down the rabbit hole until she found his attachment to Felicia's father and his company. From what she could tell, it was a financial services company. Maybe financial planning for ultra-rich people. Maybe that was why Jason had to hang out at the Hamptons and go to the right parties. Felicia would have been an asset as a wife in that lifestyle, especially since she was the owner's daughter.

"She must have felt like a pawn in that life." Angie leaned back and looked over at Dom, who was watching her. She glanced at the clock. Almost ten. She needed to go out and feed Mabel and Precious soon. Felicia didn't like talking about her family or even the time before Angie met her at Boise State. So even though it felt like an invasion, she typed in Felicia's full name. The first hits were about the County Seat, and farther down the line, el pescado, the restaurant she and Felicia had started together in San Francisco. She was down to the last page before she found an old charity event picture of her and Jason. He was grinning from ear to ear, but she wasn't smiling. The grip he had on her arm looked like it might have left bruises.

Felicia had left behind that man and that life many years ago so she could be happy. There was no way Angie would let his death ruin her new chance at happiness with Estebe. She closed the laptop and, slipping on her coat, headed outside to feed her goat and hen. Life went on, animals needed fed, and the world continued, even after one of its residents left this plane of existence. She went back into the house to wait for her visitors.

Ian pulled his old pickup into the driveway just a minute before Estebe's Hummer. The wide difference in value didn't seem to bother Ian. He loved his truck and his job even if running the local farmers market wasn't ever going to make him rich. He believed in the values of eating fresh off the farm. Angie pulled on her coat and went out to meet him.

He climbed out of the truck, frowning. "What's wrong? Is Precious all right?"

"She's fine. Mabel's fine. I just need to talk to you, alone. Can we sit in your truck for a minute?" Angie wrapped her coat around her. "It's freezing out here."

"We could go inside. Your house has heat and a living room." He waved at Estebe, who was opening Felicia's door. He turned back and nodded. "Okay, so you want to tell me something without saying it in front of them. We can sit in my truck."

Angie met Felicia's gaze. "Go inside and set up lunch. We'll be in after a few minutes."

"Wait, what's going on? Why are you talking out here?" Felicia grabbed Angie's coat to stop her from walking away.

"Felicia, leave Angie alone. She needs to tell Ian something, and he's not going to be happy with her. We will go set up lunch." Estebe nodded toward the house. "Not everything is your business."

"And yet, you know." Felicia let Angie's coat go. "You *can* talk to me if you need to, you know that, right?"

Angie smiled. "I got myself into this, I'll try to get myself out. If he breaks up with me, be ready with the ice cream."

"He wouldn't break up with you." Felicia glanced at Angie and then at Estebe, who pointed toward the house. "Okay, I'll stop prying. Good luck with your talk."

Angie climbed into the truck and put her hands against the heater vent. "Thanks for turning on the engine to keep the cab warm."

"We only have a half a tank, so hopefully, this chat won't last long. Otherwise, I'm going to be driving back to town on fumes and parking the truck until I get paid." He leaned against the door, watching her. "This can't be about our fight last night. So what did you do?"

"I didn't..." Angie stopped. She had done something. "Okay, so here it is." She told him about her visit to the Vista Bar last night and how Javier had stepped in when the drunk had decided she needed to be his girlfriend for the night. She saw his mouth tighten as she explained the situation, and one hand went from being relaxed and flat on his leg to a fist. But he didn't say anything until she'd finished.

"So you went there to see if anyone had a grudge with Estebe. Do you plan on visiting all the local bars just before closing time to clear his name, or was there something specific about this dive bar that drew you in?" He looked calm, but Angie could feel the tension in his words.

"Actually, I thought it was blue collar enough that the college kids wouldn't have taken it over, yet close enough to the community center to draw in people from events there." She shook her head. "I didn't know the community center actually had its own bar. I was upset from our fight and felt like this was something I could do to help Estebe. It was a stupid idea, but I can't let him be railroaded into taking the blame for something he didn't do. It's not fair."

"Which is why the Scooby gang is here to talk about ways we can do some research. This isn't a one-man job. You need to trust that we've got your back and will help."

"I've got no answer or excuse for that. I was wrong. Anyway, I've told you and now you're mad." She reached for the door handle, but he stilled her hand.

"You're right. I'm mad. I'm scared and thankful you weren't hurt. And I want you to promise not to put yourself in danger again." He leaned over and kissed her softly. "I'm in love with you. I don't want to lose you."

Tears fell down Angie's cheeks, and she kissed him back. "I'll be more careful."

He laughed and turned off the truck. "And I guess that's all I can hope for. You are a stubborn woman, Miss Turner."

"And you love me. You already said it, so no takebacks." Angie got out of the truck and met him in front of it. "But I won't be visiting any other bars after we close up the restaurant. Unless I've got a partner in crime. I think I've learned my lesson. I did learn something, though."

"What's that?" He took her hand in his as they walked into the house.

She held open the door and looked at him. "There's a lot of people who want to work for the County Seat. Or another high-end restaurant. It must be hard to get into a good placement. Both Hallie and this bartender, Tracy, said they would love to work for me if I found myself having an opening."

Chapter 7

Estebe had sandwiches on the table and a pot of white chili on the stove warming up. Felicia held up the muffins that Angie had set out in a basket. "Are these for lunch?"

"Yes. I made them Sunday and tried out a pumpkin apple mix. I think the spice mix might be a little too strong on ginger, but let me know. You're the pastry chef." Angie slipped off her coat and greeted Dom, who'd been standing at the door waiting for her to return. "You're such a good guard dog, aren't you?"

"Actually, he's a horrible guard dog. We came in and all he wanted was his tummy rubbed." Felicia curled her legs up under her and sat at the table. She took a muffin and broke it open, spreading a thick layer of butter on both sides. "I can't believe anyone could think Estebe would do anything like this."

And there it was again. The elephant in the room.

Estebe walked over and kissed Felicia on top of her head. "Now don't you worry about anything. We're getting married a week from Saturday, and no one is going to stop us, even if we have to do it with me in a jail cell. I think they still allow conjugal visits at the Boise pen, right, Ian?"

"Don't ask me. The last penitentiary I was in, you all were there with me. Along with some friends of both the human and former human variety." Ian took bowls out of the cabinet and set them next to the stove. "Anything else I can help with?"

"Sit down and keep Felicia from eating all of the muffins before we get the chili warmed up." He went to the fridge. "Sodas for everyone?"

"You all have everything taken care of, so I'm just going to sit." Angie held up her hand. "Root beer for me. And don't talk about the night at the old pen when Hope's in the room. She's still mad at Matt for setting that up."

"I don't think Estebe's talking to the police is something we should be laughing about." Felicia stuffed another bite of muffin in her mouth. "This is serious."

"We know it is, Felicia." Angie took a paper napkin off the pile in the middle of the table and wiped away a blob of butter from her friend's cheek. Felicia was the only woman alive who could still look amazing with stray bits of food on her face. "We're just blowing off some steam. Let's table the serious discussion until we all get some food in us, and then we'll sit down and make a plan. We're good at this investigating thing. We'll figure it out."

"Well, my uncle would disagree with this entire process, but he's not here right now. And I don't think he really trusts Roland to follow the clues that don't point to our chef here." Ian sat next to Angie. "What type of sandwiches?"

"Some deli meats. Roast beef, turkey, ham, a club, just a little bit of everything." Estebe was back at the stove, filling the bowls. "I cook when I'm thinking."

"Dude, I'm the only one here that doesn't cook to work out a problem. I use pen and paper and just write stuff down." Ian took one of the sandwiches and passed the platter to Felicia.

Estebe brought over the last two bowls of chili and sat between Angie and Felicia. He nodded to Ian. "Maybe you could bless the food. It might help us be more creative in our problem solving."

After the prayer, they all kept the conversation light. No discussion of the murder or of Angie's midnight visit to dive bars. Dom wandered around the table, but when he realized he wasn't getting table scraps, he headed outside to the back porch to lie in the sun.

Finishing lunch, Angie stood and started cleaning the table. "I'll clean up, and Ian can lead the discussion. My notebook is on the desk if you want to grab it and take notes, Felicia?"

"Let's call the Scooby-Doo team into action." Ian stood and put his plate and bowl on the counter and dunked a wash rag into the soapy dishwater Angie had just started. "Who else is done with their plates?"

In less than five minutes, the table was cleared and washed, and the only things left on the flat surface were the muffins and their drinks. Ian sat down again and tapped a pen on the table. "I guess we should start at the beginning. When did Jason arrive?"

"He texted me on Monday, but Mom said he'd been here since Friday when he took off work to come find me," Felicia said, writing the info down as she talked. She lifted her head. "Which doesn't make any sense if he didn't reach out until Monday."

"Okay, so there's a question. What was he doing from Friday to Tuesday when he met with us?" Angie stared out the window as she washed dishes. "When did your parents arrive?"

"They came in Monday night. And showed up at the restaurant on Tuesday." Felicia turned the page and started a chart. "Okay, I've got a column for Jason, my folks, me, and Estebe. Who am I missing?"

"The killer. We know he and Jason were together Tuesday night when Jason was killed. So we need five days down the other side of the chart. Your folks were in Boston Friday through Monday and on the plane Monday, right? What time did their plane land?" Angie liked this chart thing. If they could figure out where everyone was, maybe it would point to a killer.

"You're missing a column. You need to add Javier on the list. If they can't pin it on me, Roland will go after Javier. I know it. We need to prove his innocence along with mine." Estebe sipped his soda as he watched Felicia cross out one chart and turn the page so she could use the back of one page and the front of another to add additional columns. "I like that. If we find more people to add, we have room."

"I'm good with diagrams. One of my special skills." Felicia patted his hand. "Okay, so I wrote down Angie's questions. I'll have to call Mom to get her schedule. I can fill out my part, and Estebe, you list off your part and you can call Javier to get the other days filled in."

Angie dried her hands after finishing the dishes. "Estebe, the reason I was at the bar last night was to see if anyone had issues with you there. If anyone would want you out of the way. Can you think of anyone from your community center like that?"

"You are asking me if one of my brothers would stab me in the back." Estebe shook his head. "It couldn't have come from the community center. No one there would do this to me."

"Honey, you need to be a little more open-minded about this. I'm looking at my family as we're reviewing what happened. You need to look at yours." Felicia moved the notebook in front of him and tapped the column under his name. "But I'll give you some time to think about it. Fill in these blanks. If you were with someone, write their names down. Hopefully we will build solid alibis for all of us, and the police will just have to go solve the case."

"While Estebe's doing that, let me tell you about my visit to the bar last night. I really didn't get much, but I did talk to Tracy about the setup of the community center."

"Tracy Ellis?" Felicia grabbed her phone and accessed her contacts. "Yeah, he was a temp bartender for us when Jeorge took vacation last summer. From what I remember, he was good at his job. Personable."

"He mentioned that. And that he was interested in a more full-time position if we knew of anyone who was hiring. I don't think he likes his current assignment." Angie sat down at the table and watched Estebe work. He wrote in clear, tight block lettering. Time of day, setting, and who he'd talked to. He was thorough. "But other than that, I didn't get much out of the whole experience. I did think it odd that Javier was there."

"Maybe he just happened to be in the neighborhood," Estebe said, not meeting her gaze.

"Wait, did you have him following me?" Angie stared at Estebe. "Are you kidding? And I thought Ian was being parental."

"I wasn't being parental. I was being protective. There's a difference," Ian pointed out, but Angie was focused on Estebe.

"Okay, so I asked him to watch you and Felicia. When you left after that fight with Ian, I thought having him close might be a good thing. You do unpredictable things when you're mad." He glanced from Angie to Felicia. They were both staring daggers at him. "What, I didn't want you to be hurt or dead. What's wrong with that?"

"We can ask for help when we need it," Angie provided. "Besides, it's not your place to take care of me, ever."

"And you and I are going to have a long talk on the way home. I can't believe the arrogance," Felicia added.

"I was thoughtful, not arrogant," Estebe corrected, but when he saw Felicia's eyes light with anger, he held up his hands. "Okay, I get the point. I didn't think about it. And I won't do it again."

Angie took the notebook from him and started writing. "So we can add Javier to our brunch with Jason since he was there. We just need his other whereabouts. From Friday to Tuesday night. Estebe, do you want me to ask him?"

"No, I need to tell him to stop following you and Felicia anyway. I can call him for his report." Estebe grinned sheepishly. "I know when I'm fighting a losing battle."

"Actually, I'm just glad Javier was there last night," Ian said. "Which, with his reputation with the ladies, is not a statement I thought I'd ever say."

"Let's focus on what Jason did from when he arrived to when he met with us. I can't see a businessman just coming to Boise to veg in his hotel room." Angie glanced at Ian. "Can you reach out to Allen and see if the police have looked into this? Maybe find out what hotel he was at?"

"He was at the Owyhee Plaza downtown." Felicia wrote in the notebook. "My folks are staying there too."

"It has a bar in the hotel, right? Maybe after service we should *all* go and check out the bars near the hotel." Ian pulled out his phone. "I'll make a list of bars in walking distance."

"Make sure they are upscale. Jason is very picky about where he drinks," Felicia said; then she paused. "I mean he was very picky. Even though I didn't like him or our relationship, I can't believe he's dead. It seems like it's fake."

"I'm sorry, Felicia. If this is too hard, we can do it without you." Ian put a hand on her shoulder.

"No, it's fine. Like I said, it's just weird." She met Estebe's gaze. "I didn't love him. Not now, not when we were together. He's just always been in my life. I mean, my life before I left Boston behind."

"Do you think your father sent him here to get you back? To get you out of our marriage?" Estebe seemed to choose his words carefully.

"Probably. Okay, so yeah. That's what he wanted. I didn't want you to know. Dad doesn't like not getting what he wants. And he wanted me in Boston, not Boise. He wanted me married off to someone who he could use or network with. Someone with money and connections." Felicia sank back into her chair. "I thought they let me go too easily. Now I see they were just biding their time until I came back. But I wasn't ever coming back."

"Felicia, you don't think your father would have killed Jason to frame Estebe, do you?" Angie asked the elephant-in-the-room question.

She shook her head. "The dad who used to read me bedtime stories and let me play in his office while he worked? No. He wouldn't have killed anyone. But the man who won't walk me down the aisle? I'm not sure I know him. And he's definitely not the dad I grew up with."

The four of them sat quietly at the table, not talking but instead looking at the chart. "I think we have hit an impasse. We have things to get done today for our opening." Estebe stood and waited for Felicia to follow.

Angie glanced at the clock. Estebe was right. They'd done all the sleuthing they could just sitting at the table. Now they needed to talk to some people.

But first, they needed to get ready for dinner service. Matt and Nancy would already be at the County Seat starting prep. The foursome planned to talk again after service. They'd divide up the bar hopping between the couples. Ian and Angie would be one team, and Felicia and Estebe the other team. Hopefully, one of them would find the bar where Jason had been hanging out on the weekend. Then they'd all meet there and talk to as many people as possible to see if anyone remembered him.

It wasn't much of a plan, but Angie had to admit, it was better than the one she'd concocted last night on a whim. Besides, there was safety in numbers. No one would be worried about getting out of a situation like she'd been in last night.

She waited for Ian to finish feeding the zoo. They'd decided to ride in together in Angie's car since it was nicer than Ian's truck. They'd have to find a garage and pay for parking, but Ian would find one online while the rest of them were working the dinner service. Angie was going to need a lot of coffee to get through working tonight and the extracurricular activities they had planned.

As Ian pulled her car out of the driveway, he turned down the music. "I talked to Uncle Allen, and he's coming over tonight to talk to me about Jason's death. Everything he says will be off the record, but I'll use your notebook to fill in our missing pieces if possible. He really doesn't like this Roland character. He thinks Estebe is in real trouble, even if he didn't do anything. Uncle Allen doesn't like it when the wrong person pays for a crime."

"He's kind of a white knight in that way, isn't he?" Angie took the notebook out of her tote and tucked it between the seats for Ian to take with him.

"He'd deny it, but yeah, Uncle Allen is one of the good guys. The ones who go into law enforcement for all the right reasons. I'm pretty proud of him." Ian turned the car onto the road that would take them all the way into River Vista. "We have a lot of good people in our lives, Angie. We're luckier than most."

She thought about his words all night during service. She was lucky. She had a kitchen crew that were more like family than just employees. Hallie was joking with Nancy on the line as Angie expedited a table. And she had room for more in her world too. She was glad to find out that the County Seat was considered a desirable place to work in the short time they'd been in business. Angie wanted to develop a place where not only the diners were happy with their choice but also the people who worked there.

When Ian came in for dinner, he poked his head in the kitchen. "Hey, just letting you know I'm at the bar eating. What's good tonight?"

"Everything," the entire kitchen staff called back.

Angie laughed as he stepped back a bit at the response. "I'll send something out for you. Do you trust me?"

"With my life." He nodded and left the kitchen.

Estebe paused and looked at her. "What do you think?"

"He hasn't had your ribeye yet. He thinks it's too much since he gets his meals free." Angie called out an order for him. "I think I owe him a good makeup dinner after last night's fight."

"And your little trip?" Estebe added.

She shook her head. "I'm not apologizing for that. I didn't do anything wrong. My timing was just off. But I will admit, we're better when we get everyone involved in the process. We'll figure this out, and you and Felicia will have your happily ever after."

"You are a romantic, Angie." Estebe seasoned a ribeye and put it on the grill. As he did, Angie saw Hallie watching them. Her expression looked a little wistful, like she wished she was part of the conversation. She saw Angie looking and dropped her gaze.

Angie would have to make sure Hallie felt included during her time temping at County Seat. Maybe she'd ask her to enter a dish in the family meal contest next month. Angie wanted her to feel like part of the family while she was there. And from the look she'd just seen, she thought Hallie wanted that as well.

She put the idea away and drank some water. She needed to be awake after service to stay sharp and get Estebe out of the line of fire. Jason had been murdered; that was a fact. Another fact was that his killer wasn't the gentle giant grilling a steak in her kitchen. That, she knew for sure.

Chapter 8

"When did Thursday nights become so busy?" Ian pulled into the second parking garage they'd found. The first, where Ian liked to park, already had a full sign blocking the entrance. He started winding up the narrow driveway to find an open spot.

"Felicia used to come into Boise to go out after the restaurant closed, but I think now she hangs out at the Red Eye if she wants some nightlife. Me, I'm usually dead tired after a shift. I'd rather be home in bunny slippers." Angie pointed toward some lights above them. "They might be pulling out...or just adjusting their parking, but it looks like they're pulling out."

"I think you're right." Ian turned on his blinker and stopped on the ramp, giving the other car enough room to back out of the spot. "Felicia's an extrovert. And I didn't know you owned bunny slippers. How come I haven't seen these on your feet?"

"It's a figure of speech. I don't have bunny slippers." Angie bit back a grin. Ian knew how to get her to smile. "Anyway, I hope we get through these places soon. I'd like to be home before my car turns into a pumpkin."

"Once we hit the bars on our list, we're meeting Estebe and Felicia at the Basque community center to talk. Estebe's buying us a drink. Coffee probably." He pulled the car into the now empty spot and turned the key. "Let's go see if we can find out where our friend had been drinking this weekend. Do you have the picture Felicia gave you?"

Angie patted her tote bag. "Right here. Along with my notebook in case I need to make some notes. I have a feeling we're going to find something tonight. Something that's going to help clear Estebe."

"You're an eternal optimist." He climbed out of the car, but before he could get around to open her door, Angie was already out and shutting the door.

She held out her hand, and he dropped her keys into it. Clicking the remote, the doors locked and her horn blared twice. She dropped the keys into her purse. "Let's go snooping around."

"Anything you want. Of course, my uncle would say you're leading me down some questionable paths." He glanced around the empty parking garage. "The elevators down to the street are in that corner. Let's go."

They had the hotel bar on their list, so that was where they started. A bartender stood behind the wooden bar that graced the back wall. Mirrors twinkled behind the bottles of liquor, and someone sat at the piano by the lobby, playing soft music to ease the patrons' worries away. The bartender put on a practiced smile and moved their way. "Robbie at your service. What can I get for you?"

"Information, actually." Angie pulled out the picture Felicia had printed off that afternoon. "Have you seen this guy?"

He took the page, looked at it, then set it back down. He handed her a menu. "Put that away. If you were drinking, what would you have?"

Angie hesitated, then said, "I guess something sweet. Ian's my ride, so he'd be drinking coffee."

"Sounds like a plan." He pulled out a glass and a cup and made them drinks. As he pushed the finished drinks across the bar, he grinned. "Irish coffee without the Irish and a birthday surprise for the lady. Hang out for a few. My boss is still around, and she doesn't like us chatting, especially about the hotel guests."

He left and moved over to the other side of the bar where a woman with a clipboard was doing some inventory. Angie took a sip of the sweet concoction. "I'm not sure what's in this, but it's yummy."

"From what I saw, it's at most a half ounce of birthday cake vodka and a lot of juices and sparkling water. Not exactly virgin, but it won't get you drunk." He sipped his own drink. "Mine appears to be an Irish coffee, but without the whiskey. I saw him pour the liquor, but he must have dumped it before putting it in the cup. The guy is a magician with drinks."

She glanced around the room. It felt historical, like they'd stepped back in time. The lights twinkled and sparkled around the tables. It felt special, like it would be a great date night stop. "I like this place. Very magical."

"It's nice. Classy. Kind of a couples place, though. I'm thinking our bartender might have sent Jason down the road to a bar with a little more action. If I was alone, out of town, this isn't somewhere I'd hang out." He sipped his coffee and scanned the room. "There's not one table that isn't at least a couple or two."

"You're right." Angie sighed and sipped her drink. "I probably can scratch this one off the list."

"Don't give up so fast. The bartender knows Jason. Let's see what he has to tell us." He leaned on the bar and sipped his coffee again. "So how was service? Did the temp work out?"

"Hallie's terrific. If I had a full-time slot, I'd hire her on the spot. She seems to work well with the team too." Angie sighed. "So many people, not enough jobs."

The bartender came back as soon as the woman in the blue business suit left the area. "She's gone, but I don't want to jinx it, so we'll make this fast. The guy in the picture was staying here this weekend. I heard he got himself killed out in an alley down the street."

"I didn't realize where, but yes, he was killed downtown." Angie glanced at Ian, who didn't meet her gaze. Apparently, he'd known the site of the killing. They were going to have a talk about full disclosure on the way to the next bar. "Did he hang out here? Meet anyone?"

"Here?" The bartender's fake smile turned real. "Not a chance. Once I'd told him where the action was, he didn't come back in here except for Monday night when he met an older couple. They had a couple drinks, talked a lot, then left for the Gamekeeper. They had me call a taxi for them."

"Felicia's parents." Angie filled in the question. "Can I ask where you sent Jason?"

The bartender scanned the room. "He wanted to know if there was a bar in Boise that was a little more open about lifestyles. I assumed he was looking for either a strip club or a gay bar. So I gave him both. The strip club's out off Orchard. He would need to grab a cab. The gay bar is right down the street, the Front Porch."

"Do you know where he went?" Angie finished her drink.

The bartender took her glass and tucked it under the bar. He waved off the twenty Ian tried to give him. "All I can say is he didn't ask me to get him a cab."

As they moved outside, Angie studied their list. "The Front Porch is on our list. Do you want to go there now?"

He pointed to the next place on the list. "That bar is right there. Let's follow the list, just in case. We want to make sure we rule all the other ones out."

Angie didn't want to work methodically through the list. She wanted to follow the leads. The bartender had sent them to the Front Porch. They should go there next and see if Jason's picture jogged anyone's memory. But she knew Ian was probably right. Maybe Jason hadn't been looking for a hookup for the weekend. He could have been trying to stir up trouble. It felt like something the guy would have liked doing. And Angie had only met him once.

"Okay then, the Crystal Palace is next." She put her arm into Ian's and leaned close. "It's almost like a date."

"I guess if we forget the fact that we're here to walk from bar to bar trying to figure out why someone was killed, then yeah, it's just like a date." He paused and pointed down a road where the traffic was light. It appeared to be a dead end, so all the cars were turning onto the main road rather than going straight. "That's the alley where Jason was found. He was shot, and his head must have hit the dumpster he was found nearby. The head wound was fatal. The original report said he was robbed."

"But then this detective found the connection to Estebe." Angie shivered under her coat. "I can't believe someone can just say you're guilty and people have to listen."

"They have some damning circumstantial evidence, especially motive. Jason was Felicia's ex-boyfriend. He was super successful and had come to talk her out of the wedding. If someone did that to me, I'd be ready to kill him too." They started crossing the street and hurried with the crowd to make it before the walk sign turned orange.

"Except Estebe didn't know until Tuesday that he was here or that Felicia's family didn't approve of the wedding."

"That's not quite true." Ian pulled her over to the building wall to get them out of the flow of drunken foot traffic. "Look, I don't know if Felicia knows this, but Estebe flew to Boston to ask her father for permission to marry her last week. He told me it didn't go too well. The father almost had Estebe thrown out of the building. Then he acts like he's never met Estebe when they came for lunch. And this Jason, he was in the meeting when Estebe was called in to talk to the father. No one wanted what was best for Felicia. All they saw was Estebe's skin color and his accent. It hurt him. A lot."

"But he didn't tell her about the encounter." Angie filled in the missing words. "Of course not. He didn't want her to think badly of her dad. He's such a good guy. I hate that this is being pointed at him."

"He didn't kill Jason, Angie. We have to trust that the legal system is going to do its work and keep him from being convicted of a crime he didn't commit." Ian nodded toward the bar opening. "That's our next stop."

Angie followed him inside, but she didn't feel as convinced in his assurance that the system would work for Estebe.

The bartender was less than helpful when Angie pulled out the picture. He barely glanced at it before informing them that he'd never seen the guy. When they said they didn't need a drink, he shrugged and left for the next customer. This bar was bright and the music loud. Most of the people out on the dance floor looked like they were barely drinking age. Angie nodded toward the door. "We might as well leave. I don't think he would hang out here."

"You're right. This isn't his type of place." Ian took her arm and moved her toward the door. When they got outside, he took a deep breath. "I can't believe people hang out in places like that. I wanted to leave as soon as we walked inside. Too loud, too many people, too flashy."

"Some people like the flash." She took his arm, and they moved to the next bar. "Let's get moving. There are five more before we get to the Front Porch, and time's slipping away. People are starting to leave already."

"If there's something to be found, we'll find it." He pulled her close. "Don't worry about Estebe. We'll figure this out. I promise."

Angie hoped his promise was enough.

By the time they got to the Front Porch, the bouncer wasn't letting people inside. "Sorry, it's crazy in there. I'm trying to start clearing people out or we won't get out of here before three."

Angie sighed, but Ian grabbed Jason's picture out of Angie's tote. "One thing. Can you tell me if you saw this man here this weekend?"

The bouncer took the picture and held it under his flashlight. "I didn't work this weekend. Come back tomorrow night and talk to Freddie. He worked both Friday and Saturday nights. Sundays are pretty dead around here."

"Thanks, man." Ian gave the picture back to Angie, and they walked away. He glanced at his watch. "And it's time to meet the others. We got through our list except for this one, and I'll come back tomorrow while you're working at the restaurant. Maybe I'll get this Freddie to tell me who killed Jason, and we'll have solved the mystery."

"I'm not sure it's that easy, but thanks for taking on the next day's work." Angie leaned into him as they walked back to the parking garage. "It's a nice night. Chilly, but clear."

"We need to get out more. We're always just staying around River Vista. You need to see the world." He pulled her closer as they dodged a group of young people who were singing the last song they'd heard at the bar. "Maybe we should go to London this summer. You could meet my mom."

"That sounds lovely and terrifying at the same time." Angie laughed. "I'm not sure I'm ready to meet all your family. Your uncle just started liking me."

"My family loves you. Even Uncle Allen. And my mom's going to love you too." Ian kissed the top of her head.

"Well, let's get Felicia and Estebe married and onto their new life before we start talking about taking a vacation. Besides, they're taking a month to travel to Spain right after the wedding, so it's impossible for me to take off until they get back." She stepped around a trash can on the sidewalk. "I would love to go someday, though."

"Then we'll go. I might have to borrow the money to get us there, but we'll figure it out." He turned them into the parking garage. "Let's go chat with our friends."

When they got to the community center, the parking lot was almost empty. "I guess they shut down early here."

Angie climbed out of the car. "Well, Estebe's Hummer's here, so they must have gotten done with their list way before we did."

"See, I told you we were the true Fred and Daphne from Scooby-Doo." Ian locked the car and then met her on the sidewalk. "I think we're better at finding clues because we're less people orientated. We're both introverts, so we were born with the watcher gene. We see things most people ignore."

"Just don't tell them that." Angie grinned. "I agree with you, though. If this mystery is going to be solved, I'd put my money on you and me doing it."

"There the two of you are." Estebe stood at the doorway and waved them inside. "We were thinking you got lost in the party."

"I told Angie I didn't realize Thursday night was so busy." Ian held the door as Angie moved into the community center.

Instead of going into the great room, where she'd been before, they turned down a hall on the left and entered what looked like a small western-themed bar. The walls were covered with log-cabin-like paneling, the tables were round with wooden chairs, and the bar back was a full mirror and wood. If she hadn't known better, Angie would have thought she'd stepped back in time and into a western saloon.

Felicia was sitting at a table with a platter filled with appetizers in the middle and a selection of sodas in a metal bucket mixed in with ice. She stood and gave Angie a hug. "We set up some snacks for the discussion. I've got coffee made too if you want that."

Ian held up a hand. "Coffee for me. I'm not used to these late party nights."

Estebe chuckled. "I used to be. Before Felicia and I started dating, I'd come here after work and close the place down. It's just down the street from my condo, so I can walk home."

"And we have to drive back to the other side of River Vista tonight." Ian took the cup Felicia offered and sighed. "I'll probably take one to go when we leave too."

Angie grabbed a plate and filled it with different treats. "I'm starving. That was a lot of walking in the cold."

"We came up with nothing." Felicia matched Angie's plate and curled her legs up underneath her on the chair. She opened a soda. "I hope you two did better, or this adventure will have to go into the dumb ideas file."

"We found someone who saw Jason. The bartender at the hotel gave him names of a couple of specific types of bars in the area. The Front Porch wasn't letting people inside by the time we got there, so I'm going back tomorrow evening and see if I can talk to the bouncer who was on the door last weekend."

"The Front Porch?" Felicia shrugged. "That could explain a few things about our relationship. We were so young. I thought saving myself for marriage was what I was supposed to do, but looking back, I don't think Jason was ever that into me. He liked the power and prestige that came with marrying the daughter of the company president, but he really didn't seem attracted to me."

"He should have given you the 'it's not you, it's me' goodbye line," Estebe said as he took one of the egg rolls off Felicia's plate.

"The thing is, I think he would have married me this week for all the same reasons. From what my mom tells me, Carter has been taking over some of the responsibilities that Jason used to have. So with him gone, the business will just move most of his work to Carter." Felicia stared out the window and into the night. "I wish he'd just found someone he could love and had a life. It's sad that he thought I was his ticket to the business."

"I hate to ask this, but what do you know about Carter? Would he think Jason was a roadblock to his meal ticket?" Angie watched Felicia as she processed the question.

"Carter? No way. He's a sweet guy. He grew up with a single mom, and he didn't know who his dad was until he graduated from college. Then he found some letters between his mom and my dad. He went to meet him and asked for a shot to prove himself at the business. He started in some accounting position and has been moving up in the company all these years. He proved himself to Dad." Felicia ate another appetizer and leaned closer to Estebe. "I just wish Dad would give you a shot. If he got to know you, he'd love your drive and your passion. Instead, he's being a big poop."

"Sometimes people only see what they want to see." Estebe pushed Felicia's hair back away from her face. "I can handle him not liking me as long as his daughter still loves me."

Felicia's face brightened, and she leaned over and kissed him. "Then I think we're solid."

"This is way too sappy for this time of night." Angie had been making notes in the investigation book as they talked. "I think we call it a night. Ian's going to follow up with this bouncer, and what are the rest of us doing tomorrow?"

"You and I are having breakfast with my mom at ten," Felicia told Angie. "So I'll come get you."

"I have business to complete before the wedding." Estebe yawned as he finished his soda. "I've got a property I'm trying to finish the purchase of before we leave the country."

"My real estate mogul." Felicia stood and then sat on Estebe's lap. "Seriously, you're just the type of guy my dad should want me to marry."

Chapter 9

Angie woke to the smell of coffee and bacon. She got ready, then went downstairs. Ian and Dom were sitting in the kitchen. Ian was eating, and Dom was patiently watching him.

"Good morning. I hope there's coffee left."

"I would have poured you one, but I didn't hear you getting ready." Ian moved to stand, but Angie waved him back down.

"Sit and eat. I'm going to steal some of that bacon. I'm not sure what breakfast with Felicia's mom will include. The last time we went to breakfast, we left before we ate." Angie poured her coffee, then noticed Ian had the investigation notebook out. "Did you think of something?"

"Actually, Uncle Allen called. They verified that Jason had been seen with a guy at the Front Porch on Sunday, so they're looking for him to see if he can add to the timeline." Ian paused before continuing. "According to Uncle Allen, Roland's hoping this guy will tell him that Jason was fighting with Estebe. He's not giving up on pinning this on our friend."

"So as long as someone tells him that Estebe and Jason were at odds, he's going to push?" Angie shook her head. "That level of focus just doesn't make sense. Didn't his attorney give them a full itinerary of where Estebe had been once Jason came into town?"

"Yes, but there's some issue on Javier's itinerary. Estebe's upset because he had asked Javier to keep an eye on Jason, but we all know that Javier couldn't kill the guy. If we don't find out who did, Estebe thinks that this Roland might think that Javier looks like a good suspect."

"So your uncle is feeding us information because he thinks the official investigation is off the rails?" Angie reached for another slice of bacon. She might just need two breakfasts this morning to deal with the bad news.

"Unofficially—exactly. Of course, we're not any further than they are. We just know that Javier and Estebe aren't the killers. Maybe something will come up in your breakfast this morning?" Ian finished the last bite of egg with his toast and stood to put the plate in the sink.

"Well, maybe if her mom says, 'Hey, did you know Jason had death threats in Boston because of his secret second job robbing banks?' then I think we might be able to get Roland to stop massaging all the evidence to point to Estebe." Angie leaned back and sipped her coffee. "We've only been looking at what he did here. Maybe he did have something going on in Boston that followed him here."

"Like?"

Angie poured a second cup of coffee. "I have no idea. I thought Carter might be the key, but it sounds like he's just a good guy trying to deal with a crappy hand he'd been dealt."

"Has anyone besides Felicia met him? Maybe she doesn't see him with clear glasses?" Ian glanced at his watch. "I've got to get to work. I'll let you know if I find out anything after my trip to Boise this evening."

"Come into the restaurant, and I'll feed you."

He patted his stomach. "Since my planned menu was instant ramen, I'll take you up on that."

After Ian left, Angie had about thirty minutes before she expected Felicia. She cleaned up the kitchen and checked Dom's bowls. Ian had told her he'd fed Precious and Mabel before she got up, so all she needed to do was change into clothes that didn't smell like bacon and she'd be ready to go.

Dom came and sat next to her once she was back at the table, waiting for Felicia to pick her up. She gave him a hug. "Sorry I've been gone so much this week. I'm afraid next week will be more of the same since Aunt Felicia is getting married. But maybe I can bring you along for some of the prep work."

He laid his big head on her lap, and she absently rubbed between his ears as she opened her laptop. She hadn't finished researching Jason. Maybe there was something else between all the charity events and the society snapshots.

As she went back through the links she'd found before, she noticed he did a lot of work for one specific charity. An educational support charity for a private high school. Westfield Academy. Jason was an alumnus, and he was listed as one of the school's supporters on the academy's alumni website. Angie changed her search to Westfield Academy and found some issues with the local community. The boarding school had been trying to annex a property next door to add on to the campus without much luck.

The man who owned the property didn't want to sell the land between the school and his estate, saying he was already close enough to those hoodlums. Angie had just finished reading an interview with the property owner when she heard Felicia's Jeep in the driveway.

She kissed Dom, who still sat with his head in her lap but had fallen asleep. "Go take your nap in your bed. I should be home in a little bit to get ready to go to work."

He yawned and headed to his bed. Sometimes Angie wondered how much of what she said actually got through.

She grabbed her tote, stuffing the notebook inside, and went outside to meet Felicia. One of these days, all she was going to have to deal with was the restaurant. No upcoming weddings, no murders to solve, just her, Dom, and the restaurant. And Ian.

Angie climbed into the Jeep and put her seatbelt on. "Good morning."

"So why are you so happy? I figured with you being out so late you'd be grumpy." Felicia glanced at her as she turned around in the driveway and headed back out to the road.

"Check in with me after service. I'm probably going to be grumpy then." Angie turned on the heated seat and leaned back. "Tell me about Westfield Academy. Do you know anything about it?"

"Where Jason when to high school? Not much. I know we went to several fund-raising events for the school when we were dating. He loved the place. He always said he found himself there when he was growing up. He wanted to give that same experience to other kids." Felicia turned onto the road that would take them to the freeway and then into Boise. "Why? It can't have anything to do with his death, can it?"

"I don't know. Maybe. There's an issue with the school wanting to expand, but the neighbor who owns the land doesn't want to sell." Angie thought about her own experience with a company coming in and trying to strong-arm the landowners. "Maybe I'm just sensitive to this type of takeover because of what happened with the soybean factory last year."

"Not all real estate deals are run by shady characters." Felicia was quiet for a while as she drove them. "Mom might have some information on the school, though. And if there was enough of an issue for you to find a news article about it, there's probably more going around in the rumor mill. There's a reason Mom loves being part of the local clubs and golf courses. She loves her gossip."

When they pulled in front of the hotel, Felicia used the valet service to park her Jeep.

Angie pointed to the parking garage across the street. "We could have saved you fifty bucks by parking just over there."

"Mom doesn't like to be kept waiting, and we're already two minutes late. If I told her I'd parked my own car, she would think I didn't want to meet with her." Felicia checked her makeup in a small compact. "Come on, let's go play tea party."

Angie followed her into the hotel lobby and then into the attached restaurant. A hostess was at the station, but Felicia shook her head and pointed toward a woman sitting alone at a table overlooking the small park behind the hotel. They went and stood at the table.

"Mom, how are you this morning?" Felicia leaned down and gave her a kiss. Then she pointed to the third chair and nodded to Angie to sit down. "I see you got my message about Angie coming along."

Mrs. Williams nodded toward Angie in greeting. After Felicia sat, her mother lifted her hand and a waiter appeared. "Could you bring us coffee and a fourth setting?"

The man nodded and disappeared. She unfolded her napkin and placed it on her lap. "I'm sorry, I've been busy and didn't check my messages. Your brother, Carter, is joining us."

"Carter? Why? And when did you start talking to Carter?" Felicia paused as the waiter returned. She waited for the fourth setting and a chair to be set and coffee poured before speaking again. "What's going on, Mom?"

"Carter has been extremely helpful in dealing with this whole Jason thing. I don't know what your father or I would have done if he hadn't come along on the trip." She sipped her coffee. "I'm so sorry, Angie. Listening to all this family business must be so boring for you."

"That still doesn't explain why he's been invited to breakfast," Felicia pushed. "Mom, you always said that Carter was only out for himself, even when I tried to tell you he was a good guy. Now the two of you are friends? What in the world is going on?"

"Felicia, that's not true. I've always respected Carter's business savvy." Her mother stirred a little cream into her coffee, ignoring Felicia's question. Then something caught her eye, and she smiled. "Oh, here he comes."

Angie turned, and a handsome man in a suit hurried over to their table. He leaned down and kissed Mrs. Williams and Felicia on the cheek. Then he held out a hand to Angie. "I'm so sorry I'm late. And I'm afraid I haven't had the privilege of meeting you. I'm Carter Williams, Felicia's brother."

"Half brother," Felicia corrected. "Carter, this is my friend and business partner, Angie Turner."

"Nice to meet you," Angie muttered and got a glare from Felicia.

"Anyway, Carter, Mom was just telling me what a big help you've been since Jason was killed. I appreciate you helping them out." Felicia sipped her coffee. "I know this might be none of my business, but I'm going to ask anyway. So what's in it for you?"

"Excuse me?"

"Felicia, that's rude," her mother said.

"It's a logical question." Felicia turned away from her mom. "Are you Dad's successor at the business now that Jason's dead? Maybe the local police should be asking you where you were when Jason was killed."

"Felicia!"

Carter laughed as he put sugar and creamer in his coffee. "Don't worry about it, MaryEllen. Felicia was always the smart one. And I have nothing to hide. I didn't kill Jason. I was having dinner with our folks when Jason was shot." He held up his hands. "I didn't have anything to do with his death. And I've been so appreciative of the support MaryEllen has given me since I lost my own mother. I know it couldn't be easy for her to accept me."

"You've been a godsend this last year." Mrs. William blinked back tears. The waiter approached with menus, and Mrs. Williams waved him over. "Let's order breakfast and stop fighting, please. I want to talk to both of you."

"That sounds like a lovely plan." Carter took one of the menus and gave it to Angie. "I'm sure your friend doesn't want to hear about all our family's dirty laundry."

"I don't." Angie didn't know what else to say. "I mean, everyone has family issues. Well, except for me. I don't have any family to fight with. I consider Felicia and the rest of the County Seat crew as my family. So then, I guess I'm part of the dirty laundry too."

"Well, I never." Mrs. Williams shot a glare at Angie.

Carter put his hand on hers. "I think it's charming. And I'm glad Felicia has such a devoted friend here in Boise. It's hard being so far away from real family. You are very special to take her in that way."

"Seriously, Carter, why am I here? What do you want to say?" Felicia set down the menu. "Apparently it wasn't about catching up over breakfast. What's the message you're supposed to deliver?"

"Your father and mother asked me to talk to you." Carter nodded toward Mrs. Williams. "We believe it's time for you to come home and take your place at the company. It's time for you to become part of making the business successful. Without Jason, we're going to be shorthanded. We need you, Felicia."

"I'm sorry. I have a business here that needs me. And if you've forgotten, I'm getting married a week from Saturday. I love Estebe, and he loves me." Felicia held up her left hand with the ring and pointed toward it. "I can't just move back to Boston."

"I'm sure he'll understand if he really loves you." Mrs. Williams set down the menu and picked up her coffee. "And if you're still wanting to get married next summer, we can plan a real wedding. One out at the summer house. All the right people will be invited, and you can have a wedding you'd be proud of."

Felicia stood. "If I still want to be married? What are you talking about? Do you really think I can just put my love for Estebe on a shelf like a snow globe?"

"Felicia, you need to listen to your mother." Carter reached for her arm. "Sit down and let's talk about this."

"I'm not sitting down, and this discussion is over." Felicia jerked her arm away from her brother. "Look, I'm sure you can hire another paper pusher to take Jason's place. I'm not moving back to Boston. I'm getting married next Saturday at the County Seat. If you'd like to attend, I'd love to have my family there and my father give me away. If not, it's your loss, not mine."

Angie stood as Felicia stormed off. She nodded toward the table. "Nice to meet you." And then she hurried after Felicia. She found her at the valet station stewing. "Hey, calm down. I'll drive us back."

Felicia wiped tears off her cheeks. "I'm fine. It's not anything I wasn't expecting. For my family, the greatest sin isn't moving away or marrying someone outside our social circle, but abandoning the business? That's why they're mad at me. That's why my dad won't give me away at my wedding."

Angie put her hand on Felicia's back. "I know it's not the same, but we'll find someone to walk you down the aisle. And your wedding is going to be amazing. You and Estebe deserve all the best."

Driving back to Angie's house, Felicia kept the music on to fill in the blank spots of conversation. Angie didn't blame her friend. She had wanted the best for Felicia, and part of that was a wish that her parents would at least be a little happy about her upcoming nuptials. Instead, they thought she should put the wedding off so she could go to Boston and work the family business?

Families were hard. Which was one reason Angie loved her work family so much. Maybe there were fewer expectations when you weren't blood related. No matter what, she would make sure Felicia and Estebe's wedding was the storybook start of their lives together that they deserved. All she needed to do was solve a murder and keep Estebe out of jail, find someone to walk Felicia down the aisle, and keep the County Seat running for two more nights before they closed for the wedding.

Easy peasy, right?

Chapter 10

Chief Allen Brown dropped Bleak, his foster daughter, off for her shift at the County Seat, then made himself comfortable in the visitor's chair in Angie's office. She came back from the kitchen to find him scrolling through his phone and drinking a cup of coffee.

"Allen, no one told me you were waiting to talk to me." She paused at the doorway. "Let me refill your coffee, and I'll be right back."

"No need. I'll need to leave soon. Maggie's cooking something special tonight, so I'm a little worried about what I'll walk into when I get home." He sniffed the air. "I told her I could bring home food when I dropped off Bleak, but she insisted on cooking."

"Sorry about that. Do you want a plate before you leave? Our secret?" Angie brought in her coffee and sat down across from him.

"No, I've eaten Maggie's food for over thirty years. One more night of her cooking isn't going to kill me." He sipped his coffee. "Ian called me from Boise. He talked to the bouncer and got a positive ID on our guy. He was there all weekend, talking to one of the bartenders."

"The same bartender?" Angie frowned. "I thought maybe he came to meet someone new."

"I don't think this was just a random meeting. I think our Jason guy came specifically to find him and talk to him." He sipped his coffee.

"Seriously? Then maybe talking to Felicia was just a cover for him showing up here?" Angie glanced at the clock. They had thirty minutes before the kitchen would need her. She still had time to talk. "I wondered why he waited until Monday to even reach out to her."

"According to this bouncer, it appeared that the two men knew each other. He heard some strong words, voices really, but when he approached, the bartender waved him off." He pulled out his notebook. "I've got the guy's name and number. I'll call him tonight before dinner and see what connection he has to our dead guy. Then I'll turn the lead over to the Boise cop."

"Thanks for letting me know what's going on. I'm surprised you're keeping me in the loop."

He laughed. "I'm not even supposed to be working this case. So, technically, you're Roland's problem, not mine."

"Thanks for passing the buck." But she saw his point. She was glad he was sharing information, even if it was in his best interest as well as her own. She didn't care who solved Jason's murder as long as the killer wasn't someone she knew.

"I hear you had breakfast with Mrs. Williams today. How did that go?"

Angie laughed. "I think calling it breakfast is generous. I didn't even get a scone."

"So it didn't go well? I feel sorry for Felicia." He sipped his coffee.

"Me, too. I mean, it should be about her, not the business and not about that half brother of hers. I think he's a little controlling and creepy. Of course, so was Jason. Maybe it's just the way men are raised in the East. They both seemed to be Neanderthals."

Allen laughed. "That's typically a complaint people have about Idaho people. Like we're all living on ranches and riding horses into town."

"That would be an improvement over these cavemen." She held out a hand. "And don't be asking me what I know, because I don't know anything. All I know is they both treated Felicia like she was a kid or a china doll. Neither one made any attempt to actually communicate with Felicia or ask her what she wanted. Anyway, that's off topic, sorry, I'm still peeved."

"I bet Felicia is too. She doesn't seem like a woman who takes kindly to being told what to do." He stood and put his notebook in his pocket. "You've done good work so far. Just don't let me hear of you taking off on your own again. That was foolish of you."

"I know, I know." Angie held up her hands to ward off the verbal blows. "I should have taken someone with me for backup. But I really thought I'd be okay. I guess I haven't been out at closing time for a while now."

"My nephew cares for you a great deal. I hope you won't do anything to break that boy's heart." He dusted off his hat, then twirled it in his hands.

"I would never do anything to hurt Ian."

He stared at her closely. "If you wind up dead on a slab in the morgue, I think that would kill the boy."

Allen left, and Angie thought about his words for a long time that night. She had been reckless in going to the Vista Bar alone, but she'd had a good idea. One that had paid off in the lead to the bartender that Allen was probably interviewing right now. She wouldn't apologize for being curious or following a lead.

When she went out to get a water, she saw Ian at the bar. She went over and gave him a quick kiss. "No one told me you were here. Have you eaten?"

"I had the deconstructed chicken pot pie. It was amazing." He nodded to the full dining room. "I told them to not bother you. You look like you've got enough on your plate."

"I always have time for you." She sat next to him. "Your uncle said you found out something."

"Actually, yes. He hasn't been able to reach the guy yet, but he says he'll check in when he comes to pick up Bleak. And he says to leave him out a sandwich. Maggie's roast was a little burned."

"She tries so hard." She stood. "I'll put a note to make up three to-go dinners to send home with them. It's a shame to let food go to waste when people don't show up for their reservations."

"If you think she'll buy that." Ian reached for her hand. "Before you go, we have one more lead. Jason was calling an Idaho number once a day for a month before he flew out here. It's not Felicia's number or the restaurant's."

"So he did know someone. Maybe two someones here." Angie used her finger to tap on the bar. "Now we just need to get the detective to stop trying to build a case against an innocent man and do his own legwork. This should be investigated."

"Uncle Allen's on it. I just wanted you to know so you'd calm down on this. Estebe is going to be fine. There's no way anyone could seriously think he killed Jason."

A crash sounded in the kitchen. Angie leaned in and kissed Ian again. "I better go. I'll see you after service? Or are you heading home?"

"I'll wait for you." He squeezed her hand, then let it drop. "Go work, woman. You need to keep this place running. I enjoy having one good meal a day."

"That's on you. I think you should take cooking lessons so you don't starve if we break up." She headed back to the kitchen.

"I think we just shouldn't ever break up," he called after her.

The smile Ian's words had put on her face dropped when she walked into the kitchen. There were broken plates scattered on the floor. "What happened?"

"I bumped into them as I was cooking." Estebe had a broom out and was sweeping up the mess. "I'd asked for more plates, but I didn't realize they'd already been delivered. And when I turned to get one, I hit the middle of the pile."

"Totally my fault," Hallie said. "I should have told him instead of giving him more. I guess I've heard Estebe's reputation of being a little terse in the kitchen, so I didn't want to question him."

"We all make mistakes." Angie took the broom and the dustpan from Estebe. "You go cook. I'll get this."

After she'd cleaned up the mess, she went and washed her hands.

Hallie came by and stood next to her. "I'm really sorry. He just is so intimidating."

"He's a total softy. You need to learn that if you're going to work here. I don't know what happened before with you and Estebe in a different kitchen, but honestly, I don't care. We take care of each other here, and that means speaking up when you think someone is making a mistake." She studied Hallie. "Do you understand?"

"Yes. I'm so sorry." Hallie hurried over to the line and started working with Nancy.

Matt met Angie and nodded to the walk-in. "I think we need to do an order." When they got inside, Matt turned to Angie. "Hallie's lying. Estebe only asked for plates once. She took two piles over, I saw her."

"Why would she do that?" Angie leaned on one of the shelving units, letting the cold air cool her face. "Was she just trying to overstock?"

Matt shook his head. "We talked about this before service started. I told her we always keep Estebe a little low on plates because there isn't much room on the shelf. She overstocked his station so he'd break the plates, I'm sure of it."

As they walked back into the room, Angie took in the kitchen where she'd always felt happy and at home. Was her work family having issues like Felicia's real family? She needed to find out more about Hallie and where she'd worked before. Maybe she had her own reputation like the one Estebe had arrived with when he'd started.

With service finally finished, she sent Hallie home and let Matt and Nancy stay to clean up the kitchen. She asked Estebe to meet her out in the dining room for a chat.

Ian stood and greeted him with a hug. "Are you getting excited about your bachelor party? Javier called me today and invited me. I guess it's good Thursday night is rocking in Boise so we can ring you out of your single days right."

"Boys." Felicia came up behind Estebe and gave him a hug. "I thought we talked about not doing stag parties."

"My cousin has gone against my wishes and set this up. I guess I will have to be a good sport about it." Estebe grinned and put his arm around Felicia's waist.

"And I guess me and my girls will have to find something to entertain us that night." Felicia winked at Angie. "What do you think? Are you up for a night of bar hopping next Thursday?"

"If that's what you want." Angie inwardly groaned. She'd been hoping for a girl's sleepover at the house, not a wandering-through-Boise night. "Hey, we should get a suite at one of the hotels and all crash there. That way no one has to drive."

"Perfect idea." Estebe held up his phone. "I'll get two suites for Thursday night. One for the boys and one for the girls. We need to be respectable in our drunken haze."

Angie laughed as he walked away to make the reservation. She sank into a stool next to Ian, and Jeorge gave her a drink.

"Sparkling water with lime." He smiled as he went back to his closing tasks. "You look like you need it."

"What's happening? You do look worn out." Felicia sat next to her. "Were there problems in the kitchen? I heard a crash."

"We need to order a set of dishes. We had an accident." Angie bit her lip. "I'm not sure Hallie is going to work out. She might be sabotaging the other chefs. Have you heard anything negative from her other assignments?"

Felicia looked back toward the kitchen.

"I've already sent her home, so you can speak freely." Angie got a knot in her stomach. Felicia kept up on the rumors, especially in the culinary community.

"It didn't seem like much, but there's some speculation on why she hasn't been hired for a permanent spot yet. Typically, the temp pool is filled with people who want to be part-timers. People who are going to school or trying to move into another field and need to supplement their income. Hallie's been running in the temp pool for over a year now." She pointed to Jeorge, and he poured her a glass of chardonnay. She noticed Angie's look and shrugged. "It's not my fault I live upstairs and don't have to drive. Anyway, she just came off a two-month stint at Canyon Creek. Do you want me to call and find out why they didn't keep her?"

Angie rolled her aching shoulders. She really wanted a glass of wine, or a massage, or both. "I'll call Sydney tomorrow. I haven't talked to her in ages."

"You don't have to call her. She'll be at the wedding shower at the Red Eye." Felicia sipped her wine. "You forgot that Barb's throwing a party for me and Estebe at the bar tomorrow afternoon before we open."

"I didn't forget about the party." Angie finished her water. She'd have to talk to Estebe tomorrow at the event. "I forgot that tomorrow was Saturday. I'm heading home. Dom's been good this week with me being late, but I'm pretty sure if I don't come home on time tonight, he'll be eating the couch to make me pay."

"He's a good boy. He'd probably just eat the wingback chair." Ian stood as well. "I'll walk you out and then head back to my apartment too. I'm beat. You all are too much of a party crowd for this old man."

Estebe came back and tucked his phone in his pocket. "Reservations are made. And we're getting a full room service breakfast the next morning delivered to the girls' room at eight. That way Felicia can't sleep the day away."

"I can stay in bed while the rest of you eat." She leaned into his arms.

"Not if the food smells amazing. You have a soft spot for sweets, and the hotel is doing tableside crepes for us." He kissed her cheek. "If you stay in bed, you don't get huckleberry crepes."

"You're evil." She laughed and sipped her wine.

"I'll see you guys tomorrow." Angie put a hand on Felicia's arm. "Get some rest. It's been a hard week for you."

"One more day and I can sleep in for over a month. Tomorrow's service is packed. All the slots were filled last week. Maybe Estebe and I shouldn't take off for a full month."

Angie held up her hand in a stop motion. "Don't even start. If Hallie doesn't work out, I'll find another replacement. Besides, I want you to find all sorts of new recipes for us to try out. It's kind of a work vacation."

"Don't say that to Estebe; he'll be emailing you daily anyway." Felicia nodded her understanding. "Okay, we'll keep our trip, but if something happens, you need to let me know."

"I'll be FaceTiming you as soon as the disaster hits. You know I can't keep a secret." Angie patted Estebe's arm. "See you tomorrow. I want to chat a bit before service, so save me some time."

He looked at her, and she could see the questions in his eyes, but he let it go until tomorrow. "Bye, Angie. Bye, Ian. Tell Dom it's his job to watch the house while you're gone and praise him for doing such a good job."

"You know he sleeps all day, right?" Angie asked as she stepped away.

"If you praise him for what he's not doing, maybe he'll be more likely to not focus on missing you and start chewing your favorite chair." Estebe held out a hand and shook with Ian. "You'll be there tomorrow at this party so I have someone to talk to, right?"

"I've already been told I have to attend. We'll sit on the side and talk football."

"You two are horrible." Angie strode to the kitchen with Ian by her side. As they waved goodbye to Matt and Nancy, who were almost finished cleaning the kitchen, Ian held out Angie's coat.

"Do you want to tell me what happened tonight?" he asked as they stepped outside.

Angie used her remote to start her car, then walked out to get inside. "Let me call you on the way home. I want your opinion on this too."

"No, I'll call you when I get back to the apartment. That way I can have my slippers on and a cup of cocoa by my side. I'll give better feedback that way." He kissed her. "Talk to you in a minute."

As she pulled the car out of the parking lot, she saw him walking through the alley to the building where his office and his apartment were located. She'd have time to get out of town and onto country back roads before he called, so other than a random loose cow or wild driver, she shouldn't have much to worry about watching out for as they talked.

She'd already wrapped the set of cookware she'd bought the new couple. And she'd kept the receipt for the crazy expensive brand. Just in case. Estebe was particular about the pans he used at the restaurant, and he might already have a really good set at home. But if she was getting married, this set was what she'd want from a good friend.

Her phone rang and she answered it, leaving her worries about tomorrow's party in town and instead going through her concerns about her newest, although temporary, employee with Ian. He was an amazing sounding board on most subjects.

And he didn't disappoint her tonight. By the time she arrived home, she'd made up her mind. She'd talk to Sydney, but if she heard what she thought she would, Hallie's last night at the County Seat would be tomorrow.

Chapter 11

Saturday morning flew by faster than Angie wanted. Time off always did that to her. She'd spent some quality time in the sunny and warm barn with Precious and Mabel, telling them all about what had happened that week. They both agreed with Angie that the key to Jason's death had to be the calls he'd made before he'd arrived in Boise and who he'd spent time with before reaching out to Felicia.

Or at least that's what Angie thought the goat and hen would say if they could talk. Dom had accompanied her on the trip out to the barn to feed the animals, but he was staying close to the door. Just in case Precious burst through her pen and attacked the Saint Bernard, who was more than eighty pounds bigger than she was.

Precious had him fooled and she knew it. To prove her point, she nodded at Angie and bleated out several words before jumping out of the pen and out into the pasture through her private door.

Angie stood and dusted the remains of the oats she'd been hand feeding the goat off her pants. A sound alerted her that someone had pulled into the dirt driveway, and she crossed the barn to see who it was. Ian's old truck was parking in front of the garden. The truck used to be red from what she could tell, but now it was more rust brown than anything. She snapped her fingers to get Dom's attention, and they both left the barn to meet the newcomer.

Dom recognized the truck and ran over to jump on Ian. Angie smiled as she saw the effort it took for Ian to keep standing. Which was one of the reasons she'd tried to stop him from letting Dom jump on him when he was a pup. He didn't jump on her—in fact, he sat with his tail flying back and forth behind him whenever Angie came home or if he thought she had a treat. But Ian had thought he'd known best. Soon, Dom was going to be big enough to knock Ian down when he jumped, and Angie would have to be the one to rescue him from big, slobbery dog kisses.

"Hey you, I didn't expect to see you before the party." Angie crossed over the driveway to meet him at the edge of the garden.

"I thought I'd come by and drive you in. That way I can drive you home and pick up my truck after service tonight." He nodded toward the garden spot. "Not next weekend, but maybe the week after, I'll come rototill your garden plot. It's about time to plant. The snow is almost off Mount Shaffer."

"Maybe for potatoes and some of the lettuce. I hate to plant too early and have the snow freeze off the plants before they have time to root." She glanced over at the herb garden she'd moved up against the backyard privacy fence. "I do need to work on that section sooner rather than later. Maybe next week while we're closed."

"Angie, do you really think you're going to have any gardening time the week before Felicia gets married? I'm not even in the wedding, and my week is booked. You're going to have to be part of the rehearsals, rehearsal dinner, fittings, and now we've got bar hopping on Thursday to add to the fun. Although I would have rather had a slightly less over-the-top night."

"You and me both." She took his arm. "Maybe the week after, we can focus on the gardens and getting this place ready for spring. I'm so excited to show you what I decided to plant."

"I was wondering if I could get you to save a few rows for me too." He put an arm around her waist. "If you have some room. I'd love to try these heirloom tomato seeds my mom sent me from England."

"Let's go grab a quick lunch and talk about what we need to plant." She strolled with him toward the house. This was comfortable, like what a couple should be. "Grilled cheese okay?"

"Sounds amazing." He snapped his fingers, and Dom came running. He'd been sniffing at a bug in the driveway.

Angie hoped Estebe and Felicia's life would be simple and easy like hers was right now. But maybe marriage changed that. She'd been young when her folks had died, and Nona had lost her husband many years before that. So solid adult couple examples weren't part of Angie's life, and Ian had grown up with a single mom in a different country.

She washed her hands as they talked about plants and gardens. She put soup on a burner to warm as she got the sandwiches ready. "Do you think it's important for kids to have both parents around? I mean, to have a good example when they're older."

"My mom did an amazing job with raising me, and I never knew my father." Ian set aside the notebook where he'd been drawing a plan for the garden. "On the other hand, Bleak had both parents, and they acted less like adults than they expected their kids to act."

"Yeah, maybe it's not about the family you grew up in." Angie put the first sandwich in a hot pan, and the sizzle made her smile. "Estebe had both parents, and he's amazing. Felicia had both parents, and although she's amazing, I think it's in spite of her upbringing."

"So why the esoteric discussion about family ties and the people we become? Did you find out something on Jason?" Ian stood and got out bowls, plates, and silverware for lunch. They had a routine. "Or is something else bothering you?"

"I don't know. Maybe it's meeting Felicia's family. On paper, they're perfect. It's a whole 'nother thing once you meet them. I'm so lucky to have her in my life and as my best friend. I just wish they saw the amazing woman their daughter has become rather than worry about what she's not." Angie flipped the sandwich and poured soup into both bowls.

Ian took the soup bowls and set them on the table. Then he got out sodas for each of them. "You can't change what another person thinks. All you can do is be there for your friend. I'm so lucky I got to meet you. And you brought Felicia, Estebe, Matt, Nancy, and even Hope into my life. I had my friends and my church group before we met, but you brought in such interesting people."

"You're responsible for Bleak. You found her in an alley."

Ian snorted out the drink of soda he'd just taken. "Don't make me laugh when I'm trying to eat. You make her sound like I took in a stray cat."

"Technically, what I said was true. I guess I'm rethinking my work family a little, too, since Hallie may be leaving us. I didn't see these issues earlier when she worked a day here and there. Why can't people just be nice to each other?" Angie sat down and waited for Ian to bless the food before she picked up her spoon. Her mind wasn't on being grateful for what she had; it was on how wrong she could be about people.

"You don't know the whole story yet. I think your assumptions are going to be right, but don't jump to a conclusion and blame yourself until you talk to Sydney. She's got a good head on her shoulders. She'll tell you what you need to know to make a fair decision." Ian squeezed her hand. "We better get to eating or we'll have to leave everything out and Dom will have a field day."

"True." She squeezed his hand before releasing it and picking up her sandwich. "Thanks for centering me. You always seem to say the right thing."

"Except for Wednesday night when I added to the flames during our fight." He grinned as he dunked his sandwich into the soup.

"Let's not talk about that." Angie frowned as she ate her lunch. "Except we didn't get to talk to anyone at the community center bar. No one was there when we went to meet Estebe."

"And you think there's anyone who's going to say, 'Well, yeah, I'm jealous of the guy so I set him up for murder'?" He stirred his soup, then set the spoon down. "I bet Javier would know if anyone had a beef against Estebe. Probably better than Estebe would. That guy thinks everyone is as open and trustworthy as he is. He's going to rent Bleak and Hope a house down near the college so they can walk to school. Heck, I think he's actually buying a place just so it fits their requirements. He takes care of his own, even when his own isn't blood related."

"Javier will be at the party today. Can you chat with him about the guys at the community center? And then maybe drop some names off to your uncle?" Angie thought about Ian's statement. "Estebe *is* way too trusting. He blamed himself for the plate thing, even though he knew he hadn't told her to overstock him."

"A good characteristic for living life, but maybe not as far as getting out of this detective's crosshairs for Jason's murder." He finished his sandwich and took it and the empty soup dish to the sink. "Maybe Uncle Allen has talked to this bartender and has another viable suspect. He said he thought he'd get the phone number list information from the carrier today. I'll give him a call after I talk to Javier. That way I might have some information for him as well."

Angie pushed the bowl away and stood. "I'm not as hungry as I thought. Will you clean up while I get ready for the party? I need to pack work clothes to take with me as well."

He came over and pulled her into a hug. "I can do that. But you need to stop worrying. Everything is going to be all right."

Angie didn't think he was correct this time, but she nodded and went upstairs to change. When she came down, Ian was making notes in her murder book. "What did you find out? Or did I miss writing something down?"

"I was updating it from my chat with Uncle Allen. He has the owner of the phone number. It's the bartender. Larry Fortell. The phone number that the bar had was for his ex-roommate's house. Which was why no one was calling Uncle Allen back. When he called Larry, he admitted to seeing his brother. Half brother, technically. He said Jason was trying to talk him into coming home. But apparently there's some bad blood in the family. He's going over to get a statement now."

"You're telling me that Jason was here trying to get his brother to come home *and* talk Felicia into moving back. Man, they must think a lot of Boston. Or not much about Boise." Angie grabbed her larger tote and put the notebook into it along with her clothes for her work shift. "Well, we know why Jason agreed to come and talk to Felicia. He had a second agenda."

"Yeah. Uncle Allen thinks that second agenda might be enough to at least cast some doubt on Roland's theory. He's going to talk to his captain next week to see if he can get the guy to back off on Estebe."

"That's the best news I've heard today. So we're going to a party for a wedding that might actually happen." She leaned down and gave Dom a kiss. "Is he set up for the night?"

"He is, and I went out and checked on the zoo. Precious is loving this warmer weather. She's ready for summer." He glanced around the room and took Angie's keys from her. "I'll drive, and when I get there, I'll run up to the apartment to change into a suit. You look too good to have your date look like a dud."

"Mystery date is always interesting." She grinned as he looked at her blankly. "Don't tell me they don't have the game Mystery Date in England. You hit a certain spot and draw a card and then spin the wheel. When you open the door, your mystery date has arrived. And there's always a chance you get the dud."

"You had an interesting childhood." He opened the door and held it for her. "Did you play the game often?"

"I didn't have one, but my neighbor did. Sandy was my best friend until Mom and Dad died and I came to live with Nona. I should have kept in touch, but what do you say when the door for your life has opened and you got the dud?" She took a long look around the kitchen. "Nona saved my life. I was drowning in my grief, and she brought me back, one plate of food at a time."

The ride into River Vista was quiet. Ian left her alone as she thought about her grandmother and how much she'd meant to her. Maybe she was just missing Nona, which had her melancholy. Or maybe Felicia's upcoming nuptials had her worried about what adding Estebe into the mix as a permanent part of Felicia's life would mean to their friendship. But she didn't think that was what was causing her unease. Something else was bothering her. It centered around family. And now, knowing that Jason had encountered more family issues just before his death made her even more anxious.

There was something there. She just couldn't put her finger on it.

She said goodbye to Ian in the parking lot behind the County Seat. "I'll drop this off in my office and then head over to the Red Eye. I'll meet you there."

"Don't be long. I hate showing up to these events stag. Everyone thinks I'm there to pick up chicks." He winked at her as he turned and jogged toward his building.

"In your dreams, buddy," she called after him. When she got to the back door, it was unlocked and opened. Had Felicia not secured it when she'd left the apartment? "Hello?"

Two angry voices sounded in the kitchen. She recognized one, Estebe. Was he being attacked? She dug out her phone and got it ready to dial 9-1-1 if she needed to call quickly. Then she stepped into the building and slowly opened the kitchen door.

Estebe was yelling at someone standing in front of him. "Javier, you need to stop trying to fix this. You need to stay out of the police investigation."

"You were the one who sent me after Angie. You were the one who wanted me to keep an eye on Felicia. I was only helping you out."

"I know. I was wrong. Cousin, I don't want you to get in trouble just because of your relationship with me." Estebe's voice dropped, and he put a hand on Javier's shoulder. "I care about what happens to you. If you were convicted of killing Jason just because you're my cousin, I'd never forgive myself."

"Estebe, Javier, what's going on?" Angie called out, letting the door slam behind her. She wanted it to look like she'd just arrived and hadn't heard the last part of the fight. "We've got a party to get to. Why are you here at the restaurant?"

"We were just talking, Angie." Estebe shot a warning glance toward Javier. "Why are you here?"

"Dropping off my work clothes. Probably the same as you. Ian's going to be at the Red Eye before we are. Did Felicia already leave?" Angie moved around the two, keeping up her charade. "If you'll wait a minute, you can walk me over to the bar."

"Of course." Estebe's voice dropped, but Angie still heard his next words to Javier. "I warn you, cousin, stay out of this. I appreciate what you did, but now it's over."

She set her bag on the floor of the office and sat down in her chair for a minute. What had Javier done for Estebe? Had he taken it too far and eliminated the perceived competition? Javier was a hothead, and he'd been spitting mad when he'd seen Angie and Felicia eating breakfast with Jason.

Had he taken it upon himself to protect Estebe's interests? She shook her head. No use getting all upset about a theory. But, she decided, she would have Ian ask his uncle if Javier had an alibi for the time Jason was killed.

That would make her feel a little better.

"Angie?" Estebe called from the open kitchen door. "Are you ready?"

"Yep." She stood and brushed off her skirt, making sure she didn't have dog hair on her clothes. It had been one of her habits since Dom came into her life, and most times, she did carry around a bit of her pet with her, no matter how careful she had been.

Maybe that was what happened to the killer too? Maybe he carried a bit of Jason with him now that he or she had ended the Boston businessman's life.

Ian was waiting inside at the bar. When he saw her, he hurried over and greeted her. "I didn't know if you'd be coming from the front or the alley, so I stayed here in the middle." He handed her a glass of champagne. "I thought you'd arrive first. What took you so long?"

Angie didn't want Estebe to be thinking about how long she'd been standing there, listening, so she ignored Ian's question and grasped Estebe's arm with her hand. "There's Felicia. She looks lovely, don't you think? You should go be with her. This is a party for the two of you, together."

Estebe glanced down at Angie and frowned. "Are you all right? You seem...off."

"I'm fine. A lot on my mind." She nodded to Felicia. "She's waiting for you."

After he'd left, she and Ian watched as Felicia and Estebe greeted the new arrivals to the party. After a few sips, he leaned closer. "Do you want to tell me what just happened?"

She shook her head. "Not now. But I do want you to ask your uncle something."

"Okay." He turned toward her. "I'm calling him after the party. What do you need to know?"

"Ask him if Javier has a solid alibi for Jason's murder." As she uttered the words, Javier came into the bar from the back door. He glanced at her and Ian. Then he took a glass from a passing waiter's tray and held it up to them.

"I'm going to want more, you know. Good thing I'm driving you home so you can explain all this." He held up his own glass to Javier and smiled. "I'm going over to see what I can find out about other possible suspects. I'll see what Javier has to say about his own innocence as well."

"Be careful."

He kissed her cheek. "Always. Go have fun."

Chapter 12

Angie had just finished her walk-through talking to the other guests when the door opened, and Sydney from Canyon Creek stepped into the bar. She ran over to Angie when she saw her near the dance floor. "Isn't this the craziest place to have a pre-wedding party? I've never been to a dive bar before."

Angie glanced around to see if Barb was in earshot. The Red Eye's owner knew her bar was a dive, but that didn't mean others could call it that without getting grief. "The owner's a friend of ours. I'm so glad you could make it."

"I had to get lunch going, but then I took off the apron and told my crew they could deal with everything else. I'm hoping the place doesn't burn down while I'm gone." She took an appetizer from one of the passed trays. "Did you cater?"

"No, we got a company called Party Planners to handle that. I'm not sure I could have fit in one more thing. As it was, I needed to hire a temporary at the restaurant this week. Do you know Hallie Godfrey? I think I heard she worked for you."

The look on Sydney's face told Angie all she needed to know. But she waited for her friend to swallow the bacon-wrapped shrimp she'd just stuffed in her mouth.

Before Sydney said anything more, she looked around the room. She pulled Angie into an empty corner by the bandstand. "Look, there's nothing I can prove, but I'd get the girl out of your kitchen sooner rather than later. She likes to make herself at home, and in my opinion, she was working on creating her own place at my restaurant. People who I trusted for years were making mistakes. One guy 'lost' the night deposit. It set me back four thousand that night, but I don't think he lost it. I think Hallie took it."

"I've already seen her in action. She was going after Estebe and trying to drive a wedge between us." Angie shook her head. "It's sad, but I'm going to have to get rid of her tonight. I love my work family. I don't want to let a viper crawl around the kitchen."

"A little dramatic, but I see your point." Sydney waved at Felicia and Estebe. "I need to go and say hi to the bride and groom. Just keep my name out of it when you fire her and don't let down your guard. I had a tire get slashed a few nights after I told the temp service we didn't need her anymore."

"Wow." Angie pulled her phone out of her pocket. "But you reminded me I don't have to fire her personally. The service can tell her that her services are no longer required."

"Like I said, keep an eye out for the next few days. The girl is mean. Especially when she doesn't get what she wants." Sydney kissed her on the cheek. "I'll say my goodbyes now and see you at the wedding. I need to get back to the restaurant. Now you have me anxious about being gone."

Angie made the call to the temp service and then pocketed her phone. If she was going to cut the cord with Hallie, it was better sooner than later. Now, maybe she could relax a little. She went over and met Ian, who was just coming inside. "Did you forget something at the apartment?"

"Javier wanted a smoke, so we went out to the alley to talk. He says that even though a lot of people are threatened by Estebe, he can't think of one who would frame him for murder. These guys live by a code. And you don't hurt a brother, even if he is arrogant and rude."

"Well, there goes that theory." Angie walked over to a table and sat down. "I just fired the temp, Hallie."

"How did that go?" Ian handed her another flute and sat next to her. "Was she upset?"

"No clue. I let the service do it. But according to Sydney, I should expect some backlash from the action. She got her tires slashed." Angie set the glass down without tasting the drink. "I'm so tired of people who think violence solves anything."

"Well, that makes my decision—I'm not driving back to the apartment tonight. I'll be sleeping in your guest room, just in case." Ian took her hand. "Don't worry so much. You're taking on way too much stress this week."

She turned to look at him. "And how exactly do you think I should be dealing with everything that's happened this week? Just let Felicia deal with it and ruin her wedding?"

"Okay, so I said the wrong thing, again." He glanced around the room. "Can we table this to the drive back tonight as well?"

"Yeah, I'm drained, and I don't want my emotions to ruin Felicia and Estebe's party." She stood and picked up the glass. "I'm going to go make idle small talk with people. I'll see you after work."

"I just wish..." Ian's words dropped off as the door to the bar opened and Mr. and Mrs. Williams walked in with Carter in tow. "Wow, I didn't think they'd come. I knew Estebe had invited them the other day when they stopped at the restaurant, but I never thought they'd show up."

Angie watched Felicia's face as she noticed her family. She went from happy and relaxed to stone cold. It wasn't hate but more like indifference now reflected on her face. "We better get over there to navigate any issues."

Ian followed Angie as she moved through the still-chatting crowd. When she reached the main table, she stepped behind Felicia and put a hand on her back. Trying to let her friend know she was there to support her.

"Mother, Father, Carter, thank you for coming. Although I didn't expect to see you." Felicia exchanged air kisses with her mother.

"Now, Felicia, we are family. What kind of people would we be if we didn't come to celebrate your new life with Estebe?" Carter reached out to shake Estebe's hand. "I don't think we met when you visited Boston last month. I was in DC doing some lobbying."

Felicia's gaze flicked between Carter and Estebe. "I didn't realize you'd visited Boston last month. I thought you were going to New York."

He shook Carter's hand, then drew Felicia closer, leaving his hand on her waist. "I didn't tell you I was going. I went to get your father's permission for our marriage. When I was unsuccessful, I didn't want to bring up a sore spot."

"Totally my fault," Felicia's father spoke up. "I was unprepared to hear that my little girl was tying the knot. We'd gotten used to Jason hanging around after high school, but we didn't realize how much Felicia had grown in the years we've been apart. Life happens when you're not looking, I guess."

Everything that was being said was technically right, but for some reason, it felt so wrong. Angie glanced at Felicia, who wasn't showing any emotion right now at all.

"Anyway, since we may not be able to stay for the wedding, we wanted to give you your gift today. I'm sure you can put it to good use." He pulled out an envelope from his suit pocket and held it out to Felicia. When she made no movement to take it, he turned and held it out to Estebe.

He took the envelope, then laid it on the table. "Thank you for your gift. I wish you would reconsider staying for the wedding."

"With Jason's death, we need to restructure some things at the business. I'm afraid it just doesn't make sense to stay." He glanced at his wife, who didn't look at Felicia as she nodded. "My wife and I are heartbroken that we won't be able to attend."

Maybe Mrs. Williams was feeling the strain, but Felicia's father was just phoning it in.

Carter's eyes twinkled as he watched his father. "Me, too. I know Felicia has been dreaming of a storybook wedding since I met her."

Estebe glanced down at Felicia, and the love that shone through that one look made Angie tear up. "We are excited about starting our new lives, our new family together."

"Well, I guess we should be going. Our plane is leaving tonight, and we're still not packed." Mr. Williams nodded to the crowd and turned, with Carter on his heels.

Felicia's mother stood, frozen to the spot. "Felicia, I'm so sorry we can't be there."

Felicia met her gaze. "I'm sure you are."

"MaryEllen? Are you coming?" Mr. Williams stood at the door.

"I really am sorry," Mrs. Williams whispered, then hurried to catch up with her husband.

After the door closed, Felicia sank into a chair. "I can't believe they just did that. They never let me have one memory without ruining it."

"Well, they won't be at the wedding." Estebe knelt beside her. He held her glass up to her lips. "Drink this. You look pale."

She took the glass but set it down on the table. "Don't be too sure about them not crashing the wedding. They like making an entrance and then disappearing. It's the Williamses' way."

Barb came over and pulled up a chair to sit next to Felicia. "I hate to cut this short, but my Saturday crowd is going to start showing up anytime, and they'll think it's a free buffet and open bar if we don't close it down now."

Felicia turned toward Barb and gave her a hug. "Thank you so much for all you did for me and Estebe. This party was wonderful. All my friends said how much they loved visiting the Red Eye."

"They were reliving their college days, when they actually hung out in places like this." Barb laughed, and Angie mentally agreed with her. "You all go back to the restaurant, and I'll let your guests know that the party is over."

"Thanks, Barb." Estebe held out his hand. Instead of shaking it, Barb stood up and gave him a hug. "I guess since you're marrying this one and she's a part of my family, you're family now too. And I don't shake hands with family."

Angie blinked. If this moment got any sweeter, she'd think she was in the middle of one of those rom-com movies Felicia liked to watch. "I'll help you carry the gifts back to the apartment."

As they loaded up the gifts, Angie picked up the card Felicia's father had left. Felicia shook her head.

"I'm not letting them buy their way out of being parents. Whatever is in there, I'm putting away in a savings account for my kid. I'll give it to them and tell them their grandparents gave this to them. It will probably be the only inheritance they're going to see. Dad's MO is to slash and burn, even in business. I just hope they've put away enough so they'll have something to live on if he can't work."

"Our children will be fine without their money." Estebe still stood near her. Angie could tell he was worried, but he was trying not to show it.

"Of course they will. I just want my kids to have this money and for me to know that I didn't benefit from it at all. When I was growing up, everyone thought my parents were good in business, and they might be, but they are horrible at raising children." Felicia put her hand on Estebe's chest and leaned into him. "I love you, and nothing they say or do is going to change that."

Angie took a load of boxes and bags and went out the back to the County Seat. She'd leave all the gifts at the bottom of the stairs in the lobby area, and Felicia and Estebe could haul them upstairs. She had work to do, including finding a replacement for Estebe during his vacation.

Estebe came into the hallway after her and added to the pile. "I think the men can do the next two runs. Why don't you go work in your office? I'm sure you're getting behind on the day-to-day stuff since you had to deal with my issues."

"What's happening to you is worth more than the day-to-day stuff. But let me know when you need me to time travel and get you set up in the court of King James. I'm sure you'd make an excellent knight." She recentered a box that was about ready to fall. "But you are right, I need to get a temp set up for when you're gone. I thought maybe we'd be able to give you the night off, but I'll be short if I do."

"Wait, what about Hallie? She seemed to be a competent chef. She was learning the process. Did she get another job?" Estebe looked confused.

"No, I asked the temp service not to send her back. I don't think you noticed, but she seemed to be a game player. I don't want anyone in the kitchen that messes with my family." She watched him process the information.

"I wasn't going to say anything, but she came to me several times the last couple of days complaining about Matt. She said he was a slacker and forcing all the work off on her. I told her I watch everyone in the kitchen. Matt was just trying to train her in our ways." He leaned closer. "She threatened to tell you that I was playing favorites with Matt because he was male. I told her that if anyone was my favorite, it was Nancy because she's such a hard worker."

"I bet that went over well."

He sighed. "Then she went on to tell me all about the mistakes Nancy made on the line. I swear, the woman wasn't happy. Not at all."

"And you just gave me two more examples of why I don't want her working in our kitchen. We've worked hard to develop a team, a family. And we don't need to invite in a snake." She patted his arm. "I'm so happy for you and Felicia. It will be like I've gotten a brother. You treat her well, Estebe, or you'll have to deal with me."

"I think Felicia can fight her own battles, although I will treat her like a queen. And yes, you are going to be my sister after Saturday, which means if you need anything, all you have to do is ask." He kissed her on the cheek. "Thank you for bringing me into your family when you hired me. This was supposed to be a short-term job until I got my real estate holdings in order. Now, I believe I've signed up for a life stint."

"Funny, Ian said something close to that today at the house. Not about the job turning into a lifelong commitment but about the family we have." She knew she'd done the right thing in removing Hallie from the County Seat. "I guess you're all a bunch of softies when a wedding is on its way."

He laughed. "You're just as bad. We'll see who's crying on Saturday after the ceremony. I'm pretty sure you'll be on the list."

"Whatever. See you at service. Do you need help with prep?" She started for the kitchen door, pulling her keys out of the coat she'd worn over her party dress.

"Matt and Nancy came to the party, so they will be here for prep. Hope and Bleak would have come, but Chief Brown said no since it was being held in a bar. Even though it wasn't open. And since Bleak couldn't go, Hope decided to take her to get her nails done. They will be at the wedding and the reception, so missing one party isn't a problem." He followed her to the outside door. "The things those girls tell me."

"You're the big brother they always wanted to have." Angie laughed and unlocked the door to the kitchen.

"Lock the door when you get inside. There are too many people coming and going for it to be open. I don't like the idea of you being alone in there," Estebe called from the stairs.

"See what I mean, big brother is watching," Angie muttered, but she followed his instructions and locked the door. Then she turned on lights as she went through the restaurant. It was her pattern to walk through the restaurant before heading into her office. She made a pot of coffee in the servers' area, then walked out into the main dining room. When she turned on the front lights, the white lights twinkled over the wooden rails they'd installed last winter to make it look more like a Mediterranean patio. The wedding would be beautiful here.

As she surveyed the area, she watched as someone came up to the window and pulled out a spray can. She pulled her phone out of her jacket and held it up to take a video as she moved toward the vandal. As she watched through the display, she saw the woman's face as she realized she was being filmed. She shrieked and then jumped into a waiting car that sped off.

Angie hurried to the front door and unlocked it, keeping the video going. She zoomed in to see the license plate on the red sedan. "I can't believe she just did that."

She finished filming the outside of the County Seat, where one window had letters in black paint, B and I and T... She shut the video off and called 9-1-1. "I'd like to report vandalism. And I have video proof that clearly shows the suspect and the car she took off in."

"Oh, no," Cenna, the dispatcher, responded before she went into professional mode. "Where did this happen?"

"The County Seat. This is Angie Turner. Can you send a car over? I'd like to get this paint off before we start service." Angie held on the phone as the dispatcher called the deputy on duty, and Angie heard the siren start up a few blocks down on Main Street. The deputy probably could have run here faster than jumping in the car. When he arrived at the County Seat after making a U-turn in the middle of the street, Angie was glad to see it was Brandon. She hung up with the dispatcher and walked toward the car.

When Brandon got out and surveyed the damage, he whistled. "Man, did you make someone mad? I'm pretty sure I could finish the word even if you didn't give me two more letters."

"Yeah, you and all of my customers, who will be here in about three hours. Any way we can get the pictures and clean off the paint before then?"

Angie felt sick. She and Felicia had painted the front of the restaurant before they'd opened. Now, she was going to have to try to get paint off the windowpanes and the trim.

"I'll get the pictures first, then take your statement." Brandon took out his camera. "Maybe if you have some paint thinner, you can get it off the trim. You might have to touch it up again. Do you know who did this?"

"I know, and I have proof and a motive." She held up her phone. "I have video of Hallie Godfrey defacing my restaurant."

Chapter 13

Ian came out and helped Angie clean off the windows. She told the kitchen staff to concern themselves with prep. She was trying to burn off her anger at Hallie by keeping busy and talking Ian's ear off. "I can't believe any adult would act in this type of childish way."

Ian nodded and finished clearing off the last letter. "I think we'll have to let it sit, and we can look at it tomorrow to see if we'll need to repaint. Did you keep the paint codes so we can match it?"

"Yeah, they're somewhere in the office." Angie checked the time on her watch. "We need to get this stuff inside. I hope they arrest her so I don't have to worry about this happening again tomorrow."

"Angie, I don't think they'll keep her in jail for long on a vandalism charge. Even with the evidence, she'll have to have a trial." He picked up the rags and paint thinner can. He took the rag out of Angie's hand. "I know you're angry, but she won't go to jail for years for this."

"She should. And for slashing Sydney's tires. They should add that charge in too. Actions like that prove she can't take rejection as an adult."

"At least you got her out of your kitchen. Who knows how much worse it might have been if you'd fired her a month from now?" He nodded to the door. "Let's go inside, and you can get cleaned up. You should have changed before you came out here to help me clean this."

"I didn't want to get my work clothes smelling like chemicals." She stepped back and took another look at the window. "It doesn't look that bad, does it?"

"Most people won't even notice." He started toward the door.

Bleak and Hope walked around the building from the parking lot. "Hey, Matt has his music so loud they can't hear us knocking. And the door's locked. Whoa, what happened to the window?"

"Not noticeable, huh?" Angie shot Ian a death stare. "I fired Hallie today, and she was displeased, so she wrote me a letter."

"Actually, three letters," Ian corrected.

"Not funny, Ian." Angie studied the window again. "We'll get it repainted tomorrow, but hopefully tonight it won't show as much in the dark."

"Well—" Bleak started, but Hope grabbed her arm.

"Angie, I'm sure you're right. In fact, I can hardly see it now. I bet no one will notice." Hope pulled Bleak toward the restaurant door. "We need to get busy. Felicia said we're fully booked tonight."

As the girls disappeared into the restaurant, Angie dropped onto the bench they kept out on the sidewalk for overflow. "Everyone's going to see it, aren't they?"

"If they do, they'll understand. It wasn't your fault. Hallie did this, and she's the only one to blame. If you hadn't been here or if you'd waited until tomorrow, maybe she would have done something more than just spray-painting the window." Ian pulled her to her feet, and they started toward the door. "You need to get showered and changed. You have people to feed. Everything's going to be all right."

"You say that a lot. Even when all the facts go against that premise." She opened the door since his hands were full with the rags and thinner.

He kissed her cheek. "I have something better than facts. I have faith."

After chatting with Felicia, Angie grabbed her tote and headed up to the apartment, making her way through the stacks of gifts still in the hallway. The silver-and-blue-wrapped gifts made her smile for the first time since she'd witnessed Hallie's betrayal.

Of course, in Hallie's mind, Angie had betrayed her first. When was business just business, and when was it personal? The question rolled in Angie's head as she scrubbed off the chemical smells and some of the kinks that had been in her neck for the last hour. Felicia had a lavender-scented body wash that was supposed to calm the user. Angie thought it might be working; at least she hoped it was so she wouldn't bite someone's head off during service. It wasn't her staff's fault, so she needed to let this anger go before she went in to expedite the service.

A positive attitude was important in making a service successful. Going into a service with anger and pain only ensured that things would be under- or overcooked, burned, slow, or simply wrong. People needed a clear mind to create, and cooking was creating. In the best way because you got to eat the results. She wanted her customers to not even realize anything bad had happened. The County Seat needed to be a place where they could enjoy a meal with someone they loved and forget about the problems hovering in the outside world.

Ian might have faith, but Angie had something just as powerful—a positive attitude, and that created a happy, fun atmosphere for people to come and work and eat in. Hallie wouldn't steal that from her. Not today.

She checked her watch again. She still had time for a little office work, so she called the temp agency and left a message. She needed a temporary cook for a monthlong assignment starting a week from Wednesday. They would do family meal that day, so she needed them here early. And she reminded them again that it couldn't be Hallie—not after she'd spray-painted the windows after she'd been told that she wouldn't be asked back to the County Seat.

Angie didn't say that she hoped Hallie was in jail by then. It just seemed like bad karma. But she would talk to her representative at the service and let her know what had happened. It was up to Sydney to tell them why she wasn't using Hallie anymore, so she'd leave the tire-slashing story out. However, she'd seen her spray-paint the County Seat window with her own eyes. That story, she would share.

After clearing off the answering machine except for reservation requests, she got on her chef jacket and pulled her hair back into a clip. It was time to work. First up, she went to find Bleak and tell her to call back the reservation requests. She could fit that in between seating guests for the early seating.

Bleak met her at the hostess station after seating a couple near the window. "Hey, Angie, so far, no one has commented on the paint issue. I think we're good there."

"That makes me feel a little better." She smiled at the teenager. "I didn't get to ask, but how's the senior year going? I bet you're busy with all the finishing up stuff."

Bleak held up her hand. "Maggie and Allen bought me a class ring. Can you believe it? I told them I wasn't getting one so I could save for college costs, but they went ahead and got me just what I wanted. I think Hope was involved when they picked it out. They are truly lovely people."

"They think of you as family, not just some random girl who lives in their house." Angie felt a stirring of happiness and pride that the girl who had only been interested in reading when she arrived was becoming part of a community. A family. "Anyway, I've got to get to the kitchen. Can you handle the messages on the reservation line? I know Felicia usually does that, but she's been a little distracted."

"Wedding and all, I get it. I was bummed I couldn't go to the party, but I'll be at the wedding next week. And the reception. Ty and I are going to show everyone our new dance steps. He's been taking hip-hop classes." Bleak glanced at the door. "Incoming. Don't worry about the reservations line. I'll handle it."

"Heaven help us at the reception," Angie muttered once she was out of earshot. If Ian even tried to get her to dance to one of the songs Ty and Bleak would be requesting, she'd have to explain that her body didn't move like that. Especially in the mermaid-style maid of honor dress Felicia'd picked out for her.

When she got to the kitchen, several orders were already in process. She checked the tickets, then stood near Estebe. "Everything going all right?"

"Normal night in the kitchen. I told everyone about the Hallie incident, and somehow, no one was surprised. I think our staff has good instincts on people." He glanced up to the next ticket and added a steak to the grill. "We are a resilient bunch here at the County Seat. We'll get through this season without much trouble."

Angie knew he was thinking about Jason's murder and the fact that Roland, the lead detective, wanted badly for Estebe to be the one who took the blame. "You're right, as always. I have to believe that everything happens for a reason and that everything will work out in the end."

"You're a true believer in the good and Santa Claus," Matt said as he tucked a stack of clean pans under the grill area for the chefs' use. "That's why we love working with you."

Matt's comment made her smile, but she didn't have time to respond when Estebe put up the first two plates of the night. She pulled the ticket, checked the plating, and cleaned the edges of the plate, just in case. Then she called out to the server who was waiting near the door, and the night's service began. "Order up, table four."

* * * *

On the drive home, she told Ian her concerns about Hallie and the short message she'd left the temp agency. "I don't want her to be banned from the service. Okay, well, maybe I do, but the girl has got to learn to take no gracefully."

"Some people never learn that skill. They want what they want and when they want it. From what I'm hearing from Uncle Allen about Jason, he was that way too. Although he had a soft spot for the boarding school he graduated from. I don't even think anyone has said anything about how much he loved and pined for Felicia, even though he told her he'd take her back anytime." Ian turned down the radio when an upbeat song started. "The man seemed to be all about work. He had no close friends or relations in Boston. His folks have passed. Uncle Allen is trying to reach the half brother."

"I'm beginning to think his death was probably a random mugging and things just got out of hand. Have they even looked at that? Or are Estebe or Javier still high on the suspect list?" Angie had a headache. The day had been filled with highs and lows, and she was ready for it to just be over.

"Uncle Allen says that theory is still on the board, but the other detectives working the case are beginning to see that Roland is a little attached to the idea it's Estebe." He turned down the road to the farmhouse. "Quick change of subject, but I haven't seen Mrs. Potter or Erica around this week. Are they home?"

"Her daughter took her and Erica to Mexico for a week. Can you see Mrs. Potter in a swimsuit? She and Erica had me come over before they left, and we had a mini fashion show. Erica got some really cute suits, but Mrs. Potter wouldn't show us anything except the caftans she'd bought to cover up the two new suits. Apparently, cruise wear is a whole thing over at the mall."

"We should go to Mexico one day. Or on a cruise." He pulled into the driveway and parked. "Of course, that might mean I need to get a second job to pay for the trip. I'll look around, and maybe we can talk next winter."

"You know I have money too." Angie got out of the car. "I'm less worried about the cost than what I'd do with Dom and the zoo while we were gone. With Felicia and Estebe getting married, I might have lost my babysitter."

"I doubt that. Estebe loves the zoo as much as Felicia does. In fact, the last time he was here when I did the feeding, he was asking me about it. Maybe he's going to buy a ranch and have some animals now that he's settled down." Ian found the keys and unlocked the door as they heard Dom barking in the kitchen. He leaned down as he opened the door and moved the dog out of the way so they could walk through the doorway. "Hey, buddy, I've come to see you for the night."

"You really don't have to stay. I'm sure I'll be fine. And Hallie has had her hissy fit for being fired." Angie leaned down to give Dom a kiss on the head. "Besides, I've got this guy to protect me."

"No offense to Dom, but he can't dial 9-1-1. I wouldn't be able to sleep if I went home. Give me this one favor. Tomorrow night, you and the animals are all on your own." He leaned up and kissed her. "Are you tired, or do you want to watch something? We have more episodes of the western series."

"As long as it's not zombies, I'm in. I don't think I could handle anything scary tonight. I want happy and safe and maybe funny." Angie went to get the popcorn maker out of the cabinet. "With lots of buttered popcorn and some Junior Mints if we still have a box in the cupboard."

"I refilled your stash after our last movie marathon. I'm surprised you didn't see the Costco pack of boxes in there." He went to the pantry and brought back a sealed ten-pack of movie-sized boxes of the candy. He took a knife and cut through the plastic, then left two boxes out on the counter. "Movie night it is. I think there's a rom-com on Netflix you were talking about seeing."

"You really are the best boyfriend a girl could ever hope for." Angie gave him a quick kiss. "Can you start the popcorn while I change? I smell like tonight's pork chop special."

"I thought you smelled pretty amazing." He laughed and took the jar of popcorn off the shelf. "Take as long as you like, but if you're not down here in fifteen, we're watching an action blow-'em-up film."

"I'll be down in ten." She hurried up the stairs. Life was bad, then good, then okay, she realized. Today had been all of those things. She decided the important part was how you ended it. And tonight, she'd be cuddled on the couch with her guy, her dog at her feet, and snacks within reach. It didn't matter what the movie was, she was right where she wanted to be.

The phone rang at two a.m., waking her. They'd just finished the movie and had retired to separate bedrooms, one of Ian's requirements for when he spent the night. She thought it was charming. Dragging herself up to a sitting position, she answered, "Hello?"

"Sorry to call you, but you would have been mad if I didn't." Felicia was on the other end of the line and talking really fast. "Just don't freak out or drive back here. We've got it handled."

"Wait, you've got what handled?" Angie turned on the light, more awake now, and despite Felicia's assurances, she was freaking out. Just a little. "Tell me what happened."

"Estebe decided to stay over so we could move the gifts up to the apartment and talk about today's events. I can't believe how much happened today. Anyway, we were out on the balcony, drinking wine. It's really not too cold if you bundle up."

"Felicia, get on with it." Angie prayed the building hadn't been set on fire.

"I'm telling you. Just hold your horses," Felicia muttered. "Anyway, we heard a car pull up and stop. We thought it was someone picking somebody up at the Red Eye. You know, one of the *I've had one too many* calls. Estebe went to get more wine from downstairs, and he saw Hallie outside with more paint. He called the police, and they came without lights or sirens."

Angie's heart was pounding.

"Angie, they got her. She's in jail, and from what Chief Brown said, they are going to keep her for a bit. She's crazy. She was yelling about how you betrayed her and how she wished you were dead instead of Jason."

Angie stared at Dom, who was awake and staring back at her. She looked up and saw Ian standing in her doorway dressed in pajama bottoms only. She thought how great he looked as he stood there; then what Felicia had said hit her. "Wait, she mentioned Jason? How did she know him?"

"That's what Chief Brown wants to know," Felicia said.

Chapter 14

Ian called his uncle and confirmed what he could of Felicia's story. Then he talked Angie into not driving back into town. "There's no point. He's not going to let her out until they figure out how she's connected with Jason or with his murder. Felicia has the restaurant under control. You're lucky you have someone in the apartment. You may want to always rent to someone who works for you, just in case something like this happens again."

"Please don't say that." Angie sipped her cocoa as they talked at the kitchen table. Dom, who was usually asleep at this time of the morning, sat on his bed, wide awake, watching them. He'd follow anyone who got up from their chair to move. "But you're right. Driving down there tonight is a waste of time. Thank goodness Estebe caught her in time."

"I'm glad you're seeing my point." Ian went to the counter and poured himself another cup of the cocoa Angie had made while she was waiting for the callback from Ian's uncle. "I'll drive you there if you really need to go, but I don't think there's much you can do, and I suspect Felicia and Estebe have gone to bed finally."

She curled her feet up underneath her and sipped her cocoa. It was almost five on Sunday morning. "I don't think I can go back to sleep now. I'll probably crash early, especially if we go touch up the paint at the restaurant today."

"I've got to teach Sunday school, so I'll need to leave here about eight. You can ride in with me, or I'll just meet you about noon, ready to paint." Ian sat at the table, watching her. "You could try to go back to sleep. You look beat."

"Gee, thanks." She laughed as she set her cup down. "I'm just kidding. It's been a crazy week. And next week will be worse with the wedding and all. I'll tough it out, and I'll drive myself in to meet you. That way, you don't have to drive me back here. I can leave when I think I've had enough. I think I'll bring Dom along so he can get out. We haven't been hiking much this winter. It's either been too cold or I've been too busy."

"The weather should start turning soon. Then you and Dom can go climb the hills at Celebration Park." He checked the time on the clock. "Do you mind if I make a pot of coffee? I don't think the cocoa's going to keep me awake during the sermon. And that would be embarrassing."

"Especially since you're one of the teaching staff." Angie started to uncurl her legs, but Ian held up a hand.

"I'm making the coffee. Just stay still."

Angie stood anyway and went over to the desk. "I wanted to grab the notebook. I'm wondering about what Hallie said about Jason. Did she know him? It's a stretch, but if we can connect the two, maybe that would give your uncle and the other detective something to go on besides framing Estebe."

"Don't box Uncle Allen in with that Roland guy. He's certain Estebe didn't kill Jason. He just hasn't found another suitable alternative. It's been a frustrating case, especially since he's locked out of much of the information since Roland knows he's looking at alternative suspects. And it's not in his jurisdiction." Ian filled the coffeepot with water.

"If he's at church, tell him thank you for last night. I know he didn't have to go to a vandalism call himself." Angie paged through the notebook, hoping something would jump out at her.

"He'll be there. He says the Lord will excuse him if there's an emergent issue, but other than that, he's supposed to be part of the community, and that means attending." He grinned. "Bleak is starting to fit in with the other teens at church. She still holds back a little, but she went to a lock-in the other week, and Maggie said she had a blast."

"I'm glad." Angie had started adding in the notes from the last few days. "Sometimes the people you bond with during high school and college are your friends for life. Look at me and Felicia."

"I have to say, I don't have a lot of contact with my high school friends. Maybe I should reach out more. It's hard when most of them still live in London. I can barely pay for the weekly calls to Mom on my salary." Ian opened the fridge. "Do you mind if I cook some breakfast? Looks like you have eggs and some salsa. Maybe a quick Mexican breakfast skillet? I saw a recipe in our church newsletter that looked easy. You have potatoes to make hash browns?"

"In the pantry. I can look up a recipe if you want one." Angie opened the computer and typed in some general terms.

"No, I'm fine. Just tell me how long I should bake it."

"If I don't know what you're making, I can't tell you that." Angie kept looking for a recipe online. When she'd met Ian, all he'd been able to do was open a can and microwave a frozen meal. Now, he was trying all kinds of recipes when he was home by himself. Some dishes had been more successful than others. She scanned through the choices. She found one that used frozen hash browns as the base, which would account for the quick part of the recipe title. "Was it like this?"

"That's it. But I thought I could make the potato base myself. Will that work?" He peered over her shoulder at the recipe.

"Of course. I'm amazed you remembered the recipe."

He laughed and returned to gather up the rest of the ingredients and to find a pan. "Oh, ye of little faith."

By the time Ian left for church, they'd eaten, cleaned up the kitchen, and he'd fed the zoo. Angie put the notebook away, and after putting a load of laundry into the washer, she went to the living room and grabbed a book. She groaned and set it back down. Seeing Dom watching her, she said, "Look like it's a movie morning. If I start reading, I'll fall asleep."

He must have thought sleeping was a good idea, because he curled up next to the couch and did just that.

* * * *

Angie was in the office at the County Seat when Ian called to let her know he was at the kitchen door. She went to let him in, and he held up a bag from the River Vista Drive In and two milkshakes.

"After church fast food," he said before she could ask. "Before I met you, this was my go-to meal on Sundays. I got me a double with everything and got you a chicken sandwich."

Dom sniffed the bag as Ian came into the kitchen.

"Don't worry, big guy, I got you a kid's burger without any fixing." He set the bags down on the chef's table and started getting out the food. "Oh, an order of curly fries, an order of onion rings, and some plain fries for our furry friend."

"You know we could have cooked something here." Angie sat down after grabbing some paper towels from the counter and Dom's bowl they kept at the County Seat for long days.

"I didn't want you to have to cook. Let me take care of you for a bit. You've had a bad week." He nodded to the kitchen. "You should see if you have something easy you could take home for tonight's dinner. I hate to see you have to cook at all today."

"Cooking relaxes me." Angie broke the hamburger into several sections, then put it and the fries into Dom's bowl. "Do me a favor and slow down when you eat this. You could enjoy your food a bit."

Dom stared at the bowl, and as soon as it was on the floor, he ignored Angie's advice and dug in.

Angie laughed and rubbed his back. "Anyway, I've already taken out a casserole I froze a few weeks ago when I was recipe building. All I have to do is pop it into the oven, and I'm good for dinner. You could come over and eat."

He bit into his burger, shaking his head. When he'd swallowed, he said, "Sorry, I've got work to do before the board meeting tomorrow. I've been playing too much lately."

"If you call searching for a reason for murder 'playing.'" Angie took a bite of her sandwich. It was tasty. Sometimes you just needed some junk food.

"It's a lot more fun than end-of-the-year spreadsheets and reports."

She nodded. "And so is painting window trim, I guess."

"Oh, Uncle Allen said to tell you that there's been some movement on the random killing theory. They're talking to a homeless guy who says he saw Jason blindsided in the alley the night he was killed." Ian dipped an onion ring into the secret sauce container. "So that's encouraging."

"I guess." Angie opened her container of sauce and took an onion ring. "But I hate it when the motivation is just 'I needed a wallet, and this guy walked by.'"

"Sometimes that's all it is." Ian met her gaze. "Sometimes, there isn't a reason that most people can understand. It's looking like Jason's killing is one of those times."

She bit her bottom lip, thinking. "I guess I should just be happy that they aren't throwing Estebe in jail for this. I'll take random if they stop pointing a finger at Estebe."

As if mentioning his name had called him, Estebe walked with Felicia in through the kitchen back door. Dom, now finished with his meal, went to meet them. Estebe looked at the bag on the table. "You brought in food? You know you could have made anything here, including a top-level hamburger."

"Blame Ian. He wanted grease." Angie sipped her milkshake slowly to avoid brain freeze. "Thanks for being the hero last night."

He shrugged, going toward the walk-in to grab ingredients for the lunch he was cooking for him and Felicia. "I was there. That's all I did."

Felicia leaned into him and rested her head on his arm. "That's why I'm marrying him. He's so humble. Jason would have taken credit for the birth of the Christ child if he'd been around."

"That's a little over the top." Ian glanced around, hoping no one was listening.

Angie laughed, knowing that if Ian had felt it matched his current religion, he would have made the sign of the cross. "Relax, Ian, no one's going to shoot thunderbolts toward her. Besides, that's not your God's preference anyway. So did you guys just get up?"

"We've been up for a while. We were talking about next week's plans. I'd like to get in here tomorrow and start setting up for the wedding. Any issues with that?" Felicia pulled out a notebook. "I've got a meeting with the caterer on Wednesday. Our party is Thursday night, and dress rehearsal is Friday morning, with dinner that night. We're having that over at the community center. *I* wanted Canyon Creek."

"I can hear you," Estebe called from the cook line. "I will have them make things other than fried food."

"You have to promise that you won't be too busy working and following up on the food. You need be sitting beside me, having fun with our friends and family." She sighed as she met Angie's gaze. "Which is also why we aren't having it here. We want you to be part of the celebration, not working to get everyone fed."

"You worry too much about everyone else. This is your party," Angie reminded her.

Felicia raised her eyebrows and said, "Which is why I'm going to get my way with this restaurant decision."

"Yes, ma'am." Ian did a quick salute, then focused on his burger when he caught Felicia's glare.

"The community center will be lovely. I'm sure the chefs will make sure everyone's dinner is amazing." Angie stepped in between Felicia and Ian. "You've thought of everything."

A phone rang, and Angie glanced at her own. Finally, she realized the phone was Estebe's.

He picked up the phone still in the office. "Yes, may I help you?"

Angie held her breath as she eavesdropped for more information. However, Estebe took the phone and the call outside.

When he came back inside, the phone was already in his pocket. "I need to go into town. They want to question me again. That was Melvin. He says it's not looking good, and I should expect to have to post bail tonight if they charge me."

"That's stupid. Why would they charge you?"

He tried to look at Felicia but couldn't meet her eyes. "When they went back to the alley, they found a matchbox from the community center."

"A lot of people have those," Felicia responded.

He sank down in a chair. "The homeless man described seeing a man my size on the street after he'd seen Jason in the alley. They want me to take part in a lineup. If he chooses me, I'll be charged."

* * * *

Angie and Ian were outside, painting the window trim. They'd finished their lunch and come outside to give Felicia and Estebe time to be alone before she drove him into Boise. His lawyer would drive him home if he wasn't charged.

"This just doesn't seem fair. There's no way Estebe did this." Angie wiped another spot of brown off the windowpane. She'd painted more of the glass so far than the actual wood trim. If she didn't need something to take her mind off Estebe's problems, she would stop trying to paint.

"Which is why we'll find something to clear him. I'm sure of it. He has an alibi, so that helps."

Angie thought about the note she had in the book. "According to his lawyer, the detective is thinking his friends might lie for him."

"We need to have faith."

Angie focused on the painting. Faith was fine and good, but Estebe needed more than their faith. He needed them to find a murderer so the wedding next week could go off without a hitch. She paused the brush and turned toward Ian. "Tell me what your uncle has found out about this guy at the bar. You said he was Jason's brother? Maybe he went to the same school. Could someone have followed Jason here to get him out of the way for some reason?"

"I think you're stretching things a bit, don't you?"

Angie shook her head. "We're going to turn over every rock in Boise if it means we find the person who killed Jason and get Estebe out of the spotlight."

Ian stepped back and took in the window. "Well, I think we're done here. Let me buy you an early dinner in town, and we'll talk about what Uncle Allen's found so far."

"You fed me earlier," Angie reminded him.

He took the paintbrush from her and put it in a cup. Then he put the lid back on the gallon of paint and, using a hammer, closed it tightly. "You fed me most of my meals this week. Let's just say we're far from even."

"I guess I can heat up the casserole tomorrow." Angie followed him back into the County Seat. Now, she was glad she'd tucked the book into her tote at the last minute. Maybe they could put their heads together and find a real lead. One that would make Roland happy. "So where are we going now?"

"A small café I saw between the bar and the hotel. According to Uncle Allen, there's a waiter there who remembers Jason and saw him with a woman. Roland thinks it was Felicia, but he hasn't taken the time to confirm it. I'm wondering if your ex-employee actually knew our friend Jason. Especially after what she said last night."

Chapter 15

When they got to the restaurant, it was almost empty. The hostess stand was empty, and a large standing sign read: SEAT YOURSELF. Ian led her to a table near the back where they could watch the front door and the kitchen area. A waitress came out a few seconds later with a water pitcher and two menus.

Angie smiled at her. The restaurant was upscale, but she didn't know the chef. The waitress wore a white shirt and black pants, a white apron around her hips. "Are we too early for dinner? I feel like we should be ordering the early bird special or something."

The waitress laughed at her comment. "We were busier at lunch, and we'll have a crowd later, after seven, but this is pretty much a dead zone, so I'm hostess and waitress for the next hour or so. I'm Trish, by the way. Can I get you something besides water?"

"I'll have a sparkling water," Angie responded and looked at Ian.

"Hot tea. Earl Grey if you have it." He pushed his English accent just a bit.

Trish's smile grew bigger. Angie knew the effect Ian's English accent had on people and had to assume there was a reason he was using it. "I'll be right back with those. The specials are our hot roast beef dinner and a trout dish that's to die for. Our chef's pretty talented."

Angie watched her walk away. She glanced at Ian, who was studying the menu; then she got it. "She's the waitress that talked to your uncle."

"Unless there's more than one Trish with flaming-red hair. I'm thinking we found our source." He leaned back in his chair and took in the empty restaurant. "You know women are enchanted with an English accent."

"Sometimes you're so full of yourself." She studied the menu. It was good, but something was off. The menu didn't have a theme. The dishes were all over the place. She sometimes had dishes that didn't quite fit the farm-to-fork theme, but they were always seasonal. This was a menu that appeared to be the standard fare, year after year. "I think I'm going to go with the fish special. I'll have to see how it's prepared."

"I'm going with southern fried chicken. I've never been to the South."

Angie didn't want to tell him that the chef probably hadn't been either, but she was making assumptions.

When Trish came back with their drinks, she took their order, but before she could step away, Angie decided to see what she could find out. "Trish, I'm glad it's quiet in here. We have some questions for you."

"For me?" Trish tucked the menus under her arm and looked skeptical. "About the restaurant?"

"Actually, we have some questions about one of your customers. A friend of ours was in town from Boston. Jason? He ate here a couple of times last weekend."

A look of pain crossed Trish's face. "I'm so sorry. I heard he was killed just a couple of blocks from here. Was he here to visit you?"

"He was visiting family in the area." Angie figured it wasn't a total lie. "We were told he had dinner with a woman Sunday night. Did you wait on them?"

She shook her head. "I wasn't here last Sunday. I took the day off to do one last ski run on Bogus. They're shutting down soon."

Angie kicked herself. She'd taken a guess that Trish worked Sundays and that was when she'd seen him.

"Was it Sunday, dear? I thought they just said last weekend. It could have been Saturday or even Friday; we don't know," Ian corrected her blunder softly.

"Oh, I saw him on Saturday with a blonde. She was a piece of work, I'll tell you. She said she was a chef and started to complain about everything from the menu to the actual food, once she was served. I took her steak back twice because she said it wasn't medium rare. Once too over, once too under. Finally, the guy, Jason, he put a hand on her arm. I think she was planning on sending it back a third time. I hate people who just have a burr under their saddle." Trish pressed her lips together. "Look, I'm sorry about your friend, but I didn't really get to talk to him. The woman he was with didn't let anyone get in a word besides what she wanted."

Angie opened her phone and went to her pictures. She took pictures of all the temp staff. She wanted to remember them, especially if they were good workers. She found the picture of Hallie. "Was this her?"

Trish leaned closer to the picture. "Yeah, she had her hair down and a lot more makeup, but that's her. And the next time she comes in, I'm trading tables with someone else if she's set in my section. Your friend threw two twenties on the table for a tip, and she picked one up when he was in the bathroom and changed it for a five. Then she pocketed the other twenty. I tell you, she's a piece of work."

"Thanks for your help." Angie waited for Trish to be back in the kitchen before she exhaled. "I didn't think it would be that easy."

"It's not, really. So we know he had dinner with her. She's not going to talk to you since she's very mad at being fired. And he's dead. You don't know why they were together. It could have been a chance meeting."

"Could have been, but I think the possibility of that is low. She's involved in his murder. I don't know how or why, but I know she was. He met her here for dinner." She paused, thinking. Then she picked up her phone and started scrolling through a search. Finally, she set the phone on the table and sipped her drink. "Crap, I was hoping the academy was coed. I guess she didn't attend high school with him. I could see the headlines, High School Romance Turned Cold."

"Maybe she had a brother who attended the school. Or maybe she dated Jason's brother. There's a connection between her and this Jason guy. It's not a coincidence that she mentioned him when she was arrested, and she had dinner with him. She had to have known he was connected to Felicia and her family. Maybe she was trying to help him get Estebe out of the way." Ian paused as Trish delivered their meals. "This looks yummy."

"Thanks." She nodded to the other customers who had come in while she'd been in the back. "Looks like you two were good luck for me this shift. Let me know if I can bring you anything else."

"The food looks great. Thanks, Trish." Angie picked up her fork. "Shall we table the discussion about Jason until after dinner? Maybe we can even talk about some positive things. How was church this morning? I don't think I asked."

They spent the rest of dinner and most of the drive home talking about things that weren't focused on death or vandalism or mean people. Angie climbed out of the car when he parked it at the restaurant so she could switch sides. She met Ian on the other side of the car, where he took her into his arms. "Thanks for dinner."

"Thanks for going with me. I know you like to use your Sundays to decompress." He pushed a lock of hair out of her eyes and back into place behind her ear. "Are you going to be okay at home? Do you need me to drive out with you?"

"I'm a big girl. I can take care of myself. Well, me and the crew." Angie took her keys from his hand. "I'll be fine. Thanks for the offer. But having some alone time will be heaven. Especially since I'll be doing wedding stuff all next week."

He nodded. "I get it."

Angie's gaze went to the apartment window, where she saw a light on in the living room. "At least I hope we'll be busy celebrating."

"Like I said..."

She cut him off. "I know, we have to have faith. I'd be happier with an ironclad schedule and someone besides Estebe in the Ada County Jail for killing Jason."

"Maybe you should visualize what you want on the drive home. Just think of what would be the best outcome out of this whole thing and send it up to the heavens." He kissed her and then stepped away.

"You're supposed to say send it to the universe, not the heavens." She climbed into the driver's seat and adjusted it. "You just couldn't do it, could you?"

"I stand by my convictions, even when they aren't the current rage. I'll talk to you tomorrow." He shut the door, waved, and then started jogging toward his apartment.

It was only a block away, so he didn't have far, but Angie wondered why he hadn't parked in front of his building rather than her lot. Then she realized it was because he wasn't sure if she would want to go into the restaurant or not. He did a lot for her. Little things, things that sometimes she didn't notice.

Maybe, she thought as she pulled the car out onto the road, maybe she needed to be better at noticing.

* * * *

The next morning, Angie was at her kitchen table, looking at the results of an internet search on the high school Jason had been so attached to. She tried to run Hallie's name with the school, with Jason's name, and even just her name, with little luck. Sometime in the last year, Hallie had become one of Angie's Facebook friends. Since she figured that would be corrected when the woman got out of jail, Angie scrolled through the pages, seeing if she could find anything that would give her a clue.

Her phone rang, and she answered it, putting Felicia on speaker phone. "Hey, how are you? How's Estebe?"

"Home in his bed. I guess he didn't get out of there until ten last night. I am so tired of them messing with him. Anyway, what are you doing this morning?"

"Going through Hallie's Facebook posts. She thought we were the best place on earth to work." Angie stood and got more coffee.

"That's nice."

"Kind of. She thought Canyon Creek was the best place on earth to work a few months ago, until they didn't continue her temp assignment. Then the place was filled with roaches. I'm sure as soon as she gets access to her account we'll be just as disgusting. What are you up to today?"

"Nothing much. Estebe was coming over to talk about where we're going to live when we get back from Spain, but I'm not calling him until he wakes on his own. He's been through a lot."

"Do you want to come over and cook? Or we could go for mani-pedis or massages."

"We're doing that on Thursday, before we go into town for the party. Don't you have that on your schedule?"

Angie pulled out her planner. The week was filled, but she hadn't paid attention to what they'd be doing, not yet. "It's there. I'm adding the party on Thursday. So do you want to come over? We could watch rom-coms and talk about Estebe and Ian."

"Do you have vanilla ice cream and brownies?"

Angie checked the freezer. "I have two quarts, and I could have brownies by the time you get here."

"Sounds like heaven. I'll text Estebe and let him know I'll be at the farm. See you in a few."

Angie hung up and saw that Dom was watching her with a grin on his face. "Don't think you're getting any brownies. But Aunt Felicia will be here soon, so at least you'll get lots of hugs."

Setting aside the phone, she started working on her brownie batter. It might not be the healthiest brunch, but it would be fun.

After the batch of brownies was in the oven, Angie sat back down to scroll through Hallie's Facebook posts. She was just about to give up when she recognized a face in one of the group shots. There were several people gathered around a table, a bottle of tequila and shot glasses all around. The neon light above the table looked like a bar, and as she studied it, it actually looked like the Vista Bar she'd visited last week.

Hallie was sitting with a man who had his arm around her shoulder. Next to that guy was the bartender she'd talked to that night. Tracy.

Angie was still trying to figure out if it meant anything besides being a coincidence or that Boise was still a small town, even as large as it had grown in the last few years, when Felicia's new Jeep pulled into the driveway.

She left the laptop open and went to unlock the door. She probably was being overcautious by keeping the house locked when she was home, but with the week she'd had, she'd take paranoid over being robbed or attacked.

"Hey." Felicia shoved a bag from the drive-in toward her. "You probably want to eat the fries before they get too cold. I already ate mine, but I left the burger so I'd have something to eat with you."

"I feel the pounds coming on this week. Hopefully, we'll both be able to fit into our dresses on Saturday." Angie took the bag and set it on the table, then grabbed some napkins from the counter.

"It smells like chocolate in here." Felicia leaned into the smell, enjoying the future joy that is brownies. Then she sat at the table.

Angie unwrapped her fish sandwich. "Now it smells like chocolate and grease. My two favorite food groups."

They ate in comfortable silence for a few minutes. Finally, Felicia wiped her mouth. "You know, my mom called me last night to talk. She asked me if I was sure about marrying Estebe. I got to thinking about the question and realized I've never been as sure of anything in my life. I mean, I trusted we could do the restaurants. But was I sure? No flipping way. Anything could have happened. But with Estebe, I know it doesn't matter what happens, because he'd never put me, or us, in jeopardy. All we have to do is get through this witch hunt about Jason. Did you come up with any theories yesterday?"

"No, but I found something weird." Angie turned the laptop toward Felicia and pointed to the picture. "Do you know that guy?"

"The one next to Hallie? Sure, that's her boyfriend. I wouldn't doubt if he was the one who drove the getaway car on Saturday night. He's a piece of work. I had him work for Jeorge one night, and our receipts at the bar were down over thirty percent. On a night where we were slammed. I think he skimmed." Felicia finished off her burger and then wiped her mouth. "So I never hired him back."

"The other guy is the bartender at Vista Bar I talked to last week. He knew who I was. He told me that he'd subbed in one night at the restaurant." Angie stared at the picture. "You didn't tell me about this skimming bartender. What did he say when you confronted him?"

"I didn't confront him. We've been lucky with our hires. Well, not really lucky, we vet everyone we bring into the County Seat. Most of our temps are there because one of their friends works for us. So when we have an opening, we work off referrals. A friend isn't going to mess with another friend's job. And they work hard. They like working there." She wrapped up the paper the hamburger came in and did a shot into the bag that still sat upright on the table. "All accusing him would have done was a 'he said, she said' argument. I know how to deal with problem people, just the same as you do. They don't get invited back to the sandbox to play."

"I hope you put someone in charge of the front-of-the-house crew while you're gone. You know I have no clue what happens out there."

"Of course you do. And you'd be fine, but yeah, I'm having Bleak and Jeorge tag team the crew. Jeorge is old enough he knows what to do, and Bleak's young enough that she has the energy to do it. They'll be fine together. You won't even miss me." She took several onion rings out of the paper tray and set them on a napkin.

"That's not true. I'm going to miss you horribly. Are you sure you guys want to be gone a full month? You should cut it short to, let's say, two weeks, and then come back. I don't know what I'm going to do without you." Angie finished her sandwich and stood to put her trash in the paper bag.

The buzzer on the stove went off, and Felicia stood and grabbed potholders. "I'll be back before you know it. Let's stop thinking about this mess and find some movies. I'm voting for *Sleepless in Seattle.*"

"You always do." Angie finished the last onion ring and cleared the trash from the table. "What about *The Holiday?* I love that one."

"It's not Christmas." Felicia opened the door, and a wave of warm chocolate smell filled the room. She used a toothpick to check the middle of the pan. "All done. Now to let them cool. Good thing I brought lunch so we don't have to burn our mouths on this."

"Remember the time we made brownies in a cup in the dorm?" Angie rinsed her dishrag and then cleaned the table off, closing the laptop and putting it on the desk. She'd make notes and comments in the notebook later. For right now, she was going to spend some time with her best friend before she got married and took off for Europe for a month.

"I couldn't taste anything for a week. Of course, you didn't want to taste campus food. I can't believe how bad it was there. And they had a culinary school. Seriously, BSU needs to put their kitchen staff through some classes with our professors."

They moved into the living room and started looking through Angie's DVD library. They had several choices set out within a few minutes, but Angie let Felicia have first choice. She was the upcoming bride, after all.

Angie and Felicia with Dom between them curled up on the couch and talked about their past together. All the fun. All the challenges. Soon, there would be new memories, but these ones belonged to them. Two friends who'd found each other through their love of food.

Chapter 16

Estebe and Ian arrived at the farmhouse at six, Estebe's Hummer leading the two-car caravan into the driveway. Angie was in the kitchen, looking out the window as she and Felicia talked about dinner plans. They'd decided on just finishing the pan of brownies when Angie spotted the newcomers. "I think they came to get us so we'd eat real food tonight."

"What are you talking about?" Felicia came into the kitchen and watched as the two men crossed the driveway, walking toward the barn. "I can't believe it. It's like the man has a sixth sense about when I'm going to dive into a bag of chips."

"Chips and salsa would have been a good dessert with the brownies." Angie glanced at Dom, who was standing at the door, waiting to greet the men. "Ian's feeding Precious, so I guess I have time to get out of these yoga pants and into jeans. I'll be right down."

"I'll let them in. Maybe." Felicia broke off a piece of brownie. "We could just hide in the house and pretend we're not home."

"Both of our cars are out there." Angie stood at the bottom of the stairs. "Besides, Dom would rat us out. Be right back."

Angie hurried into her bedroom and found some jeans. She pulled them on and then found a much cleaner and cuter shirt to put on. Pulling a brush through her hair, she put on some tinted lip gloss and called it good.

When she got back downstairs, Felicia narrowed her eyes. "Lip gloss, really?"

"I didn't put on foundation or eye makeup." Angie tried to defend herself.

"That's because you don't need it." Felicia stood by Estebe. "The boys want to take us to dinner."

"Great, where?" Angie went over and gave Ian a kiss. "Thanks for feeding the zoo."

"No problem. You look lovely." He glanced at Estebe. "We thought we might hit Canyon Creek tonight."

"I'm not really dressed for it." Felicia glanced at her jeans and T-shirt. "Maybe we should just grab Chinese."

"Angie can loan you a different shirt," Estebe said. "I think we need to talk to Sydney about Hallie's time there."

"She already told us about the flat tire." Angie looked from one man to the other. "What do you know that we don't?"

"Rumor is that Hallie was or is dating Jason's brother. Uncle Allen let it slip, accidentally, today after he got off the phone with Roland." Ian grinned like he'd won the lottery.

"And how is talking to Sydney going to give us more information?" Angie felt like she was missing something.

"Larry, Jason's brother, worked for Sydney at the same time as Hallie. Maybe Sydney knows something else." Ian looked at Estebe. "It might be a long shot, but the cops aren't even talking to them about their interaction with Jason. We need to find a new suspect, so my man here isn't the only one with a bull's-eye on his chest."

"Okay, if you think so." Angie nodded to Felicia. "Do you want to look in my closet?"

"I'll just run up and grab that red blouse I borrow from time to time." Felicia kissed Estebe. "We'll figure this out. The Scooby-Doo gang always does."

Once she was upstairs, Estebe looked at Ian and Angie. "I want to thank you for your help with this. I don't know what's going to happen, but you need to be there for Felicia, just in case."

"You're not going to jail for this." Angie got the notebook out. "We may not have any evidence on anyone else, but we do know who you are. And we will fight to keep you out of jail. I need my head chef."

"You could get along without me." But he smiled as he said it.

Ian slapped him on the back. "Let's just do this and figure out who killed that jerk. He was horrible to so many people, they must have been lining up to get a crack at him."

"You would think so. Maybe we need to widen our search area." Angie opened the notebook and wrote something on the last page. "I'll call the school and see if they can tell me why Jason supported them for so many years. Maybe there was a specific reason."

"I can reach out to a relative who works at Boston PD. Maybe they know our friend Jason." Estebe pointed to the book. "Write that down."

"I don't know anyone in Boston, but I can reach out and see if anyone knows this homeless guy who saw the incident. Maybe he knows more than the detective is writing down in the report." Ian nodded to Angie.

"Okay, so we have our assignments."

Felicia's voice sounded behind her. "Actually, write down one more thing. I'm going to meet with Carter. Maybe he knows something."

"Are you sure? He'll try to get you to go back." Estebe watched as she walked over and put her arm around him.

"He can talk all he wants. I know where I belong."

Angie shut the book and tucked it in her tote. She winked at Ian. "Just in case. Okay crew, let's go find out stuff."

"Someone on television says that." Ian frowned, trying to remember the show.

Angie gave Dom a hug, then met Ian at the door. "Are you sure it's not Scooby?"

They took two cars, Angie's and Estebe's. Both Ian and Felicia would ride back with her to gather their vehicles. Estebe would head over to the community center after dinner to see if there was any chatter about the killing and to finish plans for the rehearsal dinner.

This driving arrangement also gave both couples some privacy on the way to dinner.

"How is she doing?" Ian asked as they pulled out of the driveway, following Estebe.

Angie didn't look at him. Instead, she focused on Mrs. Potter's empty house and blinked back tears. "She's worried. She won't say it, but she's scared."

"We'll get the wedding done. She doesn't have to worry about that."

Angie wiped a stray tear. "It's not the wedding. She's worried about Estebe. He's so trusting sometimes. She's scared he's going to say something stupid and get caught in this guy's web."

"He's smarter than that. He may not appear that way to people who don't know him, but you and Felicia need to trust him. He's not going to do anything to risk this marriage." Ian reached out and took her hand. "He's crazy in love with your friend. I understand the feeling."

Angie met his gaze, and for a second, the world made sense again. She relaxed into the seat. "So your uncle is still feeding us information and leads?"

"Why would you say something like that?" Ian grinned. "My uncle is a pillar of virtue in his position. He just wants justice to be done."

"And he kind of hates that detective, Roland," Angie added.

"Hate is a strong word." He turned up the music. "I love this song."

When they arrived at the restaurant, the hostess moved them straight into the side room that was usually rented out for parties and events. A table had been already set in the middle of the room.

"Sydney said not to worry about menus. She's doing a tasting menu for you, since you're with the County Seat. She told everyone you were coming and to be on the top of their game." She covered her mouth with her hand. "I probably wasn't supposed to say that."

Angie laughed as she sat between Ian and Estebe. "Don't worry, we won't let on that you forewarned us."

"Thanks. I'm new here, but I really like working for Sydney. She's the best." The woman nodded and stepped away. "I'll let her know you're here."

"So anyone else think Sydney's giving us some privacy to talk?" Ian glanced around the room. "Maybe she's worried that Hallie and Larry have spies in the crew."

"Possible. I think Hallie makes friends with the 'poor me' attitude, then keeps them after she's canned." Angie glanced at Estebe and Felicia. "Was she friends with anyone on staff?"

"I saw her talking to Bleak a lot, but no one else gave her much notice." Felicia looked at Angie. "You don't think she would have brainwashed her against us, do you?"

"Bleak's been through better brainwashing and lived." Angie picked up her phone and texted a note. "But if she did develop a friendship, Hope will know."

"Now who's sounding like a cult?" Felicia asked.

"Not a cult. I just don't want Bleak to think we're in the wrong here. If she needs the full story, we can give it to her."

"Bleak saw the damage Hallie did to the restaurant. I don't think she's going to side with that kind of behavior." Ian squeezed Angie's arm. "Remember, she was there on Saturday when we were cleaning up."

"You're right." Angie's phone buzzed. She read the message before continuing. "Hope confirms your assessment. Bleak thinks Hallie's crazy."

"And she wouldn't be wrong." Sydney came into the room and shut the door after herself with a kick of her foot. She was carrying a tray that had several types of appetizers on plates. "Here's your first course. Sorry about the setting. I figured we didn't want this conversation at the typical chef table. There are too many listening ears." Sydney pulled up a chair.

"What do you want to know? I heard what she did to the restaurant. Can't say I'm surprised."

"Thanks." Angie glanced around the table. "Tell me about Larry Fortell? He worked for you? Maybe as a bartender."

"Wow. That's specific. Yes, he bartended here around the same time as Hallie worked here. Don't tell me they're a couple? They never said anything. Of course, I try not to hire couples. No offense." She laughed as she saw shocked looks from Felicia and Estebe. "It's just if one person has a problem, so does the other. Scheduling gets to be a bear too, especially if they both want the same day off."

"Yeah, we think they're a couple," Angie admitted. "He's in a picture on Facebook with her, and they're pretty chummy."

"Well, that would explain some things. Hallie called in sick around a weekend and so did Larry. I thought they'd both caught some bug here. I was worried the rest of the staff would get sick, but they didn't. Go ahead and eat. I'd like a second to think." She sat quietly while the others tried the appetizers. Finally she shook her head. "I guess I can't think of anything else. Except maybe one thing."

"What's that?" Angie set her fork down and focused on Sydney.

"Well, two things actually. Hallie called Larry 'Boston.' I thought it was because he liked to drink a type of beer, Sam Adams. He always had one after shift while things were winding down."

Angie took in a breath. It was another connection since she didn't think the nickname was because of the beer. "What else?"

"He didn't quit right after I terminated Hallie. If I have my timeline right, he quit the night my tires were slashed. And"—she met Angie's gaze before she continued—"he didn't have a beer that night. He just quit and left. Asked me to send his last check to his address on file."

"Did you tell the police about the tires?" Ian asked.

"No, I didn't want to make a big deal of it. And, I hate having police calls to the restaurant. People look at those stats to see if it's safe to come here. We're on the edge of a bad neighborhood. We're also on the edge of an upscale neighborhood. So we keep the police calls down to a minimum. I had someone give me a ride home; then we came back the next day and got my car." Sydney looked crestfallen. "I screwed up, didn't I?"

"You did what you thought was best for your crew and your business. That's never screwing up." Angie ate the last scallop from the plate. "And these are heaven. What did you cook them in?"

Sydney brightened as she described the food. Then she stood. "Your main courses are probably ready. I told the staff I'd handle bringing dishes out, so I better get back there. Let me know if you have any more questions or if I can do anything. I feel awful about what she did to the County Seat."

"It was bound to happen sooner or later. But if we can keep her from just walking on this, maybe she'll leave the area and go find another city to play her games." Angie handed Sydney the plate the scallops had been on.

After gathering the empty plates, she disappeared, closing the door after her.

"So that was interesting. We think this bartender Larry was part of the problem?" Estebe glanced at Felicia. "You should have called the cops when the receipts went down that night."

"I know. I just didn't want to get in a fight." Felicia sipped her wine as she looked uncomfortably at the door. "I'm just as bad as Sydney. We're so focused on being pro-customer and giving people the benefit of the doubt, we let bad people walk all over us."

"You fired him. That was enough." Angie rolled her shoulders. "Well, unless we have more questions for Sydney, let's table the criminal investigation and enjoy a peaceful dinner. It's going to be a madhouse the rest of the week."

"You can relax on Thursday. After a massage, we'll be ready for a few drinks." Felicia rubbed her arms.

"Are you cold?" Estebe reached out to still her hand.

Felicia shook her head. "No, not cold. I'm just wondering what's going to be the next shoe to fall. I'm not looking forward to talking to either my mother or Carter, so keep your phones nearby. I might need a reality check as I'm driving back into River Vista."

Angie thought it might be just as hard on the rest of them. But they needed to figure out who killed Jason and soon. Or the honeymoon might have to be to a country that didn't have extradition.

Sydney came back into the room just then with another waiter. As they set the plates down, she explained each dish, asking who wanted it. Then she left another set of the same dishes on a nearby table. "Just in case you didn't get your first choice."

The waiter who'd come in with her glanced around the room, his gaze lingering on Estebe. Angie was just about to ask if he knew the waiter, when he left the room, taking the trays with him.

Sydney frowned and watched him leave. "Martin is usually more talkative than that."

Estebe picked up his fork. "It's my fault. He's the son of one of my friends. I'm afraid he doesn't like me much since I kicked him out of my kitchen at the community center."

"Was there a problem?" Angie glanced back toward where the young man had left the room.

"Nothing that concerns today." Estebe took a bite of the pork loin. "This is wonderful. My compliments to the chef."

Sydney blushed and tucked her hands together. "Thank you."

After she left, Angie questioned Estebe one more time. "Are you sure there's nothing with this Martin kid that could be part of the problem we're looking into now? Did he work with Larry when he was there? Or maybe here?"

"I don't know about here, but no, the issue between him and me was years ago. I can't imagine him still holding a grudge. Not liking me or talking to me, I get. But his dad gives me good reports on his current life, so he has turned a corner."

Angie heard the 'we're not talking about this' subtext in Estebe's voice, so she dropped it. But she was going to call Sydney and find out what she could about Martin tomorrow. Despite Estebe's confidence in the young man, Angie hadn't liked the way he'd looked at her friend.

Chapter 17

The next morning, Angie stirred her coffee and looked at the two phone numbers she'd written down on the notebook in front of her. One was the foundation's director of the boarding school that Jason and his brother had attended. When she'd called the school, asking about him, she'd lied. She'd told the woman on the other end of the line that she was a reporter from the *Idaho Gazette*, a paper she hoped didn't actually exist so the school couldn't verify her identity. Of course, she could have said the *Idaho Statesman*, and the school might not have checked anyway. She hadn't gotten much except a phone number for the donations manager and a name. Maybe this woman knew Jason and would actually talk to her.

But she'd given herself a new last name when she'd talked to the school—McNeal—which was Ian's last name, yes, but that wasn't weird. She could have said Williams, but that was too close to where he'd worked and Felicia, so she'd borrowed Ian's name. She'd give it back after this. Or maybe she'd always use it when she was investigating. Give her some time to get used to it in case Ian actually proposed. Or maybe she'd keep her name if they got married.

Questions she didn't have time for today. She was stalling and she knew it. Today was for investigations and getting Estebe off the hot seat.

She checked the clock again and decided it was too early to call Sydney. Most chefs weren't up this early, especially when they closed out their restaurant. Of course, Sydney had a young child, so who knew what time she'd actually be awake. Angie would call around noon. That sounded reasonable. Even though she herself had been up since seven.

Getting up early was a habit she'd had since she'd moved in with Nona. Up with the chickens, her grandmother used to call it. Angie had scheduled her classes at college early too. It was better. She got into the ones she wanted because no one else wanted to be there that early. One summer, she'd worked as a line cook in a chain breakfast place. Well, it served other meals, too, but breakfast and the in-restaurant bakery were what it was known for. The muffins had been to die for. Angie still liked stopping in there every once in a while to grab a big breakfast when she didn't mind the drive into the other side of Boise.

Still stalling. She glanced at Dom, hoping he wanted something, but no, he was asleep. Her angst about making the call apparently didn't even faze him. She wrote down a few notes to keep herself on script and then dialed the number.

One ring, two rings, Angie was hopeful the woman wouldn't pick up, but then she did.

"Opal Parks, may I help you?" The woman answered the phone in a friendly yet businesslike tone.

"Good morning, Ms. Parks. My name is Angie McNeal, and I'm with the *Idaho Gazette.* We're doing a story on Jason Roberts and his untimely death here in Boise. It's just awful what happened. I understand he was a big donor and even attended Westfield Academy. Do you have some time to chat with me about your connection with Mr. Roberts?" Angie held the pen upright, hoping she wouldn't just get hung up on.

"Oh, my, yes. We just heard yesterday about his death. I'm sorry, I'm still a little in shock. What was your name again?"

"Angie. I've heard from others that Mr. Roberts was uncommonly generous with your school. I've done some research, and it looked like he attended your fundraisers every year without fail."

"Jason was very generous with the school. He said that being here saved his life after his brother died. It was a tragic swimming accident when the boys attended the academy. The school is situated on the banks of a nearby river. Unfortunately, as many times as you tell a teenage boy that the current can be dangerous and to stay away, it's never enough. In fact, I think it just makes them all the more curious."

"Oh, I didn't see mention of his brother's death. We should have that information too." Angie rattled papers like she was looking for something. "No, darn it, I don't have that info. What was his brother's name?"

"Jack Roberts. I've been part of the school for many years, so I was here when Jack died. Jason and his friend came running back to the office, frantic. Jack had tied a rope to a tree and swung out. I think they were just planning on playing chicken, but he must have slipped. Jason was inconsolable. It was painful to watch."

"I assure you, I don't want to bring up painful memories during this time of grief." Angie paused a beat before asking a question she thought she knew the answer to. "I'm sorry, I must have missed it. This other boy, what was his name?"

"Larry. I probably shouldn't give out his last name. Our students have a right to privacy, you know. And I'd appreciate being able to read the article when you finish."

"I don't know if my editor will allow that." Angie pondered her imaginary editor's stance on the freedom of the press argument. "But what if I send you the section where I quote you or refer to the school. Would that help?"

"That would be perfect." Opal gave up easy, which led Angie to think she should have held fast to the freedom of the press fanfare.

"Did you know if Mr. Roberts was seeing anyone special? I saw him photographed with so many beautiful women at your fundraisers." Angie threw out the question, wondering what gossip she'd get.

"He said he was playing the field until his high school sweetheart realized what she'd missed and came home to him. He must have been very much in love with that girl."

Angie doubted it from the way he'd treated Felicia, but she let the comment slide. "If you could have one encounter with him again, what would it be? And why?"

"That's an unusual question, but I guess I've never been interviewed about someone who passed so early in their life." She paused, humming into the phone. "Oh, I know, we went to the beach for a brainstorming session to plan last year's gala. Jason was funny and happy. I've never seen him that happy."

"Do you know why he was happy?"

"Actually, I do. His boss had just told Jason that he was going to take over the company when this guy retired in a few years. I guess now they're going to have to find someone else to run the company. That's really sad now, thinking about it. He would have had his dream job if he'd lived that long."

Angie wrote down everything Opal had told her. Was Hallie's Larry the same guy who'd attended this boarding school with Jason? And if so, why was he working as a bartender? Wouldn't someone who attended an upscale prep school be more likely to be in some sort of white-collar profession? Or a doctor or lawyer? And what happened to Jack? Was it an accident, or did one or more of the other boys push him into that water?

She sat for a long time staring at what she'd written. Then she started an internet search on Larry Fortell. Who was the man who seemed to be following his girlfriend from job to job around the valley? And was he the same guy who had gone to school with Jason? If not, it was weird that Jason and Hallie would have had dinner. And if not, there had to be another connection between the two that Angie hadn't found. Yet.

A few hours later, with a splitting headache and not much more to go on, she closed her laptop and went to the fridge to get out ingredients to make lunch. She made a salad and sat down to eat. Just as she did, her phone rang.

"Hey, Felicia, what's going on?" She took a bite of the lettuce, hoping she wasn't crunching in her ear.

"Estebe and I are picking up Ian and heading out to your place. We're stopping at the drive-in for food. Do you want something? Or have you already eaten?"

"I'm eating a salad, but if you're bringing over food, get me a fish basket with tots. I'll see you in a few." She hung up and looked at her salad. She covered it with wrap and put it back into the fridge. She could eat salad for dinner.

"All your favorite people are coming by," Angie said to Dom and got a wag and thump of his tail. Apparently, they had news about the investigation. *The Scooby-Doo gang rides again.* She grinned and went about straightening the house. She even put in a load of laundry and started baking cookies for dessert from dough she'd frozen last month during a weekend filled with cookie recipe development. Hopefully stress burned calories, because if not there was no way she was going to fit in the dress she was picking up tomorrow. Maybe she'd only eat one cookie.

When the Hummer pulled in, she had two dozen cookies baked and on a plate in the middle of the table. She'd also started another load of laundry. *Betty Crocker's are us.*

Felicia was first through the door, and she handed her a drive-in bag. "Delivery at your service. Ooh, chocolate crinkle cookies. I love those."

"Thanks for the food." Angie waited for Ian to come in and gave him a quick kiss. "Did you take off work?"

"Done for the day. I closed up shop when Estebe came by with his news." He nodded to the table. "Let's get lunch out, and then everyone can report. I take it you've completed your assignment?"

"Of course." She hadn't called Sydney yet about Martin, but she wouldn't admit that in front of Estebe. Especially since he didn't want to explore that lead. "And I've got interesting news."

"Who wants to go first?" Ian asked, and the other three all raised their hand. "Okay, hold on."

"What are you doing?" Angie watched as he went to the desk and grabbed a notebook.

He sat back down, wrote something on the second page, then looked at everyone. "I'll take notes. I've written down a number between one and ten. Closest number without going over goes first, next closest goes next, and Angie will go last."

"Hey, why do you think I'll lose the guess?" She took her tots and sandwich out of the bag. Dom came over and put his head on her lap. "No, big guy. No junk food for you."

"You treat that dog better than you do your own body," Felicia commented.

Ian laughed. "I was just kidding about you losing, Angie. So you can guess first. What's my number?"

She thought about the rules and then guessed, "Seven."

Ian wrote it down by her name. "Felicia?"

"Five."

He nodded and made another note. "And Estebe?"

"Six."

"You all went big for this. Interesting. I wonder what that means about your personalities?" Ian turned over the page, and a large 2 was written on the page. "So you all lose the going over part, but if I take that away, it's Felicia, Estebe, and then Angie. Who predicted that? Oh, yeah, it was me."

Angie threw a tot at him, which bounced and fell on the floor. Dom moved faster than she thought possible and snatched it up off the wooden plank floor. "I don't know how you do that, but you always outthink me on these things."

"Do I? Or do you just think I do?" Ian made a scrunched-up face. "Anyway, Felicia, you're up. Tell us what Carter said."

"Well, now, that was interesting. I asked what Jason's role had been in the company and what was going on between the two of them." Felicia dipped a fry into the secret sauce. "He said that nothing had changed. Jason was next in line to take over the company, just like he'd been for years. Carter was just there to try to help out. That Dad was working with him to teach him the business. Which he guessed was a good thing since now Jason's gone."

"The real question is, did you believe him?" Angie asked, thinking about how excited Jason had been about being chosen to take over the company.

Felicia dipped another fry. "My father has a really big ego. If he thought he could keep control of the company in family hands, he'd do it in a heartbeat. That's why they wanted me to come back. So they had a spare, just in case something happened to Carter. And Carter's the same way. He's smug about taking over. Like it was his birthright all along."

"So did Carter believe he'd be running it? Or did he make sure he would be the only logical choice?" Ian asked.

"You're asking if Carter killed Jason for control of the company?" Felicia shrugged. "It doesn't make sense, especially since I'm still around. Dad could decide I'm the logical choice, and if I come to my senses and come back, I'd be in control."

"Which means if Carter did this, you're in danger. He might just want to get all the opposition cleared away now, while everyone's off kilter," Ian pointed out.

"I knew you shouldn't have met with him alone today." Estebe took her hand. "Let's not take a chance like that again."

"If he wanted a clear path, he could have killed me today. Maybe put something in my coffee. Or even cut my brake lines on the Jeep." Felicia shook her head. "Don't get me wrong, Carter's happy he's next in line, but he doesn't have what it takes to kill someone to get there. He's soft, according to Dad. He must get that from his mother."

Angie saw the pain in Felicia's face as she talked about her half brother.

"My family is messed up, but if jealousy had been the reason for all of this, I would think that Jason would have killed Carter. He hated him, and he was devoted to my mother. Carter's existence proved that her marriage wasn't the perfect story she liked to pretend it was."

They all sat with that information for a minute. Then Estebe wiped the hamburger sauce off his mouth. "I talked to my friend in Boston. Apparently, Jason was involved in an accidental death when he was a teenager. At the boarding school."

"His brother, Jack," Angie added. At least this confirmed what she'd heard from her interview.

"My friend said the name, but not that they were brothers. That loss must have been hard," Estebe said. "There were some questions on how the boy died, but the other two boys' statements matched, and it happened late on a fall day that had turned cold with a storm brewing."

"My contact didn't say it was fall. She said summer. But she did say that there was another boy there. She'd admitted to his first name being Larry, but due to confidentiality, she wouldn't tell me the last name."

"You think it's Hallie's Larry," Ian stated. It wasn't a question, more like a confirmation.

"It ties her to Jason," Angie said. "But would you stay friends with someone who you'd witnessed a death with? Or maybe committed murder with?"

"Personally, I wouldn't know. But there's one problem with the theory," Ian pointed out as he finished his burger.

"What's that?" Angie waited for him to finish chewing.

"Uncle Allen said that Hallie was dating or had dated Jason's brother. If this guy is dead, she must have dated him in high school."

"Not totally improbable. Then she turned to Larry when Jack died," Estebe guessed.

"Maybe, but I feel like we're missing something." Ian absently rubbed Dom's head as he talked. Then his phone went off. He glanced at the display. "I need to take this."

He walked into the living room to talk, and Angie moved the notebook to Felicia and told the others what she'd found. "This woman thought Jason walked on water."

"Not an unusual reaction. Jason could be charming, especially if he wanted something," Felicia pointed out.

Estebe looked at her but didn't comment.

"He thought he could sell ice to Alaskans." She paused. "What if the missing item's right here? What if he was being blackmailed by Hallie and Larry? If he'd killed or thought he'd killed his brother, maybe his guilt was making him pay off Larry so he wouldn't tell."

"And what? He decided to stop paying right before he was named CEO of a very large and profitable company?" Angie shook her head.

"No, he told his blackmailers that he wasn't paying their increased charge. If they knew about his upcoming raise, maybe they were tired of working at restaurants. Maybe they wanted to open their own and needed seed money." Estebe put his half-eaten burger back into the bag. "Which would explain the calls to and from Boise before his arrival. They were trying to talk him into giving them a big payoff."

"We had plans at the Health Department months before we were planning on opening. We did our own funding for the restaurant stuff, but for the building I took a loan from the bank. I wonder if there is any way to see pending filings?" Angie mused.

Ian walked back into the kitchen. "Sorry to do this, but I need to get back to my office. Can I get a ride back into town?"

"Sure." Estebe glanced around the table. "I think we're done with the reporting part of the day. Now we need to do more digging. I'll reach out to my funders and see if anyone has been trying to get a backer. And I'll talk to Nancy and Matt to see if they know anything."

Angie still needed to find out what Martin's story was, but again, she wasn't going to blurt it out. "Sounds like a good plan. I'm not sure we can go from wanting to open a restaurant to killing Jason, but at least it's a motive."

"And one that would rival the jealous fiancé theory that is being bandied about," Ian reminded everyone. "Sorry to cut the brainstorming short, but I have an angry vendor issue. We go live with our first farmers market of the year in two weeks, and he's upset about where his stand is located versus another rival farmer. Seriously, sometimes I feel like I'm herding high schoolers who all want to be near the popular kids." Ian gave her a kiss as they put on their coats to leave.

When they were gone, Angie sat for a while, thinking about the information they'd found out. Several points were contradictory. One, there was a death in the past; that was certain. The boy's name was Jack, but was it Jack Roberts, like her source had said? She'd been connected with the school, so that seemed the more likely answer. But if that was true, why had Allen Brown mentioned Jason's brother dating Hallie? Was there a simple case of mistaken identity? Or was blackmail a more likely answer?

She decided to see if she could find out more about Jack Roberts and Larry Fortell. It seemed like the answer to today's murder lay in the past around these two men.

She checked the clock and decided to go out and feed Precious and Mabel first. Maybe spending some time with her goat, talking out the many different fingers of this investigation, would help give her some clarity. It had happened before. There was nothing like a goat to give a person some perspective.

Chapter 18

Wednesday morning, Angie fed the zoo first thing. Yesterday's long chat with Precious hadn't done anything around brainstorming who killed Jason, but it had calmed her mind. Precious was good that way. Mabel, on the other hand, didn't involve herself in the issues of humans. She was more concerned that there was food to eat and a warm place to roost. Angie liked that about her hen. She put things in perspective for her at times.

With their breakfast done and Dom's food and water dishes cleaned and filled, Angie decided to feed herself. Today she was going into town with Felicia around noon to pick up the dresses, and if they still fit, they'd have a nice lunch at one of the restaurants in town. There was a new Basque restaurant near the community center where Estebe volunteered his time. Angie had been hoping to go there and check out another chef's versions of the Basque food Estebe loved so much. Although the County Seat was focused on the farm-to-table lifestyle, often Estebe's recipes made the menus because of their ability to fit into the theme—plus they were tasty.

Either lunch would be awesome, or they'd be drinking protein shakes to make sure the dresses fit on Saturday. Which made her breakfast plans crucial. She decided on a high-protein breakfast that would fill her up and not affect weight loss plans if they were implemented later. She didn't think she could lose much in three days, but a pound or two might make the difference in the dress fitting.

Angie wondered if other people thought about food as much as she did. Normally, she didn't worry about what she ate because she and Dom were active hikers when the weather was good. Which was most of the year for southwestern Idaho. Not California sunny good, but good enough that they could get in a walk every few days. Walking Dom was like having a cardio and arm and core workout all in one. He liked to hang out at the end of his lead, which meant Angie was always pulling him back toward her when other people were in sight.

He liked to visit, but oddly enough, some people weren't excited to meet a dog that might weigh more than they did.

Food was her job and her passion. She thought about it a lot. There wasn't anything odd in that, she decided as she seasoned the eggs with a little paprika to give them just a touch of spice. The sausage patties were from a local butcher who had his own spice mixes in the meat. This was a breakfast sausage that made a mean milk gravy. But sadly, biscuits and gravy were not on today's menu. Maybe Sunday, when she didn't have to worry about her waist size.

As the sausage cooked, she sat down and opened her laptop. She decided a deeper search on the accident during Jason's school years might give her some ideas on why he was killed. She wondered if the school had online yearbooks. She hoped her high school never went that way. She didn't like remembering that time in her life. She'd been trying to fit in for years until she realized those kids weren't her tribe. She'd found one or two friends during those years. But they'd moved away as soon as high school was over. The ones who'd stayed around didn't have the same interests as she did now. Well, except the guy who ran the Southside Winery. He'd gone to school with her, but she couldn't remember his name. Felicia would know. His winery was supplying some of their wines.

She scrolled through the Google hits and surprisingly found an article written about the river where the accident had happened. The author, a journalist from the local paper, had gone back and told the story of several deaths in the river. When she found the paragraph regarding the accident with Jason and Larry, she read it twice before writing down the name on the byline and the paper's name.

Then she called Felicia.

"Hey, I thought we were meeting at noon. Are you driving in, or am I coming to get you? You're not calling to cancel, are you? You have to be at this fitting." Felicia rambled as soon as she picked up the phone, not giving Angie time to answer even one of the questions.

Finally when she paused for air, Angie spoke into the phone. "Calm down. I'm not canceling. I'll drive in and pick you up. You don't seem like you're up for driving right now."

"Okay, good, that will work." She paused. "So if this isn't about the dress fitting, why are you calling at nine on a Wednesday?"

"I found something. According to this article, the accident where Jason's brother died was particularly sad because there were three brothers there that day. Neither of the other two could save Jack." She paused and let the information sink in. "So did you know Larry attended the same prep school as Jason?"

"No. He didn't talk about his family at all. He always said how lucky I was to have my parents together." Felicia paused. "Seems logical. But looking back, it seemed like he was embarrassed about his family."

"Larry told the police they were half brothers. Then this reporter from Plantersville mentions a third brother at the accident. Maybe we should do more research on that angle. Do you happen to know anyone from Jason's family we could talk to, besides Larry?"

"No. I never went to Plantersville when he was going to school there. We started dating when he was just graduating from college. The one dance Jason took me to was held in a hotel outside of Boston, and that was for his college frat."

"Well, I'll see if I can find out anything before I pick you up." Angie went to hang up, but then Felicia spoke.

"I wonder if that's why Carter bothered Jason so much. If he'd had to live with the half brother issue when he was in school, having Carter represent that betrayal for his own family, that would be tough."

"Did he say anything about his family?" Angie needed Felicia to remember as much as possible, even if it was painful.

"He adored his mom. His dad, well, he said he was gone. His mom died a few years after he graduated from college. I assumed his dad had died before that." Felicia huffed out a strangled laugh. "But then again, he never said he had a brother at all. I met Jason the summer before my senior year. He was doing an internship with my father. After that, he was always there."

"Felicia, it's all right. Sorry I'm making you relive this."

"Angie, I let him into my life because my dad liked him. We dated because they thought we'd be a great power couple. I never even considered I had a right to be loved and to love someone like I do Estebe. When I finally picked up and moved to Boise for college, I think that was the first time I'd ever done something I wanted to do. Everyone was shocked. I'm not the most reliable narrator for that time in my life."

"But look at the amazing life you have now. You found yourself in food. That's not a bad thing. And you have an amazing fiancé who loves the same things you do. And of course, your ultra-fabulous best friend."

Felicia laughed. "The yoga class would think you were describing them."

"I know where I stand with you. Relax about the past. We'll figure out what happened to Jason; then you can shut that door and lock it. What you do about your folks, well, that's another story for another day. Today you only have to worry about one thing."

She paused before she answered. "If my dress fits?"

"Okay, two things. If your dress fits and if your fiancé is going to be available for Saturday's wedding ceremony. Everything else goes on the back burner."

"You're right, as always. Hey, Estebe's calling. I'll see you around noon?"

"Sounds good." Angie hung up and went to the stove. The sausage was almost done, so she used some of the grease in another pan and started scrambling the eggs. Yes, she needed a good breakfast to get through today. And tomorrow. And every day until the wedding was over and Estebe and Felicia were on a plane to Spain.

After breakfast, she called the Plantersville paper and was told that Sally was not there anymore. The woman who answered the phone said she thought she moved to Pittsburgh. When Angie asked if she knew anything about the article, she laughed. "Girl, I only started working here last week. If anyone knows, it's Ed. He's the editor in chief, and he's been here forever. I'll give him your message, and maybe he'll call you back. He seems really busy all the time."

"Thanks, I'd appreciate it." Angie left her name and number. She spent a few minutes trying to find a Sally Ernst at a Pittsburgh paper, but either the receptionist had given her bad information, or Sally had decided that journalism wasn't her bag.

She went back to researching Larry Fortell, but she hit a wall there too. There was nothing on the internet about the guy before ten years ago. It was like he just appeared. She tried combining the name with Plantersville or the school, but the results were the same. Nothing relevant. She closed the laptop and went to pick up a mystery to spend the rest of the time reading before she had to leave to get Felicia.

When she arrived in town, Felicia was sitting on the back stairs of the County Seat, waiting for her. When Angie pulled up, she ran to get into the car and turned up the heater. "I'm freezing."

"You didn't have to wait outside. I would have called you." Angie turned the car around and headed back out to Main Street, where she turned left toward Boise.

"I know. I just couldn't stay in the apartment any longer." She glanced at Angie. "After we get back from Spain, I'm moving in with Estebe."

"I figured. You two will be married, remember?" Angie let the car plod along at the low speed limit that didn't make any sense since there was never any traffic on this stretch of road.

"We're having a house built out on the river cliff. He showed me the plans last night. It's huge. I think I'm going to get lost in it as soon as we move in. But Angie, you should see the kitchen plans. It's heaven."

"It sounds perfect for you two." Angie glanced over at her friend. "So why the long face."

"I guess moving out of the apartment is hitting me. I love that apartment. It was the first time I've lived on my own. We shared a house in San Francisco. Before that, I lived in the dorms or with my folks. This apartment was all mine."

"I get that. Nona's farmhouse is that for me. I know I lived there with her before, but now that it's just me, it feels different. Well, just me and Dom and Precious and Mabel."

Felicia laughed, the warm and happy sound echoing in the car. A laugh that sounded like happy Felicia and one that Angie hadn't heard in a long time. "So you get what I'm feeling."

"I do. Are you sure you're ready to get married? Sharing your life with someone is a big step. They want to do things when you don't. They make messes. And they're always there, wanting to talk about stupid stuff." Angie turned onto the highway that would take them to the freeway and sped up to the thankfully higher speed limit. "Not that I'm saying Ian does any of those things, but Estebe might."

"I'm sure Estebe will be lovely to live with, but you're right. It's different than being alone. I was never lonely in my apartment. If I wanted company, I'd go to the Red Eye and chat with Barb or one of the regulars. Or if the restaurant was open, I was downstairs working. The apartment was my den of solitude."

"Why don't you make a place for you in this huge house? An office or exercise room. One just for you. Where you can go and put up a please-keep-out sign on the door. Well, maybe not a real sign, but an agreement with the two of you. I'm sure Estebe's going to have an office, right? You need a space too."

Felicia grinned. "I think you're onto something here. When did you get to be so smart?"

"I have had lots of time watching my smart best friend," Angie responded. "So tell me what you want in your fantasy house. Maybe we can get some ideas developed so you can give them to Estebe to incorporate into the house design."

"He said he wanted to know what I thought, but when I said something about the yard, he kind of told me it was impossible." Felicia closed her eyes. "Oh, no. I've become someone who settles."

"Settling is not a word that describes you. It's more like an unstoppable force meets an unmovable rock. You just have to explain to him that this is important. That it's your house too and you want—no, need—to be involved in the planning, or the two of you might just as well move into your apartment together." Angie liked the sound of an ultimatum. "Estebe just doesn't like taking advice."

"Boy, isn't that the truth." Felicia laughed as she slipped on her sunglasses to block the glare from the sun reflecting off the car in front of them. "So this is what I was thinking..."

By the time they got to the wedding dress shop, Felicia was feeling better and had a list of things she wanted in the new house. Estebe wouldn't know what hit him. As they got out of the car, Angie saw Hallie walking out of the shop. Luckily, she turned the other way toward the parking lot on the east side of the building. "That's odd."

Felicia turned and looked at her, then paused and walked back to the car. "Are you all right? Do you need a drink? You look like you just saw a ghost."

"Not a ghost, but Hallie. She was just in the dress shop. I wonder why?" Angie locked the car and waited until she didn't see Hallie's anymore. A red sedan pulled out of the parking lot and drove east, away from the building.

"Let's find out." Felicia waited for Angie on the sidewalk, and when they entered the store, the floral scent of soft perfume surrounded them. Felicia headed up to the counter. "We're here for a fitting. Felicia Williams bridal party?"

"Oh, yes, Miss Williams, we have you on the calendar." The girl's smile faded as she glanced at the doorway. "I'm so happy you could make your appointment."

"The woman who was just here, I think I went to school with her. Hallie something. Is she getting married? I didn't attend the last reunion. I'm so bad at those things." Felicia leaned down and whispered conspiratorially with the receptionist.

"Yes, that was Hallie. She's getting married in a hurry. I guess her fiancé is moving back east to take over some business. She didn't understand that we're just not an off-the-rack kind of place. Anyway, I sent her down to David's Bridal. They should be able to get her a dress for this weekend." She glanced at the clock. "Do you want champagne with your fitting? I have a bottle I just opened for another booking, and they didn't want it, so no charge."

"That would be lovely." Felicia smiled and then joined Angie on the white chairs in the waiting room. She glanced over to make sure the receptionist was gone. "So they're moving back east? Does Larry think he's getting an inheritance?"

"He probably will unless he's found guilty of murder," Angie muttered. "And Hallie is just making sure she's in on the payout."

"That's what it feels like." Felicia stood as the receptionist handed them each a glass of wine and nodded to the fitting room area. "Let's go, Angie. Time to pay the piper."

"I'm not sure that's the correct quote for this. Maybe something about seeing where the chips wound up." Angie followed Felicia into the reception area.

"Actually, I think it's getting ready for the rest of your life." The receptionist opened a door to a fitting room and ushered them inside. "The gowns are hanging up in the dressing rooms. Let me know if you need something else. I'm sure you're going to be a lovely bride."

Felicia nodded and waited for the woman to leave before pulling off her jacket. "I will be as long as I have a groom waiting for me at the altar."

Chapter 19

After taking Felicia and her dress back to the apartment, Angie stopped by the farmers market office to see Ian, but the door was locked and the lights out. She dialed his cell, but no one answered. She left a message: "Hey, I was here, but you weren't. Call me if you get bored tonight."

She drove home and thought they had just enough time to carve out a short walk at Celebration Park if she ran inside to change really quickly. And Dom hadn't eaten anything in the house that he shouldn't have. Like the couch.

Angie got cuddles from a non-evil Dom, so she got changed and got his walking bag ready. It always had his leash, an extra collar, just in case, and water and a bowl. Then they headed over to the park. She'd feed Precious and Mabel as soon as she got back.

They'd made their first lap around the flat river trail when she saw another walker coming her way. She usually didn't meet up with people on weekdays in the winter. Most people tended to be at work or exercising inside where it was warmer.

When the figure got closer, she realized it was Allen Brown. Her heart sped up. Had Ian been in an accident? Was that why he hadn't been at work? She held back Dom, who'd also recognized their visitor. "Hey, Allen, what brings you out here?"

"When you weren't at home, Ian mentioned you might be walking Dom. I knocked on the door and no one answered, so I figured he must be right." He leaned down and gave Dom a rub on the head. "When you're not at the house, I can't get out of my car without hearing him bark."

"He's a good watchdog, what can I say?" Angie nodded to a bench. "Do we need to sit for this chat?"

"What? No, I'd rather walk around with you if you don't mind. It helps clear my head, and Maggie checks my watch every day to see how many steps I've taken. She hates inventory day. I hardly have any." He fell in step on the other side of Dom, and they started on another lap.

"What did you want to chat about?" Angie asked. She figured it was about the case, but she wasn't going to be the first person to say something.

"I wanted to see what your theory is about why this Jason guy was killed. You have a good knack for this kind of thing. You seem to put together puzzles well." He stepped around a post in the middle of the path to keep cars from driving on the walking path. "So in your opinion, who's the killer?"

"Would you believe me if I said I didn't know?" Angie sighed as she hurried Dom from a spot that was particularly smelly, at least for a dog. "I feel like we're missing a clue. Or twenty."

"Don't I know it. I know Estebe didn't do it, and anyone with half a brain looking at the evidence knows that too. He'll never be convicted, but he could be charged and have to go to trial to prove his innocence. Which would play havoc with his honeymoon. I doubt he could get permission to go to Spain." He took off his hat and rubbed his hand over his thinning hair. "I don't want to hurt that friend of yours. She's a good person. She doesn't deserve to have her wedding day disrupted like that."

"You're right, she doesn't." Angie went through the things they'd found out about Jason and his connection to Larry and Hallie. "Now, I can't prove that Larry killed Jason, but it's the only thing that fits."

"So why would he kill Jason?" He turned toward her. "Unless you're thinking he was blackmailing his own brother?"

"Half brother, and yes, that's the only play that's on the field. Maybe Jason said no more. Maybe they asked for a big score and were planning on letting him go after he'd paid them what they needed." Angie rubbed her thumb across her palm. "I know, it's stupid."

"Not stupid. But right now, not verifiable," Allen pointed out. He paused by the exit to the path and looked up at the setting sun. "Are you heading home now? Or one last lap?"

"I'm freezing, and I want a cup of hot cocoa. My dress for the wedding actually still fits, so I don't have to worry about starving myself for three days, then falling into a vat of brownie chocolate chip ice cream." She pulled out her remote and unlocked the car door. "So, yeah, heading home."

"If you think of anything, don't hesitate to call." He paused as he watched her load Dom in the back seat; then she turned toward him. "I wanted to tell you how happy we are that Bleak's doing well, not only at the restaurant but at school. She's an amazing girl."

Angie climbed in the driver's seat and started the car. Dom's head came between the seats, and he watched her and Allen as they talked. "Bleak's special. And she's very lucky she found a family who cares about her like you and Maggie."

"Maggie's going to go crazy when she goes to college next year. I guess you've heard she's going to move into a house with Hope." He shoved his hands into his jacket pockets. "I'm going to have to call in some favors to make sure the campus police make the house a regular drive-by place."

"They won't have a chance to do anything bad." Angie considered the man standing next to her car. A man who had only become a father a few years ago; however, he was taking his new role seriously. "She'll be fine. I plan on keeping her busy at the restaurant. Between working there and classes, she won't have time for trouble."

"Divide and conquer. I like it." He tipped his hat toward her. "Have a good evening, Ms. Turner."

"Angie. Just Angie," she responded and rolled up the window. She turned up the heat and backed out of the spot. Time to head home and feed everyone. Including herself. And now, after talking to Allen, she hoped she had chocolate brownie ice cream in the freezer.

* * * *

The next morning, she packed her bag. Hope and Bleak were coming over and staying the night to feed Precious, Mabel, and Dom. She hated to be away from him, but Dom loved the girls, and he'd have fun with a movie night. Her dog had friends, and it made her happy. Especially since he didn't like many other animals.

She'd finished her chores for the day. She'd changed sheets on both her bed and the guest bedroom in case the girls didn't fall asleep in the living room watching television. She'd baked cookies and told Hope that she could use anything in the fridge, freezer, or pantry for dinner. Angie kept a variety of quality ingredients, just in case she had a craving for a specific recipe. Besides, she did a lot of recipe testing here in the kitchen. She didn't need to be driving to the store every time she decided to make something.

Glancing around the kitchen, Angie realized there wasn't much more to do. So she opened the laptop and started looking for anything on Larry,

Hallie, or even Jason. Two hours later, all she had for her effort was a raging headache and tired eyes.

It was time to drive into Boise and to their hotel. She was supposed to meet Felicia there at five. They were doing dinner first, then some bar hopping until someone tapped out. Then they'd return to the hotel room and crash. Angie just hoped she could hold on until they got to the hotel room. Maybe she should take a nap when she got there before dinner. It was a thought.

Tires crunched on the gravel drive outside the kitchen window. She needed to run upstairs and change into party clothes. She went to the door and waved in the girls. She waited for them to gather their overnight bags and hurry into the house.

"I don't envy your bar hopping tonight." Hope shut the door after her. "It's cold today. I would stay in the hotel room and order room service."

"It's an option, at least in my mind." Angie gave each of them a hug. "Thanks for babysitting tonight. I don't mind leaving them alone to go to work, but overnight is just a little more than I feel comfortable with."

"No problem." Bleak knelt on the floor next to Dom. "We'll have fun together."

"You know where everything is. I put clean sheets on the beds if you want to sleep upstairs, or you can get blankets out and crash in the living room. Food is all up for grabs, so if you want to cook, my recipe books are over there." Angie pointed toward the desk. She was taking the notebook with the investigation into Jason's murder, so that wasn't an issue. "No one delivers this far out, so you'll have to go into town if you want takeout food."

"We brought snacks." Hope eyed the recipe book. "And who knows what we'll find to make."

"I've got to get dressed and get out of here. Think of any questions for now, but if you need me, just call. I'll have my phone on." Angie ran upstairs and decided on cool boots, jeans, a pretty shirt, and a fun but heavy ski jacket. If they did go walking, she'd be warm. She checked the pockets for a hat and gloves, then went into the bathroom to glam up.

Ten minutes later, she was driving to Boise with party music blaring through her speakers. She really needed to get in a better, more fun mood.

She beat Felicia to the hotel, so she asked the front desk to hold her bag and her coat, and she went to the bar to wait.

"What can I get you?" Robbie, the same bartender they'd spoke with about Jason, was on duty.

She smiled as she settled on a stool. "How about coffee and a soft shot of something."

"So you need a pickup but also need to relax. You're asking a lot from one drink." He laughed at his joke and then held up a finger. "I'll fix you up, just hold on a second."

The piano player was either not on duty or it was too early, so a soft instrumental song flowed through the hidden speakers. There were other people in the bar, mostly couples. She checked to make sure Estebe and Felicia weren't among them.

"Here you go." Robbie set a cup of what smelled like hot chocolate in front of her. "It's an espresso in hot chocolate with a shot of Kahlua. You do look tired. Hopefully, this will give you some umph."

She sipped the drink and smiled. "I love whipped cream. It's perfect."

"Did you figure out your case?"

"Excuse me?" Angie set the drink down even though she really didn't want to.

He leaned on the counter. "The guy who died. Did you figure out why?"

Angie shrugged. "Not really. It's looking like he was just in the wrong place at the wrong time."

"Really. That's unfortunate." He nodded to a table behind her. "He came in the bar with that girl several times. Very cozy, if you know what I mean. Which is one of the reasons I thought it odd he was looking for the Front Porch. But now she's with that other guy. I guess I read the signs between them wrong."

Angie turned so she could focus on the couple in the mirror. The man, she knew. It was Carter. And he had his arm around a woman who, from the back, looked familiar. It wasn't until they broke the kiss they shared that she realized who the woman was. Hallie.

She opened her phone and set up the camera. Then she waited a few seconds until she could see both of their faces in the mirror. She spun around and clicked the picture, then tried to spin back, but her phone rang, and she saw Carter look right at her.

She turned to face the bar and answered the phone. "Hi, Hope."

"Hey, Angie, I was just checking. There should be two bags of feed, right? One for Mabel and one for Precious. I only see one."

"That's the goat food. Mabel gets into her bag if I leave it out. Go to the wall by her roost, and there's a door. It's back there. I should have showed you." Angie kept an eye on Carter and Hallie as she talked. Hallie was putting on her coat and leaving via the side door. Apparently, they thought she hadn't seen who the woman was. And she'd keep it that way. "Anything else?"

"No, we're good. Hope I didn't disturb you."

"The party hasn't even started." Angie hung up and saw Felicia coming toward her out of the corner of her eye. She sipped her drink as her friend slipped onto the stool next to her.

"That looks amazing. I'll have what she's drinking," Felicia told Robbie.

"Okay then, one cozy special coming up." He glanced back at Carter but then moved over to make the drink.

"This is going to be so much fun. Nancy's on her way. She called. And I know you sidelined Hope to help Bleak watch the zoo." Felicia chatted about the two friends from her yoga class, who were also coming. "Don't look like that. You'll love them."

A hand clasped her shoulder, and she looked up into Carter's eyes.

"What are two lovely women doing out without chaperones?" He kissed Felicia on the cheek. "Maybe I should stay here with you, just in case."

"I think you're the 'just in case' we're both worried about," Felicia teased. "Seriously, Carter, get out of here. You're wrecking my bachelorette party."

"Not much of a party with just the two of you." His eyes glittered as he looked between them. "It's a beautiful bar. Lots of amazing architecture, right, Angie? That was what you were taking pictures of earlier, right?"

"I wanted to get the grand piano in my picture. I'm thinking of getting a baby grand for the restaurant and wanted to have something to reference when I get back to the County Seat." It wasn't the best lie, but it was one she could remember. And that was crucial when you started a lie chain. You had to remember what the first lie was.

Felicia turned back toward the piano. "How big is a baby grand? I think we might have to take out the hostess stand and move it to the end of the dining room to get enough room."

"Okay then, if you're just going to talk shop, I'll leave the two of you. I've got to meet our father and your mother for dinner." He nodded to Robbie. "Put their drinks tonight on my tab."

Neither one of them said anything until Carter was out of the bar. "Sorry, Angie. I should have had Estebe put us up somewhere else. I thought they would be gone by now. I don't know why they aren't."

"Maybe your dad changed his mind, and they're coming to the wedding Saturday." Angie tried to sound hopeful, but it seemed to make Felicia wilt even more.

"Heaven help us. They'd probably try to pay Estebe to walk away before the ceremony started. At this point, I'd rather they didn't come. I'm sorry I even invited them." She took the drink from Robbie and sipped it. "Wow, this is great."

"Thanks. I invented it for a pick-me-up when I needed one." He paused by Angie. "Was he mad you took a picture of him and the girl?"

"Actually, I lied and said it was of the piano, but I'm not a very good liar. I'm sure he doubted my story. Felicia coming saved me from an uncomfortable conversation with him." Angie curled her trembling fingers around the warm cup.

"What girl? What did I interrupt?"

Angie started to tell her, but then Nancy swept in, and after that, the two yoga friends. They ordered a drink and told Felicia that the group needed to hurry to make the dinner reservations.

Angie, Felicia, and Nancy hurried to the front desk to get checked into the suite. When they reached the top floor, they dumped their bags on the beds. They looked around and got ready for the evening.

Nancy came out of the bathroom and grabbed her coat. "It has a clawfoot jacuzzi tub. I call dibs as soon as we get back. You two can bring me bonbons and refill my wineglass."

"If I'm even awake by then." Angie liked hearing Nancy laugh. The woman had three kids and worked her butt off. Less lately than when she'd been paying off debt from her ex-husband, but she still ran circles around anyone else Angie knew.

"That's the problem with being pampered. It's so hard to get good help anymore." Nancy fanned herself with a hand, then burst out laughing. "I'm so glad you invited me to come play with you. I've taken pictures of the entire suite so the kids can see how the other half lives."

"You think that's wise?" Angie held the door open as they filed out.

"I'm also going to tell them the only way to get this is to go to college and get a real job. Not work for the state or some restaurant. No offense, guys, but if I'd decided to be a lawyer instead of a chef? Even with the lower wages due to the gender gap, I'd be living in my own house by now and not renting from a friend." Nancy pushed the button for the elevator. "I'm leaving out books about famous doctors and lawyers and talking about ways to save for the future. They're going to be a lot smarter than their mom was at eighteen when they start making their own decisions."

"You're a good mom." Angie leaned into the back of the elevator. The adrenaline rush from the run-in with Carter was starting to fade, but the caffeine was starting to kick in. As long as she kept caffeinating every hour or so, she should be okay. Of course, tomorrow she'd sleep until checkout at the hotel. They walked out of the elevator and toward the bar. "But tonight we're a bunch of wild and crazy guys—I mean, gals—out to show our friend what she's giving up by marrying one of the most wonderful men in the valley. Ian excluded."

"Well, thank you," a male voice said from the lobby.

Angie turned, and Ian and Estebe stood watching them.

"I don't know, dude. Should we let them out without one of us to guard them?" Ian asked Estebe.

Somehow the question echoed Carter's statement, and it chilled Angie to the bone. She met Felicia's gaze and saw a look of understanding.

"We'll be fine." Felicia held up her purse. "I have Mace."

Chapter 20

"Mace will not help you in your purse. You need to carry it in your hand while you are walking." Estebe stepped over and gave Felicia a kiss. "Maybe we should get you a gun and a concealed carry permit instead."

Felicia shook her head. "I still have to get it out of my purse before anything happens. And then I'll have to shoot someone. I like the idea of Mace. It makes someone's eyes burn, and they'll think about what they did or tried to do for a long time. A gun might just make them mad."

Estebe and Ian shared a look. Then Ian shrugged. "What can I say, dude? You're marrying her, not me."

"My Felicia is a study in contrasts." He leaned over and kissed her. "We're heading out to eat. I see you have friends in the bar."

"Yeah, we need to get to our own reservations. Have a fun night, but not too fun." She pushed back a lock of his hair behind his ear.

He took her hand in his and kissed the palm. "I am counting the hours until we are man and wife. I will do nothing to mess that up."

Nancy nodded to the bar and then left Angie and Felicia standing in the lobby, watching the men leave.

"He's a catch." Angie put a hand on her friend's back. "I'm so happy for both of you."

"I can't believe I'm so happy." She wiped at her eyes as Angie dug in her purse for a tissue.

As she handed a pack to Felicia, she paused. "I hate to bring this up, but did Carter know Jason before he came to work for your dad?"

"Carter went to the same boarding school as Jason. He said that was the one gift Dad gave him, his education. I think it was more about keeping him away from Mom until he could figure out how to tell her. Carter was born after their fifth wedding anniversary." Felicia rolled her eyes. "Which is why I still don't understand why Mom is getting so cozy with Carter. I thought she hated him, or at least the idea of him, because of the bad memories."

"Carter went to school with Jason and Larry and Jack?" Angie pulled Felicia back to the question at hand.

"Yeah, I told you that." Felicia turned toward her and shook her head. "No way. Carter isn't like that."

"But what if he and Larry knew about each other. That they were the unwanted kids. It could lead to bad feelings," Angie pointed out.

"How do you know Carter knew any of the others?" Felicia asked, as if she were trying to wrap her head around what Angie was saying.

She pulled out her phone and found the picture. "Because I saw Hallie cuddled up to Carter just now. For someone who's supposed to be getting married in a few days, she looks pretty chummy with another man."

"Yes, she does." Felicia sent the picture to her phone. "But we don't have anything but suspicions at this point. And it could have been Carter or Hallie or Larry who was the killer. Or maybe all three of them were involved. We need to find out where everyone was on Monday night."

"I can help you with Hallie's whereabouts," Nancy said as she walked up to them with a beer in her hand. "Everyone wants to go to dinner. I got tasked to come tell you."

"Okay, you told us. Now what do you know about Hallie?" Angie turned to focus on Nancy while Felicia waved at the others and motioned for one more minute.

"Hallie told me Saturday that she had a date on Monday. That was why she was glad we were closed at the first of the week." She sipped her beer. "She said this guy had just come in from Boston and she was dying to meet him."

"Okay, so she's not off the list." Angie worried her bottom lip. "Now we just have to see if we can track down Carter and Larry."

"Carter was on a plane. Mom said he flew commercial because he needed to stay for a meeting. Actually, I don't think he would have come for the wedding, except for Jason being killed." Felicia made a checkmark in the air. "I know he could have said he was flying in later, but Dad needed him to talk with some investors early Monday evening. Carter wouldn't have put the business in jeopardy by missing that meeting."

"Ian's uncle can sort out the validity of the alibis, but yeah, I think Carter's off the list for actually having shot Jason." She tried to remember if she had heard anything about Larry and where he was. Nothing was coming up. "So we're down to two."

"And out of time." Nancy pointed to the bar where the two yoga friends were pulling on coats to meet with them. "At least you found someone and some other reason for the killing than Estebe in a jealous rage. That was playing way too well for the mainstream media."

"If we don't leave now, we're going to miss our reservation. Let's go," the blond woman said. She reached out a hand to Angie. "I'm Tasha, and this is Meg. We met at yoga once. I'm sorry you didn't come back. Even busy career women like us need to take care of ourselves."

"That's right. I remember meeting you." Angie smiled and nodded, even though she didn't remember meeting the women the few times Felicia'd dragged her to the yoga class. "I guess we better get walking. Where are we eating?"

The meal was filled with talk about the upcoming wedding and honeymoon. Meg and Tasha were telling Felicia how unfortunate it was that Estebe wasn't taking her to this private island vacation spot where Meg had just spent a week. Nancy and Angie chatted about the food and the restaurant. And Felicia tried hard to bring the two groups together. It wasn't working.

When they left the restaurant, Meg and Tasha begged off the bar hopping, as they had a yoga class first thing in the morning.

Angie glanced at Felicia and Nancy after they left. "What about the two of you? Are you ready to call it a night?"

"You're kidding, right?" Nancy shook her head. "I don't get a lot of girls' nights, so we're doing this one up right. Besides, every bride needs some fun before taking the plunge. It doesn't matter how much you love your man, you always need your girlfriends around to keep you sane."

"That is so true." Felicia put her arm in Nancy's. "I'm in for some bar hopping. And I'm sorry about those two. I really thought out of all of that group, they might make an effort to get to know you guys."

"Sometimes worlds just don't match up." Angie shook her head. "Besides, they were fine. They just had different things on their minds."

"Like their next manicure. I swear, not counting the one I'm getting Friday, I don't remember the last one I had." Nancy glanced at her mitten-covered hands. "My nails thank you for getting married, Felicia."

That got them all laughing, and they started down the street. Felicia stopped in front of a dueling piano bar. "This looks fun."

"Okay, let's try it." Angie nodded to the bouncer who was watching the door. "Is there a cover?"

"Not tonight. Or not for you, anyway. It's ladies' night." He held the door open for them. "Enjoy the music, but stay away from the island punch unless you want to get hammered."

"Good hint." Angie made her way into the darkened room and pointed to what looked like a table freeing up. Two men were throwing money on the table. Angie hurried over and slipped into one of the chairs, waving the others over. A woman at the bar huffed when she saw them sitting down; then she turned back to talk with the bartender some more. "You snooze, you lose."

Nancy moved the empty beer bottles over to the edge of the table along with the tip. Soon, a waitress stopped by, grabbed the empties and the money, then wiped the table. "What can I get for you gals? Island punch?"

"Actually, no. I'll have a Woodhouse Riesling." Angie looked at the others.

"Frozen margarita, with salt," Nancy said.

Felicia nodded. "I'll have the same."

Angie held up a hand. "Fine, make it three. Cancel the wine. Who wants to be classy at a bachelorette party?"

The waitress laughed. "Who's the bride?"

Felicia held up a hand. "That would be me."

"First round's on the house for the table. Thanks for coming here to celebrate the big day. We love bridal parties." She winked at Felicia and left them to talk.

"That was nice," Angie said as she watched Nancy fumble in her purse. "What are you doing? The first round is on the house. You don't need money."

Nancy pulled out three tiaras and a sash. She gave a tiara to Angie and one to Felicia with the sash. She put the last one on her head.

"What's this?" Felicia held up the sash.

"It says 'I'm the Bride!'" Nancy got out her phone and snapped a selfie. Then she looked at the other two. "Go on, get them on so I can take one of all three of us. And believe me, that sash is going to get us free drinks all night."

Nancy's prediction wasn't wrong, and since the music was good and the drinks were flowing, the group just stayed at the piano bar the rest of the night. When it started to wind down, Angie stood and put a twenty on the table for a tip for their waitress, who'd kept the free drinks coming by pointing out their group to every table she served all night. "Come on, princesses. The coach is leaving. Which means we're walking back to the hotel now."

"Already?" Felicia straightened her crown. "I really like this song."

"We can turn the stereo on in the hotel room," Angie offered. "And order some room service."

"Brownies?" Felicia sighed. "I seriously won't fit into that dress on Saturday."

"Yes, you will." Nancy pulled Felicia to her feet. "Besides, our chaperones should be outside."

"What are you talking about?" Angie asked, but Nancy took Felicia's arm and walked out of the bar without answering. When they got out of the building, the cold air failed to clear Angie's senses. She must have been dreaming because Ian, Matt, and Estebe stood there, leaning on the wall of the building, waiting. She shook her head and closed her eyes. When she looked back, they were still there. She turned back to Nancy and Felicia. "Okay, who called the guys?"

"Matt texted me and asked how it was going. When I told him where we were, he said they were down the street and to let him know when we were ready to leave. That they'd walk us to the hotel." Nancy took Matt's arm. "Wasn't that sweet?"

Angie gave Ian the cross-eyed stare. "We *could* have made it back all on our own."

He pulled her into a hug. "Of course you could, my dear, but isn't this a nice way to end our night out? Together?"

Angie saw Estebe and Felicia meld together like they had magnets in their sides and start walking toward the hotel and warmth. "I guess so. Just so you know, we were fine."

"Never doubted it." He adjusted her tiara. "This is nice. You should wear it at the restaurant and make the crew call you Queen Angie."

"That's a great idea." She took Ian's arm, and they followed the others. As they passed by the alley where Jason's body had been found, a chill ran up her spine. She peered into the darkness and thought she saw movement. She froze in place.

Noticing her full-on stop, Ian leaned down, staring into the alley as well. "What's wrong?"

Angie stared into the blackness. Nothing moved now. "I thought I saw something."

"Hey, slowpokes. We're going to stop at the café on the corner for pie," Felicia called back to them.

Ian raised his eyebrows. "I could go for some coffee and pie. What about you?"

Angie looked one more time into the alleyway. No one would be hanging out there this time of night, not in this weather. She took Ian's hand in hers and nodded. "Coffee would be good. Especially hot coffee."

He chuckled as they hurried to catch up with the others. "I totally agree."

They sat at a large booth by the front window. The waitress brought a pot of coffee and six cups when she first approached the group. Apparently, this wasn't the first late-night shift she'd worked. She poured and passed the cups around. "What can I get for your highnesses?"

Angie frowned, then remembered the tiaras. "We were celebrating my friend's upcoming wedding."

"I see that a lot. We have an amazing dessert menu and more types of pies than any other restaurant in town. Do you want menus?"

"I'm having apple with ice cream," Angie said.

"Brownie with ice cream and hot chocolate sauce," Felicia called out.

As the rest called out their dessert order, Angie studied the street. There weren't very many people out in the cold. One man, who appeared to be homeless, stopped to check a trash receptacle for cans and then moved on. Then a woman dressed in black jeans and a coat jaywalked across the street and got into a newer red Honda. She started the car and pulled it out into traffic. The driver looked into the window directly at Angie, then twisted away.

Angie swore she recognized the woman driving the Honda. And she'd seen the car before too. In her parking lot. It had to be Hallie. Had she been the shadow in the alley?

Chapter 21

"You're kidding, right?" Felicia sat on the couch in pajamas, drinking hot chocolate they'd brought and heated in the mini microwave. "I think you had one too many margaritas. Why would she be in the alley? Are you saying the murderer always returns to the scene of the crime?"

"Maybe?" Angie went to the fridge and got one of the bottles of sparkling water she'd brought along. The hotel hadn't expected them to bring their own party supplies. While the trio might still get some late-night treats from room service, they'd each brought their favorite dessert packed in their suitcase. Which was why they'd actually brought a suitcase rather than a tote for a change of clothes. "I don't know anymore. But if that wasn't her car, it looked just like it."

"How many late-model red Hondas are in the Treasure Valley? Hundreds? Thousands?" Nancy ate a truffle and passed the bowl filled with popcorn toward Angie. "You may just be seeing what you expect to be seeing."

"I didn't imagine her having a cuddle-fest with Carter earlier today in the bar. And according to Felicia's wedding dress designer, Hallie's getting married this weekend. Maybe we just assumed it was Larry. Maybe she's been seeing Carter long distance and they're getting married in Boston." Angie pulled out the murder notebook she'd brought along. She'd grabbed it as an afterthought, but now she was glad it was here. "Why did we think Larry and Hallie were dating again?"

"You saw them on her Facebook page looking chummy." Felicia turned the notebook to the page where Angie had written the fact down. "I guess we jumped to conclusions. Especially since he drove the getaway car when she came to deface the County Seat. We don't have another fact that corroborates her relationship."

"That's right, he was there too. Maybe he's just a good friend." Angie went to cross out the detail, but Nancy reached out to still her hand. "What?"

"Wait. I have your second verification or whatever. Hallie told me that she and Larry were living together and she was sure he would propose before the end of the year. In fact, she'd already found the ring in his sock drawer when she was putting away laundry last week." Nancy took the book away from Angie. She scanned the contents. "This is crazy good. You guys should be private investigators or something."

Angie and Felicia shared a glance. Angie held up her hand and counted out facts on her fingers. "So at least Larry thought they were going to get married. Larry is Jason's half brother, and they all went to the same high school. I checked the alumni list a few nights ago when I couldn't sleep."

"Boarding school, not high school. Besides, all that means nothing when you're trying to prove who killed him. Unless you can find a blackmail note or fingerprints or the gun that shot him." Felicia groaned and fell backward on the couch.

"But maybe Allen can push on this. If he can cite probable cause or some legal stuff, maybe they can search Hallie and Larry's place for a gun," Angie pointed out. "I'm going to email this theory to Allen and then text him to let him know it's there."

Felicia held out her arm, and her watch sparkled. "It's almost three in the morning. Email him now but wait to text him until at least eight. Or whenever we get up."

"Okay, I get it. Not everyone is a night owl." Angie pulled out her laptop and put all the information about the connection between Larry, Hallie, and Carter to Jason. She also listed off the fact that Carter had been on a plane when Jason was killed. She finished the email with who she thought was the killer because of what she'd seen tonight.

Felicia yawned and pulled a blanket over her. "Who do you think killed Jason?"

Angie put her laptop back in her bag and took another handful of popcorn. "Hallie. She's mean to the bone. And if for some reason Jason had told her no or stood in the way of what she wanted? She'd do anything to get her way. I know it was her in the alley tonight. I think if the boys hadn't come to walk us back, we'd all be dead in the alley."

"Wow, that's crazy. Your theory is freaking me out a little." Nancy ate another truffle. "And on that cheerful thought, I'll say good night and sweet dreams. The kids will be at school when I get home, but I'll have to pick up the little one at noon since she only has a half day tomorrow. Teachers in-service day."

"You're an amazing mom," Angie pointed out as she watched Nancy head to the bedroom.

"I'm just keeping my head above water. Some days, I even get to swim a little." Nancy smiled and disappeared into the bedroom.

Felicia reached for the truffles. "Estebe is talking about kids. When, how many, where we should send them to school. Is that crazy talk or what?"

"You don't want kids?" Angie stood and brought the popcorn and her water over to the couch. "I thought you would want a tribe. You're like that. You'd be a great mom."

"I do want kids, but I still feel like a kid myself. I know we're in our thirties, but somehow that feels really young to be having the responsibility of not screwing up someone's life in your hands." Felicia finished off her cocoa and looked in the bottom of the cup to make sure there wasn't more. "What if I raise someone who acts like Hallie? Even if she didn't kill someone, the girl is off her rocker."

"You won't. You're going to have one of those saga families you read about where everyone is happy and successful and loved even if they just want to raise horses." Angie took Felicia by the arms and squeezed. "You're getting married in two days, and I can't be happier for you. Just tell Estebe you want it to be just the two of you for a while. He'll think that's romantic and take you all over the world. Just live one day at a time. That's all you can do. Just don't quit the business. I need you there."

"I promise, even if I have a tribe of kids, I'm still going to work. I'll have to have some excuse to get out of the house, right?" Felicia yawned again. "I either need coffee or bed."

"I think we need some sleep." Angie stood and put the popcorn on the coffee table. "We have the rehearsal where you'll cry through the whole thing, then the rehearsal dinner where I have to figure out something nice to say about you and Estebe."

"You haven't written your speech yet?" Felicia's eyes widened in surprise. "Angie. You told me you were done."

"Of course I've written it. I'm just not sure where I put it." Angie laughed at the look of horror on Felicia's face. "Just kidding. It's on my desk in the kitchen."

Felicia threw a couch pillow at Angie. "Fine, now I am going to bed."

Angie dodged the pillow and stepped toward the bedroom. "This was a fun night. I'm so happy for you and Estebe. And now you can tell the boys we had a pillow fight like they imagine all good sleepovers have."

"You are so bad." Felicia laughed as she followed Angie into the bedrooms.

* * * *

Angie left the hotel right at eleven after a quick shower to push away the alcohol and lack of sleep from the night before. The guys had come into the suite for the large breakfast Estebe had ordered, and the talk had been about the upcoming festivities and all the things they needed to do before the wedding the next day. A wedding planner had been hired to decorate the County Seat, and Angie and Felicia were meeting her there at one to make sure everything was going according to plans. The florist was also supposed to be there today and would leave the bouquets and boutonnieres in the walk-in to stay fresh for tomorrow's ceremony. The rehearsal would be at four, and then they were all going to the Basque community center for the dinner.

Their day was set. Now, it just needed to happen the way it was planned. Driving home, Angie was going through all the things she needed to do before meeting Felicia when her phone rang.

"Hello?"

Felicia's voice filled the car. "You won't believe it. They're staying for the wedding."

"Your folks?" Angie had wondered if they would since they had still been in town last night.

"Yes. I ran into Mom as we were leaving the hotel this morning. She said Carter talked Dad into staying, and he's going to give me away on Saturday. She wanted to know about the rehearsal time and place and the dinner afterward. Of course, she made a face when I told her the arrangements, but then she just said, 'It's your wedding.'"

"Which it is. And it's going to be beautiful." Angie wondered if having Felicia's parents there today and tomorrow would be a blessing or a curse, but she figured they might be able to keep their feelings about their new son-in-law under control for the few hours they'd be around. At least she hoped so.

"I'm glad you think so. I'm a little worried about what they might say. I'm used to their sideways comments, but Estebe might be offended." Felicia admitted her fears about the change in plans.

"The man would walk through coals to marry you," Angie reminded her. "Besides, it's two days, and then the two of you will be in Spain."

The line got quiet for a second, and Angie knew Felicia was thinking as long as Estebe wasn't charged in Jason's murder. Which reminded Angie she hadn't texted Allen about the long email she'd sent him last night.

"Oh, Estebe's calling me. I better answer and see what he thinks. He didn't say much when Mom told us the news."

"He's probably overjoyed. Not." Angie laughed and hung up.

Then she called Allen Brown.

He answered on the first ring. "Hey, you know email isn't an appropriate place to write a novel, right?"

"Good, you got it. Now I don't have to wait for you to read it. What do you think?" Angie hoped it was enough.

"Jason and Larry *were* half brothers. I verified this. His dad remarried after he divorced Jason's mom, and the baby was born a few months later. Now Dad and new wife are deceased too. This family hasn't had the best luck in the longevity department. He sighed. "Anyway, the familial relationship isn't enough for a search warrant, but I am going to be chatting with Carter this morning about his relationship with Hallie. Maybe I can get him to say something stupid."

"Sounds like a plan." Angie drummed her fingers on the steering wheel. "This is so frustrating. I know it was Hallie in the car last night. She didn't like the fact I'd taken a picture of her and Carter together."

"You're putting a bull's-eye on your back if she or Carter is the killer. You know that, right?"

"I think I explained it away," Angie said weakly.

"You and I both know that's not true." He paused. "Look, just stay out of trouble and get your friend married. Do you need me to stand in today at the rehearsal?"

"Her dad says he's going to be there, so no. But you're coming to the wedding Saturday, right? You might want to get there a little early, just in case."

"I'll be there in my tux. Maggie's crazy excited that we get to dress up. She likes how I look in that monkey suit."

Angie laughed and thanked him again for his willingness to step in for Felicia's dad.

"The girl's special. She deserves the royal treatment for her wedding. Hopefully, it's the only one she'll have." He sniffed, then disconnected the line.

"Well, Chief Allen Brown, aren't you the softy?" Angie said to herself in the empty car.

When she got home, Hope and Bleak piled their stuff into Hope's car. They both looked like they hadn't gotten much sleep last night. But they promised the animals had been fed, and the kitchen didn't look like a tornado had gone through it. She opened the fridge, where Hope had said they'd left her a surprise, and found a container of soup for her lunch. She opened the top and sniffed. "Creamy chicken and tortellini?"

Dom huffed out a sound, which might have meant yes. But it could have also meant they didn't feed *me* any. Angie's Saint Bernard thought anything cooked in *his* kitchen should be fair game for him. She spoiled him, but she bet Hope and Bleak had kept the treats to a minimum hoping they wouldn't get him sick.

"Sorry they didn't spoil you. And I'm only here for a while today. Then I'm heading back into town. Tomorrow night when I get home, I'll be here to stay until Wednesday when I reopen the restaurant." She poured the soup into a pan and sat at the table, letting Dom come and give her loves. She rubbed behind his ears. "We should have had Aunt Felicia use you as a ring bearer. If I get married, I'm totally doing that. You can wear them around your neck in a fake barrel like the Swiss dogs do on the Alps."

Dom lolled his tongue to the side and panted happily. He was a bright spot in her life. Dom was always happy to see her. No matter how long she'd been away.

Angie opened her laptop to check her email while her soup warmed up. She'd have a couple of thick slices of bread out of the loaf she'd brought home from the restaurant on Saturday with it. And maybe a small salad. She mentally planned her meal as she went through, deleting the junk mail that seemed to grow if you didn't weed it out daily. Suddenly she stopped. She had an email from a reporter at the *Colorado Examiner*. It was the woman who'd done a piece on the school, but she'd changed her last name.

Angie opened the email and started reading. The woman started talking about what a blast from the past it was and that one of her friends from the Massachusetts paper had forwarded Angie's email.

She scrolled through the email until she found what she was looking for. "I always thought there was more to the drowning story than the boys had told. One woman told me the fight had been over a girl who lived in town and had been dating both of the brothers. Until one of them found out."

Angie glanced at Dom, who had moved over to his kitchen bed and lain down, but he was still watching her. "I wonder where Hallie met Jason and Larry. I bet she was the girl the brothers were fighting over."

She scanned the rest of the email, but there was no mention of the girl's name. She responded to the email and asked if the reporter had heard a name attached to the rumor. And if it was Hallie Godfrey.

She made a note in the murder book and read through her notes. What if Jason had been calling to talk to Hallie. Or maybe he was talking to Larry and trying to make amends for letting Hallie get between them.

She should be upstairs, getting ready for the rehearsal and the rehearsal dinner, but she had a few minutes. She keyed Hallie's name into the internet search and tried to see if she could find out where she was born. After clicking too many links, she was no further than she'd been twenty minutes ago, and now she did have to sign off. Time to go play peacemaker between Felicia and her family. If they even showed up.

Angie shut the laptop and headed upstairs. It was going to be a long night.

* * * *

When she got to the restaurant, all the lights inside were shining through the front windows. She could see people milling about, and she glanced at her car clock, wondering if she was late. She parked in the last parking spot in her small lot behind the restaurant, glad she'd claimed her spot with a metal sign last summer. She'd thought Felicia had been silly, having the signs installed, but today, she was glad she didn't have to find on-street parking.

The back door to the kitchen was unlocked, and when she entered, she found people moving around. Estebe called out to one of the men to set the glasses up on the table and open the wines in the kitchen. Angie stepped over to where he stood, directing everyone. "What are you doing?"

"I'm getting the catering set up for the rehearsal." He opened his hands and shrugged. "What does it look like?"

"Typically, we don't cater the rehearsal. That's what the dinner's for. And we can't have people drinking, then driving to Boise for the dinner." She glanced at the boxes of wine.

"I have also taken care of that. There is a bus coming to pick us up at five to take us to the community center. Then, people will either be dropped off at their hotel or at their houses. I have drivers to deliver their cars back home. So don't forget to give me your keys." He nodded to one of the waiters, who poured a glass of champagne and handed it to Angie. "Relax and enjoy yourself. I'm getting married in the morning to the woman I'll love the rest of my life. It's time to celebrate."

"As long as your classmate doesn't arrest you for Jason's murder." Angie didn't want to remind him, but he needed to be realistic. "I think I figured out a possible motive."

He held up his hand. "No talking about death or murder or jail. Today and tomorrow are for Felicia and me. We will not talk about this problem. We will not bring trouble down on ourselves by thinking bad thoughts. Drink. And give me your keys. Your man is already in the dining room with the others."

"Estebe, I just..."

He took her by the shoulders and moved her toward the door. "Go talk, eat, and drink. It is time to celebrate."

Angie paused in the doorway, holding open the door, then held her keys toward Estebe. "Here you go. They better be careful with it."

He chuckled. "They will be careful, and if not, they are insured. Go have fun."

She moved her foot and let the door shut behind her. Estebe was probably living in a fantasy world where Jason's murder wouldn't be pinned on him, but it was his wedding. She tucked her coat and purse into her office and kept her phone out to take pictures. She knew the couple had hired a professional photographer, but she still wanted to have her own pictures of this special weekend.

Felicia met her at the edge of the dining room. It was breathtaking. The white roses that lined the room gave it a floral smell, and the white wooden chairs they'd rented made the room look like it was made for weddings. A floral arch was where the hostess stand typically sat, and Hope and Bleak stood next to it, talking. "It's better than I could have imagined. Of course, the farmhouse would have been lovely too."

"No, it would have been cold and dirty. This is magical." She took in the room and saw Ian standing with the minister and his uncle. "Excuse me a minute, I need to talk to Allen."

"No murder talk. Estebe has put down the rule. This is going to be about the wedding and nothing else." Felicia smiled, but Angie saw the sliver of fear go behind her eyes when she'd mentioned Jason's murder.

"I promise. I just need him to tell Maggie something." She lied smoothly to Felicia and wondered when she'd been able to do that before. But Felicia's attention was being taken up by one of the yoga girls who'd come to the party. Angie couldn't remember her name, but she knew she was Felicia's bridesmaid. Angie was the maid of honor.

She moved over to Allen and pulled him away from Ian and the minister. "I need to tell you something."

He nodded, and they went over to where the guests would enter tomorrow and pretended to check out the flower arrangements. "So what did you find?"

She handed him a slip of paper with the reporter's name, email address, and phone number. "Talk to her about Jason's brother Jack's death. She's going to try to find her notes about the girl who they were fighting over."

"You think it's Hallie." He didn't frame it as a question but as a statement.

She nodded. "I think that girl has been playing with these guys and their heads for years. Now, she's taken another one out."

Chapter 22

Thirty minutes into the rehearsal, they had to start all over. The rehearsal had gone off without a hitch right up to the time Felicia's mom and dad showed up with Carter. Felicia already stood at the altar with Estebe, rehearsing the vows, when Mr. Williams insisted that they start the rehearsal again so he could walk his baby girl down the aisle. As they walked back to the serving area, Felicia turned to Angie and hissed. "The man is infuriating."

Angie took Felicia's arm and moved her away from her mom and dad, who were following them to the back. She opened the office door, and they quickly went inside, shutting the door behind them. "Okay, now breathe. You don't want them to know they got to you. Don't give them the satisfaction."

Felicia took a tissue from Angie's desk and patted at her eyes. "You're right, as always. I just need to get through this weekend; then Estebe and I will be on a beach in Spain. At least for a week."

"There's my girl. What doesn't kill us, right?" Angie moved a strand of hair out of Felicia's eyes. "No crying, this is just a rehearsal. Save your tears for tomorrow when you've realized you made a horrible mistake by marrying him."

"You're awful." Felicia started laughing, breaking the sour mood.

Angie nodded. "Yes, but at least you're laughing now."

A knock sounded at the door. Meg called from the other side, "Are you two ready?"

"Yep, we'll be right out." Angie smoothed her purple cocktail dress and checked her hair in the mirror she kept on the door. "Seems weird being here and not in my dress whites. Hey, did we have Hallie fill out an application for full-time?"

"Sure. But you're not considering hiring her after what she did." Felicia paused with her hand on the doorknob.

"Are you crazy? I was just wondering if we were missing something about her." Angie held up her hands. "I know, no murder talk today or tomorrow."

Angie followed Felicia out into the dining room area, then got in position behind Meg to walk down the aisle. Again. If she found time before they went to the rehearsal dinner, she'd find that application and see if it said where Hallie went to high school or college. A girl could only hope.

When they arrived at the community center, the party had already started. A group of people greeted them as they left the bus. Angie grinned at Ian as an older man grabbed him and kissed him on both cheeks.

"Welcome to our family," he cried as he gave Ian and then Angie a big hug.

Angie stepped back and shook her head. "We're just friends of Felicia and Estebe; we're not related."

"Nonsense, you are now our family too." He put his arms around them and started walking inside. "I'm Estebe's uncle. You can call me Ander, or Uncle Ander, it's up to you. I'm his father's brother. My wife, she helped with the cooking for tonight. You won't get the full family experience tonight. Estebe asked for us to not overwhelm you, so we're just helping out. You'll meet his mama and papa, and his brothers and sisters will all join you for dinner. We would have come for the rehearsal, but it was important to get the food right for tonight."

"Uncle Ander, please bring Ian and Angie over to their table. I'm sure you've told them far more than they needed to know." Estebe waved them over to a table where another couple already sat.

Angie sat and smiled at the older woman next to her. "I'm Angie Turner. I'm Felicia's friend."

"And my boss, so you two be on your best behavior." Estebe leaned down and kissed the woman on the top of her head. "Angie, Ian, this is my grandmother, Mikel, and her husband, George."

"Nice to meet you," Ian said.

The older man leaned closer. "What? What did he say?"

"He said it was nice to meet you, Papa," Estebe yelled over the table. "Sorry, they're both a little hard of hearing. Mostly they will just eat and enjoy your company. You will not have to do a lot of talking. Especially once the music starts."

"The music is the best," the woman yelled at Estebe, who smiled and nodded.

"Yes, Mama, it is." He glanced at the head table. "I better go rescue Felicia. She looks like her family is surrounding her. And not in a loving manner."

Angie's gaze followed Estebe as he made his way to the head table. Mr. Williams's face was beet red, and her mother had a hand on his arm, trying to get him to calm down. Apparently, he hadn't liked his table assignment, which from the raised voices, Angie could hear was in the back near the kitchen. She rubbed her face and was surprised when Estebe's grandmother leaned in and whispered.

"It will all be fine. Families are supposed to be loud and messy. Felicia will fit in well with our group, and her parents will learn to accept her love, eventually." Mikel patted her hand. "And we're not deaf. We just let the family think that so we don't have to listen to their complaining. Sometimes, they complain so much."

"Everyone wants something they can't have," George filled in. "A new or better car. A different job. A better wife."

She elbowed him, and he chuckled.

"But it's true, Mama. Those children are spoiled. We built a good life here, and all they want is more. Except, of course, Estebe. He is a good man, and Felicia will make him a good wife. They came by and spoke with us after they got engaged to get our blessing. Not something you see a lot with the younger generation." George glanced up at the waitress, who set several platters of food in front of them. "Yes, it's time to eat. I'm starving."

"You're always hungry. And yet you stay so skinny. I try to be careful and eat like a bird, and I balloon out like a water buffalo," Mikel complained.

George leaned over to Ian. "See, everyone complains. I would pretend not to hear her, but alas, she's my wife so she knows all my secrets."

"Of course I do. And I'm not complaining." She dished up food on Angie's plate, then her own. "Just please keep our secret from Estebe. He would be heartbroken to think we lied to him. He's a good boy."

Angie's and Ian's gazes met, and they smiled at each other. It was going to be an interesting night. That was certain.

Later that night, she excused herself from the table and got up to find a bathroom. She ran into Carter near the bar. "Nice party, isn't it?"

"Why are you looking into Hallie? Hasn't the woman suffered enough without you insinuating she had something to do with Jason's death?" He moved and blocked her into a corner.

"Did she?" Angie met his gaze. He wasn't going to bully her.

"No. She's heartbroken that Jason's gone. They dated in high school." He sipped his drink, which from the whiskey smell coming off him, wasn't his first.

"Thanks for confirming that she also lived near the boarding school. So did she date Jason before or after Jack was killed?" She reached for a waitress's order pad and pen that was sitting on the bar. "Let me write this down."

"Just stay away from her." He leaned closer. "Or else."

"Angie, can I talk to you about next week's temp assignment?" Tracy, the bartender she'd talked to at the Vista Bar, leaned over the edge of the bar into Carter's line of sight.

Carter took two steps back. "Mind what I said."

As he moved back into the larger room and to the table with the Williamses, Angie sank into a stool by the bar.

"Thanks for the save. I can't believe he was so aggressive." Angie felt her hands shaking.

Tracy shrugged. "No problem. He's been slamming back drinks for the last hour like he was the jilted bridegroom. I was about ready to cut him off."

"Probably a good idea." Angie started to leave. "Are you really working next week at the County Seat?"

"Nah, I just said that to break into your convo." He opened a bottle of soda water and took a drink. "You looked like you needed rescuing."

Typically, Angie didn't admit she needed rescuing to anyone, but he was right this time. "Don't tell me you're friends with Larry and Hallie?"

"With Larry, yes. But not Hallie. She's a piece of work." He sipped his water. "Anyway, it's all probably moot now. Larry told me he was leaving for the East Coast in a few days. He came into some money. If I was him, I'd take off without leaving a forwarding address so I could get away from the girlfriend from hell, but I guess everyone has a different vision of the person they love."

Angie laughed and pointed to the water. "Anyway, I can get one of those?"

"Of course. And for clarification, I *was* Larry's friend. But not anymore. Word travels, man. I want to work in this business for a long time. To be honest, I suspected that Hallie talked him into slashing Sydney's tires, but he never admitted it. I heard you caught him and that crazy witch painting the front of your place. That's cold. Everyone loses a job now and then. It's the way things are." He handed her a bottle of water and waved away her offer to pay. As he did, he glanced around the bar. "When Larry turned this job down, I was next in line for the position. I guess your friend pulled some strings when he saw my application. He's a good guy. I hope his wedding goes well."

"Me too. So you didn't know Hallie well?" Angie set the pen and paper down.

"The black widow? I stay as far away from that..." He paused, and then he blushed. "Sorry, but I'm really not a fan."

"Why do you call her the black widow?" Angie leaned over the bar.

Tracy waved at a guy at the end of the bar who was holding up what must have been an empty beer bottle. "Look, I've got to go, so I'll make this quick. But again, it's rumor, so take it with a grain of salt."

"Like Larry slashing tires, which I believe he did?"

Tracy nodded. "You're right, of course. Anyway, Larry told me she killed her first boyfriend. Or she got him killed. He said he thought it was hot. I told him he was crazy. That's when I started calling her the black widow. Larry just thought it was funny."

Angie left the bar and went to find the bathroom. When she returned to the table, Ian leaned close.

"Are you okay?" He looked worried.

"I'm fine." Angie forced her face into a smile. She was probably looking like she felt. Scared and confused. She'd spent a minute in the bathroom texting the information to Allen. Now, she looked around the room to find him. He was sitting at a different table with Maggie, Bleak, and what looked like Estebe's parents. She met his gaze, and he pointed toward the bar.

She nodded, letting him know he'd find Tracy there.

"Angie? What's going on?" Ian started to stand, but Angie waved him down.

"Nothing that we can't deal with later." Angie poured some wine into her glass. She smiled at Mikel. "So tell me about what Estebe was like as a kid."

* * * *

On the way home, Angie sat in the back of the bus next to Ian and behind Allen as he explained what he'd found out.

"You're sure he said she knew Jason when they were kids?" He glanced at his phone. "According to Roland's notes, when he talked to her, she said she just met him this week."

"She's lying. I saw her car by the diner when we walked by the alley where Jason was killed. It's the same type of car that the homeless guy saw speeding away. I think she was waiting for us to walk back from the bar. I bet that's how she got Jason alone." Angie started nodding, thinking about the actual murder. "Yeah, that had to be it. She comes up to him on the street late at night and says something about Larry or even Jack. He follows her because she's upset, and then she shoots him."

"That's a great story. Do we have anything but your story-weaving skills to back it up?" Allen turned his head and made eye contact with Maggie, who was sitting close to the front, helping to direct the driver to their house. "We're almost to where I'm getting off. I'll take this and see if we can verify anything. I would love to find a note or something from Jason saying he knew Hallie. But Larry's holding fast on his story that his brother never met her. Maybe your reporter friend will find something useful."

Angie leaned back as she watched Allen Brown walk toward the front and stand by the driver, holding on to the railing as he directed him down their street. "I don't think your uncle believes me."

"He believes you, but like he said, we need to find proof if we want to put Hallie behind bars for doing more than just painting your wall." He saw the look on her face and held up his hands. "Fine, painting your wall, not just painting your wall. I need to get ready to bail too. Main Street will be the next stop."

Felicia had walked home with Estebe, so she didn't have to ride the bus with her parents and Carter. She'd gotten flak on that too, especially since it was the night before the wedding. Angie had to promise to come get her exactly at six, and Estebe had to promise to stay out of the guest room and in his bedroom until she left. Angie smiled as she thought about how carefully her friend had set up the rules for her overnight stay.

She kissed Ian and watched as he walked up to stand by the driver. She would be the last one on the bus once they dropped off the Browns and Ian. She stared out into the blackness of the night. Why would Hallie kill Jason? Angie was certain that she had; however, the reason why continued to elude her. She was marrying his brother soon. Maybe the thing with Carter was just a pre-wedding fling.

"Good night, Angie," Ian called as he got off the bus.

She called out a greeting and moved up to the seat behind the driver. "Sorry I'm so far out."

"Don't be. I'm making a ton tonight, and it's all going into my college fund. I've almost fully funded my room and board for next semester." He nodded to the radio. "Do you mind if I turn on some tunes?"

She gave him directions to the house and permission for the tunes. Then she curled up and stared out the window, watching the night pass by. Usually, she was the one driving home after a long night at the restaurant.

It was nice being a passenger for once. She could sit and think and take in the scenery.

"So was the woman in the red car with your group? She hung out in the parking lot forever tonight."

Angie sat up straighter. "Excuse me, what did you ask me?"

"There was a woman sitting in the parking lot at the community center. I figured she was waiting for her boyfriend. You know, being the designated driver? I went over to talk to her, and she told me to buzz off." He shook his head and met Angie's gaze in the rearview mirror. "Some people just don't know how to talk to people. Then when you all came out, she watched for a minute, then took off out of the parking lot like she was freaking mad. Tires squealing and such. Didn't you hear that?"

Angie shook her head. She hadn't heard anything, but she'd been talking to Felicia at the doorway and had run to catch the bus before it left. "What type of car, did you see?"

"One of those foreign sedans. It's hard to tell a Kia from a Honda, but something like that. It sure wasn't that Hummer I got to drive earlier. That's a sweet car."

Angie nodded, then pulled out her phone and texted Allen. Maybe the community center had cameras in the parking lot. Being downtown, they probably did. Allen needed to get someone to pull the files before they got dumped.

Chapter 23

Angie's alarm went off at four thirty. Dom raised his head as she got up, then went back to sleep as she showered and got dressed. She'd get ready for the wedding at Felicia's, so she needed to pack her dress, shoes, and assorted other things in a bag to take with her this morning. Dom was still half asleep on the bedroom floor when she zipped up her duffel bag. She sat on the bed and gave him a hug. "Don't worry. I'll be home after the reception, and you and I will spend all day tomorrow together watching rom-coms."

He stared at her with those big brown eyes, and her heart hurt to have to leave him alone for the day.

"I'll even make popcorn."

With that, she got a quick yip from him, and they made their way downstairs. Of course, Angie thought Dom believed he was getting popcorn now, but she gave him a treat instead as she made some coffee for the road. As that brewed, she pulled on her coat and went out to feed and check on Precious and Mabel.

Both the goat and hen were still asleep when she delivered their food and checked on their water, but they watched her move around the barn with sleepy curiosity. Angie bet they both went right back to sleep as soon as she'd shut the barn door.

Back in the house, she took off her barn coat and put on a cleaner, cuter one for her drive into Boise. She fed and watered Dom, then checked on his dog door to make sure it was open and the gate coming out of the backyard was shut. Then she went back into the house; got her bag, dress, and coffee; and with one last look around to make sure she wasn't forgetting anything, locked the door.

Lights were on at the Potter home when she pulled out of the driveway, which meant that either Erica or Mrs. Potter had returned from their visit to Mexico. Angie would drop by tomorrow with some food and spend time with her neighbor catching up. Happiness bubbled out of her as she drove into town. Felicia was starting a new adventure today. Mrs. Potter was probably home. She had three days off before she had to open the restaurant. Life was good. It just needed one thing.

She turned up the stereo and started singing along with the music. Today was going to be amazing.

* * * *

Felicia was waiting outside on the porch when she arrived. She hurried into the car as soon as Angie pulled over to the curb.

"How long have you been out here?" Angie turned up the heat as Felicia clicked her seatbelt.

"About ten minutes. I didn't want you to knock and wake Estebe up. He might forget and come out and see me." She held her hands against the heater vents and eyed Angie's coffee. "You stopped for coffee?"

"No, I made coffee at home before I went outside to feed the animals." She picked up the cup and handed it to Felicia. "Here. It's almost gone, but you can have what's left. You seem like you need it."

"Sorry, I'm a little tense. Having my family close by does that to me." She took the coffee and sipped it. "That's so good. I needed that."

"Good because I need breakfast. We're going to the Pancake House and eating carbs." Angie grinned at her friend. "And I'm having a hot chocolate and orange juice."

"We'll make mimosas when we get to the apartment. I could cook you breakfast instead of going out if you want." Felicia sipped more coffee. "No one's even out this early. I can't believe how quiet it is here. When we walked back to Estebe's last night, there were people all over."

"I think Hallie was at the community center when we left." Angie hadn't planned on telling Felicia. It just slipped out. "Sorry, I promise, no murder discussions on your wedding day."

"Tell me what happened." Felicia set the cup down and stared out the window while Angie drove and told her what the bus driver had said.

They pulled into the parking lot of the restaurant. Angie turned off the engine and turned to Felicia. "Anyway, that's it. No more talk about Jason's murder."

Felicia grabbed her arm as she went to open the car door. "Angie, this woman sounds deranged. And she's acting out in violent ways. You need to be careful and stay away from her. When Estebe and I leave for Spain, I'm going to be worried about you. Tell me you won't go off investigating on your own."

"I promise. Besides, she's scaring me a little too." Angie squeezed Felicia's hand. "Nothing is going to happen to me."

* * * *

Breakfast over, they went back to the apartment. Felicia was using her bedroom as the dressing area. Hope and Bleak had already left their dresses and bags in a corner. With a long table filled with mirrors, the room looked more like a backstage set than a bedroom.

"Yvonne and her assistant will be here at noon, which gives us two hours to get pretty and dressed. The wedding starts at two thirty. I told my mom two, so hopefully they'll be on time." Felicia read off items from her extensive and inclusive to-do list she'd made for the day.

Angie looked at her watch. It was only nine. She had time. "Hey, I'm running downstairs to check on payroll for this week. Sorry, I was going to do it this morning, but someone had to be picked up from Boise."

"I can be alone for a couple of hours. Besides, I need to finish packing for our trip. Estebe's limiting me to two suitcases. I have enough swimsuits to fill one. What does he expect me to do? Buy new clothes while I'm there and ship them home?"

"Not a bad plan." Angie paused by the door. "I have my phone if you need me."

"As long as I don't have to open another bottle of champagne for the mimosas, I'll be fine." She ran over to the door and hugged Angie. "I'm getting married today."

"Yes, yes you are." *And it's a modern miracle,* Angie thought as she made her way downstairs. Somehow, Allen had gotten Roland, or at least Roland's supervisor, to look at the facts and realize neither Estebe nor his cousin Javier had killed Jason. She didn't think her theory of the killer being Hallie was making much progress, but in her mind, the woman was crazy enough to do it. And if the stories were true, she might have gotten away with murder when Jack died.

She opened her office door and opened the file cabinet where the job applications were kept. She found the file and set it on her desk. If she was really going to work on payroll after this fishing expedition, like she'd told Felicia, she'd need some coffee.

Angie used the one-cup brewer they kept by the bar, and while the coffee was brewing, she took in the dining room. Even without the lights on, the place looked and smelled magical. Floral with the scent of good food underneath. In an hour, Estebe would have the caterers set up in the kitchen getting ready for the reception. They'd set up the banquet or classroom for the reception, and they'd move people into there for a drink or two while the wedding planner redesigned the dining room into a reception hall. A little back and forth, but the one thing this had shown her was they could rent out the building on days the restaurant wasn't open. And even cater events. The wedding planner was coming in when Felicia got back from Spain to finalize some summer events.

The business was becoming successful. With the added catering jobs, she could offer the kitchen and serving staff more hours and make most of them full-time, if they wanted it. Felicia was starting her new married life with Estebe. Angie had fought off a land grab for Nona's farmhouse. And she and Ian were solid.

Life was good.

She picked up the hot cup of coffee and made her way back into her office, where Hallie sat at her desk, reading an application. Angie started to turn to run, but Hallie had heard her walk up. She held up a gun. "Come inside and close the door behind you. Then have a seat. You and I need to talk."

Angie considered her options. If she ran, Hallie would shoot her before she got to an exit door. Felicia might hear the shot and come downstairs. Then they'd both be dead. This way, maybe she could talk Hallie out of killing her. She shut the door and sat down, setting the coffee on the desk. "You made a copy of the kitchen key before I let you go, right? What do you want?"

"You're brighter than I expected." Hallie eyed the coffee, then reached over and took it from the spot close to Angie. She took a long sip. "This is good coffee. I appreciated the fact you allowed staff the same coffee as what you served the customers. That was classy."

"My staff is my family." Angie leaned back in the chair, watching Hallie.

Hallie set the cup down, nodding. "Yeah, I realized I moved too quickly with you. I would have been better just biding some time and making myself indispensable while Estebe and Felicia were gone for a month."

"You're a planner, aren't you?" Angie had almost used the word *scammer*, but she'd changed it before it came out. "You play people."

"Play is a hard word. Let's just say I set myself up for the windfall. Of course, that's not important now that Larry is going to inherit Jason's money. That boy sure was lucky on the stock market. He saved every dime he made with your friend's father. I made the wrong choice all those years ago when I picked Larry over Jason. I could have been a socialite wife for years now. A role your friend turned down." She picked up her application. "Are you looking to hire, or just reviewing my application?"

"We may be adding a chef this summer. I wanted to see what my options were or if I needed to run an ad," Angie said.

"You're not a very good liar." Hallie laughed. "You think too much before you speak, choosing your words carefully."

"Being an honest person is a virtue, not a vice." Angie glanced at the clock. By the time Hallie got done here, she'd be able to run out the back door and leave before Estebe arrived with the caterers. "So what's on the application you were afraid I'd see?"

Hallie grinned. "Nothing much. Just my high school. I figured you'd put it together if you knew I was a town girl for that fancy boarding school."

"Actually, I found that out without it. Carter told me. And someone else called you the black widow." Angie didn't want to put Tracy in her crosshairs, but she needed to keep her talking in case someone did show up. She wasn't sure how she would get out of this, and she didn't want anyone else hurt, but then again, she didn't want to die either.

"Tracy was always a little shit. He didn't like Larry being with me. They worked at the Front Porch for a few years together." She took the application and pulled out Angie's metal trash can. "I hope the sprinkler system isn't really sensitive or that beautiful wedding chapel you set up is going to be trashed in a few seconds."

Which might also bring the fire department, which could be a good thing, Angie mused as she watched Hallie take a lighter and set the application on fire.

"Since you're going to kill me, tell me why you killed Jason?"

Hallie was watching the fire take the paper and held on to the edge right up to the end, when she opened her fingers and the burning paper fell into the empty trash can. "Jason was rich. And he wanted to reconcile with Larry. If they did, the boys would talk. They always do. And Larry might not like the things Jason told him about me."

"That was it? Because he wanted to reconcile with his brother?"

Hallie stood and leaned forward over the desk. Her face burned with anger. "Larry was supposed to be loyal to me. I chose him; he should choose me. But no, I hear him talking to Jason night after night. Laughing together. Larry is mine. He just needs to remember that."

Now Angie was totally confused. "But what about Carter? You two looked pretty chummy the other day."

Hallie leaned back, her anger subsiding and a soft smile replacing it. "Carter is my forever lover. He and I will be together—after I marry Larry and we get Jason's money."

Realization hit Angie, and she almost gagged at the thought. "You're marrying Larry so you can inherit his money when you kill him?"

Hallie stood and waved the gun at Angie. "Precisely. I knew you'd figure it out. Now get up. I have the perfect place to shoot you and hide your body."

Chapter 24

Angie found herself standing in the walk-in, next to Felicia's wedding cake. She hoped Hallie wouldn't shoot her here; the spatter would ruin the cake.

Of course, finding Angie's body in the walk-in would probably cancel the wedding anyway. She swallowed, hard.

Why was she thinking about these things when she was about to die? She couldn't raise a ruckus hoping someone would hear the noise, because the walk-in might not have been designed to be soundproof, but its design meant practically, it was. Even if Estebe was standing in the kitchen, he wouldn't know she was there unless he opened the door.

Then Hallie would shoot him instead of or probably in addition to Angie. She just didn't see a way out of this.

"This time they will find you for the murder," Angie commented, moving across the room and behind the cake.

"No, I'm with Larry, on our way to pick out wedding rings. He'll swear to it." Hallie's eyes shone, and Angie realized she was enjoying this. It was part of the thrill she got out of killing. Playing with her prey, like a cat with a mouse. "Face it, Angie, you might be all high and mighty with your culinary degree, but this time, I outsmarted you."

She wanted the praise. The glory. To be the best. This was Hallie's Achilles' heel. "Yeah, but Jason outsmarted you. He sent an email to the cops saying if he wound up dead, you were to blame."

"He did not." Hallie stepped closer. "Take that back. He loved me."

Angie shook her head, a hand on the metal shelving they'd just put in last quarter. The guy who'd installed it was supposed to come back and attach it to the floor of the fridge. Angie had wanted to just screw in supports, but apparently it invalidated the fridge warranty if they didn't have a trained person do the work. She thought it had been stupid when Estebe told her, but right now, she was thinking the workman's delay might just save her life.

She glanced down at her foot. There weren't any supports she could see. Of course, that didn't mean the guy hadn't done it some other way that she hadn't thought about. Which was one of the reasons he was the specialist. She focused on the angry woman coming closer. "Nope. I don't lie. He sent an email on Monday after we had brunch with him. He was scared of you. He didn't love you. He loved his brothers. The one you killed and the one you're planning on killing. He knew you were trying to obliterate his entire family."

"Liar, liar, liar." Hallie held the gun out and stepped even closer.

Angie thought about how angry Felicia was going to be if this escape plan ruined her cake, but she shook it off. She could either have a nice cake or her maid of honor. And this was Angie's decision. Angie's life.

She grabbed onto the shelf railing and pulled it in front of her.

Hallie saw what was happening right before two boxes of canned tomatoes fell on top of her, knocking the gun out of her hand and out of reach. At least she hadn't been able to shoot it as she went down. Angie stepped through the now grounded shelves and around the boxes and loose vegetables. She reached for the gun just as Hallie's hand snaked out of where she was lying. Angie stepped on her arm, and Hallie screamed in pain.

Angie grabbed the gun, which was just out of Hallie's reach. She stepped back away from the woman and out of the maze caused by the fallen shelving unit. She stepped out into a wide-legged stance and pointed the gun at Hallie's chest. "Stay down. Don't move."

"Screw you," Hallie yelled back.

Light from the kitchen poured into the walk-in, making Angie's eyes burn, but she didn't blink.

"What the heck?' Estebe stood in the doorway. "Angie? Are you okay?"

"You idiot. I'm the one with a ton of shelving and boxes on top of me," Hallie complained. "Not to mention a gun pointed at me."

"You probably deserve it." Estebe leaned back and called to someone else in the kitchen. "Call 9-1-1. We have trash that needs to be picked up and taken out of here."

Hallie screamed as she struggled against the shelf. "You can't do this."

Angie smiled at Estebe. "Actually, we can. At worst, you're on the hook for trespassing and attempted murder. Larry might not be happy I saved his life, but he will be after they get a confession out of Carter.

He's going to throw you under the bus so fast you're going to think you're standing on ice."

After Deputy Brandon came and took Hallie out from under the shelving and thankfully took Hallie's gun from her for evidence, Angie sank into a chair next to the chef table.

Estebe stood in front of her. "I've called Ian. He'll be here in a few minutes. I haven't called Felicia yet."

"Don't. I'll tell her when I go up to change." She checked the time on her watch and smiled shakily. "I still have thirty minutes before I have to start. Time slows down when you have a gun pointed at you."

* * * *

Angie opened the door to the apartment and saw Felicia's suitcase sitting by the door. She had a light raincoat laid on the cases and a new hardback release on top of that. Angie picked up the book. It was a mystery. Fitting. First, Felicia needed to know the full story that Hallie had bragged about to Angie and why her first boyfriend had been killed. Angie knew she'd promised no murder talk, but Felicia needed the story so she could put this issue to bed before she married the love of her life. A man who would have never killed anyone, much less someone who'd once meant something to his new bride.

"Angie? Is that you? We need to start getting ready. I can't believe you took so long with payroll. My hairdresser and the other girls will be here in a few minutes—" Felicia's words broke off. "What is in your hair? Is that frosting?"

The cake had survived the walk-in incident, but it had taken some hits. Estebe and the wedding planner had assured Angie that they could angle it so no one would see the patch that had to be made before the reception started. Angie reached up and found the clump in her hair. "I'll take a quick shower in a minute, but first, we need to talk."

"Just tell me first. I do have a groom for my wedding today, right?" Felicia reached over and took a second clump out of Angie's hair. "And a cake. The groom's the most important, but it took me forever to explain my vision to the cake decorator."

"Estebe's fine." Angie paused and took Felicia's hand and led her to the couch. "And the cake will be fine by the time the reception starts, but let me tell you the story my way."

After Angie told Felicia everything, the hairdresser arrived, and Angie took that time to get into the shower and wash her hair. Again. When she got out and dressed, there were more people in the apartment.

Felicia was sitting on the couch with her mother, and her father was standing close by talking. Angie moved closer into the room. She didn't want Mr. Williams to get away with bullying Felicia and trying to talk her out of the wedding. Instead, his words surprised her.

"I'm very sorry for the trouble I've caused these last few days. And to be honest, for the way I treated you before you left. I should have known my little girl had dreams for her life outside the business I'd built. I was just so focused on growing the business, I treated you like an ungrateful employee. Not like I should have treated my daughter. If it's not too late, I'd like to walk you down the aisle. And dance with you at the reception. And do all the wedding traditions a father is supposed to do to give away his daughter."

"Daddy, I love you." Felicia stood up and flew into his arms. "Of course you can give me away. We had a stand-in just in case, but you were always my first choice."

A hand squeezed Angie's shoulder. She turned, and a woman in bright pink hair grinned at her. "Come on, deary, we need to get you dried and styled if you're going to look your best for the pictures today."

Angie gave one last look at her friend and her family. Felicia was happy. And that's exactly how any woman should feel on her wedding day. Not a care in the world. She turned and followed the hairdresser. "I'm in your hands. Make me beautiful."

"Impossible." The woman laughed as she pointed to a chair sitting in front of a mirror. "I can't make you beautiful because you already are. I'm just here to make sure everyone else sees your true beauty."

* * * *

Ian was sitting across from her as the wedding party began to wind down. He took out an envelope from his suit pocket and passed it to Angie.

She frowned and set down her glass. "What's this?"

"You're going to be on vacation the first week of May. I've already talked to Estebe, and he and Felicia will be back by then, so you won't have to worry about the restaurant. Hope and Bleak are staying at the house to take care of Dom, Precious, and Mabel. I've taken care of all your excuses." He met her gaze, his eyes filled with caring and love. "Angie, you need a break. And I need you to meet someone."

She opened the envelope and pulled out a sheet of paper with hotel reservations in London, England.

"My travel agent needs your information to get us the airline tickets, but we should be there those dates from what she told me. And we can adjust the hotel days if we need to due to some appointment you have that I don't know about." He moved his chair closer and pointed to the paper. "This place is within walking distance to all the tourist stops. And I hear there's a ton of great restaurants for you to check out."

She looked up from the paper. "You're taking me to London to meet your mother?"

He nodded. "I think it's time. But there's one more question I need to ask you before we go."

She scanned the paper. "Yes, I have a passport."

He shook his head. "That's not the question."

The music changed from a fun dance tune to a slow ballad she loved from a long-ago country-western star. Love songs like this were perfect for a wedding reception, and she was glad the DJ had included this song in the mix. She watched as Ian stood from his chair, then knelt down in front of her.

"Don't freak out, because I've already cleared this action here at this moment with Felicia and Estebe, so we're not stepping on their toes." He grinned up at her.

"What are you talking about?" She glanced around, and all of a sudden, everyone's eyes were on them, not on the bride and groom, who were sitting at the head table. They all were watching her and Ian. Realization hit, and her stomach flipped. This couldn't be happening.

"Angie Turner? Will you marry me?" Ian's voice seemed to come from a long way away.

She looked down at the ring, then at him. This man knew her to the core and still loved her enough to be her family. Her heart filled with love, and she nodded. "Yes. Yes, I'd love to."

He slipped the ring on her finger and stood, pulling her up into a kiss. Then he held their joined hands up in a salute. "She said yes. We're getting married!"

The crowd in the dining room roared their approval, and then Maggie, Allen, and Bleak were at her side.

"Welcome to the family, Angie." Maggie pulled her into a hug.

Allen kissed her on the cheek, then put his arm around his wife. "Don't think this means you can get involved in my investigations, young lady.

In fact, this is the perfect time for me to remind you that you're not in law enforcement. You run this restaurant."

Bleak squealed and hugged her. "You're going to be my cousin. Well, foster cousin, but that's still cool."

"Actually, Bleak, Allen and I wanted to know if we could adopt you. We already feel like you're family. We might as well make it legal." Maggie grinned as Bleak threw herself into her arms. "I think that's a yes."

Allen petted the top of Bleak's hair like he still wasn't sure what this child was doing in his life, but the love he felt for the young woman was evident. They were family. Legal papers signed or not.

After the guests and the caterers left, Angie sat at a table alone with Ian chatting about the day. Felicia and Estebe, who had left the reception earlier, came back through the back stairs. They were dressed in jeans, a big change from the tux and white wedding dress they'd been in just an hour before. They sat at the table.

"Shouldn't you be getting to the airport?" Angie glanced at the clock on the bar.

Estebe shrugged, his hand entwined with Felicia's. "We have time. We just wanted to say goodbye and congratulations."

"And thank you," Felicia added. "The Scooby gang solved another mystery, but mostly it was you this time. You were the one who kept focusing on Hallie."

"I thought it was just because I was mad that she spray-painted our building." Angie admitted her fear regarding her motivation. "But the pieces didn't make sense without her. She was the glue that made it all fit."

"She killed Jack and Jason and was planning on killing Larry. I think Carter dodged a bullet. Who knows when she would have gotten tired of him too?" Felicia shivered a little. "And she almost killed you because you wanted to do payroll."

Angie scrunched her face a little.

"Wait, you *were* doing payroll when you were down here, right?" Felicia eyed her friend suspiciously.

"I was going to after I read through Hallie's job application to see if she mentioned living back east at all." Angie shrugged. "I wanted another piece of evidence for Allen to work with."

"Unbelievable. On my wedding day, when you're supposed to be thinking about me. And only me. My best friend goes hunting killers." Felicia stood. "We've got to go, but I'll call you when we get to Spain. We need to talk."

"Sorry?" Angie stood and hugged her.

Felicia laughed and hugged her back. "And congratulations on the engagement. When I get back, we'll start planning the wedding. Hopefully Ian can stay out of trouble until then so we don't have to keep him out of jail too."

After they were gone, Angie stood. "I told Dom I'd be home early."

"I'll walk you to your car." Ian stood and followed her to her office to get her stuff. "Unless you want company tonight."

"I could use a driver." Angie smiled as she grabbed her tote bag. "I'm beat. And if you don't mind rom-coms, we could watch a movie."

"Honey, our lives are much more interesting than any movie." He turned off the light and closed the door. "You ready to lock up?"

Angie nodded. "Time to go home and enjoy our lives."

She made sure both doors were locked and engaged the alarm system. She'd do payroll on Monday when she had to come in and lead a crew tearing down the wedding chapel look and re-setting up the restaurant. When life would be normal again. Next month, she'd be dealing with running the restaurant on her own while Estebe and Felicia were gone. Then, she'd be in London, meeting Ian's mother. But those were worries for another day. Today, she was just happy. And that was enough.

Workday Quick and Easy Risotto

As soon as you get home, put a pot of chicken stock on the stove to warm; 3–4 cups should be enough. If you don't have chicken stock, boil water and add 3–4 bouillon cubes to make a stock.

Chop assorted veggies—I usually chop the onions pretty fine, but the others can be coarsely chopped or sliced.

Onion (or green onion)
Mushrooms
Asparagus

Heat a large skillet, and when warm, add a touch of olive oil (1–2 tbsps.)

Sauté the onion and mushrooms until the onion wilts but doesn't brown. Then add a handful or two of arborio rice (about a cup/cup and a half) to the skillet. Keep stirring as the rice browns (think Rice-A-Roni) for a minute or two.

Then add a ladle or two of the chicken stock. Stir to mix. Add asparagus now.

Let risotto cook as you prepare your meat.

Continue to stir and add stock when rice appears dry.

When the stock is all added, and the rice is creamy, you're done. Takes about 30 minutes total.

If you want a veggie boost, add a handful or two of spinach leaves with your last bit of chicken stock. The leaves will wilt into the risotto and give you a nice color and extra nutrients.

And that's it!

ABOUT THE AUTHOR

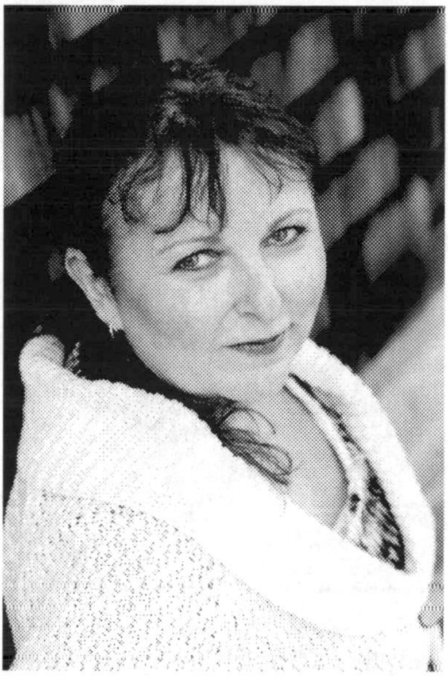

New York Times and *USA Today* bestselling author **Lynn Cahoon** is an Idaho expat. She grew up living the small-town life she now loves to write about. Currently, she's living with her husband and two fur babies in a small historic town on the banks of the Mississippi River where her imagination tends to wander. Visit her at www.lynncahoon.com.

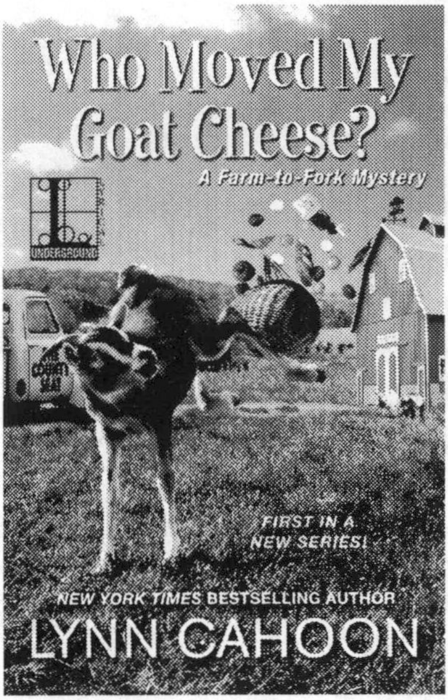

WHO MOVED MY GOAT CHEESE?
A Farm-to-Fork Mystery

Angie Turner hopes her new farm-to-table restaurant can be a fresh start in her old hometown in rural Idaho. But when a goat dairy farmer is murdered, Angie must turn the tables on a bleating black sheep…

With three weeks until opening night for their restaurant, the County Seat, Angie and her best friend and business partner Felicia are scrambling to line up local vendors—from the farmer's market to the goat dairy farm of Old Man Moss. Fortunately, the cantankerous Moss takes a shine to Angie, as does his kid goat Precious. So when Angie hears the bloodcurdling news of foul play at the dairy farm, she jumps in to mind the man's livestock and help solve the murder. One thing's for sure, there's no whey Angie's going to let some killer get *her* goat…

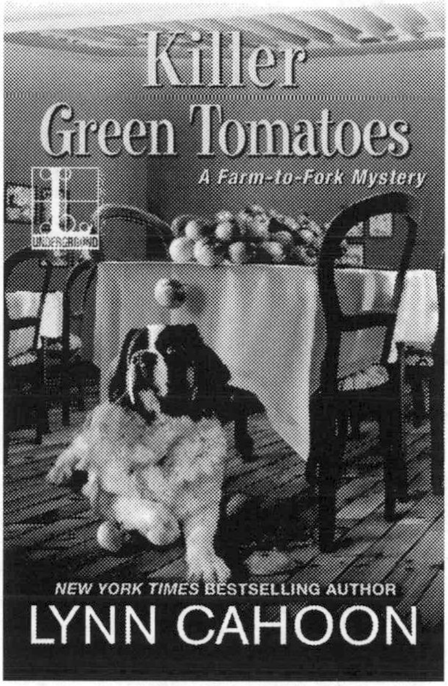

KILLER GREEN TOMATOES
A Farm-to Fork Mystery

The time seems ripe for success as Angie Turner opens her farm to-table restaurant in her Idaho hometown—until her new tomato supplier is accused of murder and Angie has to pick the real killer...

To Angie, nothing tastes more like summer than her Nona's fried green tomatoes. Eager to add the recipe to the menu at the County Seat, she's found the perfect produce supplier—her sous chef Estebe's cousin, Javier. Just one problem: ladies' man Javier's current hot tomato, Heather, has turned up dead, and he's the prime suspect. Somehow, between managing her restaurant and navigating a romantic triangle between Estebe and Ian, the owner/manager of the farmer's market, Angie needs to produce evidence to clear Javier—before this green tomato farmer gets fried...

ONE POTATO, TWO POTATO, DEAD
A Farm-to Fork Mystery

Angie Turner's restaurant, The County Seat, is conveniently located near a first-class farmers market—so her menu is full of fresh ingredients. But a visiting culinary professor has just had a taste of something very unhealthy…

Angie first meets Daniel Monet at a local mission, where she and her chef-in-training, Hope, are serving barbeque chicken poutine to the homeless. Monet is one of Hope's teachers—but Angie's boyfriend thinks he knows him from his youthful days in England. But soon, the bon vivant is no longer *vivant.* When Monet is found dead, with Hope's prints on the wine glass next to him, it will be Angie who has to sauce out the real killer…

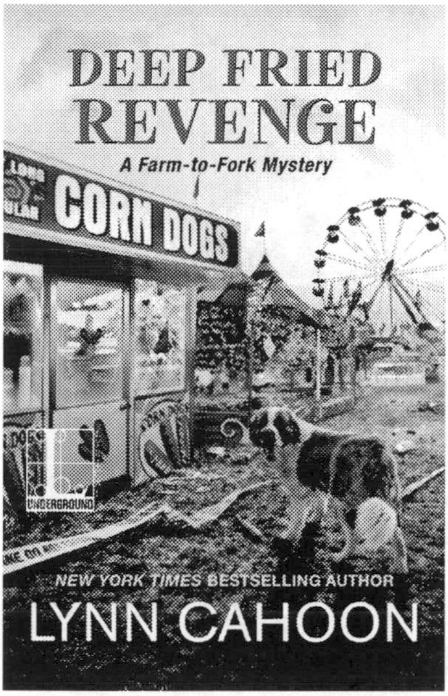

DEEP FRIED REVENGE
A Farm-to-Fork Mystery

Angie Turner is all prepped to face Boise's culinary best when she enters her restaurant, The County Seat, into a big State Fair challenge. Instead, she gets dunked into a new murder investigation after a killer starts scrapping her competition…

The Idaho State Fair is in full swing and chefs are lining up to enter Boise's Best Restaurant contest, including Angie and her County Seat crew. They might be the hometown favorite, but the competition is steeper than a funhouse floor. And when a top contender is felled following a heated confrontation over a corn dog recipe, winning suddenly becomes a matter of life or death. With a foul foodie on the prowl, it's up to Angie to dig into the case and put a murderer on ice.

KILLER COMFORT FOOD

A Farm-to-Fork Mystery

Angie Turner's Idaho restaurant, the County Seat, is known and loved for its fresh food. For Angie, it's also meant a fresh start. But when big agriculture comes to town—along with whispers of foul play—Angie could lose more than the farm…

A soybean processing plant is trying to buy up the land around the small farm Angie's beloved Nona left her. If Angie doesn't sell, she'll be surrounded by the plant and the congestion that comes with it. On the other hand, it's Nona's farmhouse. What is Angie supposed to do without it? Move into a condo in town with Precious, Mabel, and Dom—respectively, a goat, chicken, and dog. Worse, a troubling rumor is circulating about the lawyer who's heading up the development: His socialite wife seems to be missing. When Barb, owner of the local bar, asks Angie to look into the woman's disappearance, she's hesitant—until Barb reveals her surprising connection. Now it's up to Angie to find the woman, uncover a shady plot, and hang onto her home—before she becomes a criminal's final course…

HAVE A DEADLY NEW YEAR
A Farm-to-Fork Novella

Chef Angie Turner of The County Seat—Idaho's finest farm-to-table restaurant—is preparing a private dinner in the mountains during ski season, but the trip's about to go downhill...

It's a rockin' New Year for Angie and her crew as they cater a bash for a famous band—and as a bonus, they'll get to stay at the singer's Sun Valley house for a whole week once the party's over. But there are hints of discord, and the event hits a sour note when one of the musicians is found with a drumstick in his chest.

Is this a case of creative differences turned lethal or is there another motive at play? Angie's jumping out of the frying pan and into the fire as she and her fellow foodies try to solve the case before the killer comes out for an encore...

PENNED IN

A Farm-to-Fork Novella

Angie Turner, chef at Idaho's finest farm-to-table restaurant, has organized a team-building event at a haunted prison, only to find a real-life murderer in their midst....

Contented employees make for a successful restaurant, which is why the County Seat's crew goes on a quarterly out-of-office meeting. This time, the location is the Old Idaho Penitentiary near the Boise Foothills, a prison brimming with ghostly lore. The lock-in features actors role-playing as guards, fascinating prison stories... and an unscripted murder.

Who sentenced one of the faux guards to a very authentic death? Angie, her boyfriend, and the County Seat gang are locked in with a killer—excellent motivation for a little sleuthing. Between ghostly apparitions and flesh-and-blood suspects, Angie's plate is full, but will her luck, and her life, hold out until the gates reopen at dawn?

A PUMPKIN SPICE KILLING
A Farm-to-Fork Novella

Angie Turner's Idaho restaurant, the County Seat, owes its success not only to its farm-fresh fair, but also to its devoted and passionate staff. But a team-building retreat turns into much more than they bargained for...

Angie and her County Seat staff are all prepared for some much-needed R&R. Hope's been hinting at an arts-and-crafts themed retreat. Instead, they end up at a military veteran's home, where it's their job to get it spic and span for summer. In between weeding the garden and painting the rooms, Angie starts up a conversation with an older vet who wants to make amends with his son before it's too late. Unfortunately, he has no idea of his son's whereabouts. It's the perfect side job for the County Seat team, but someone keeps blocking their efforts. And the more they try to find out why, the more they're certain someone's life might be in danger…

Printed in the United States
by Baker & Taylor Publisher Services